D1248284

Legends of Lost Man Marsh

For Tim —
the solver of
mysteries,
mechanical and
electronic —

Best regards —

Gerald Duff

Legends of Lost Man Marsh

An Alabama-Coushatta Tale

Gerald Duff

LITERARY PRESS
LAMAR UNIVERSITY

Copyright © Gerald Duff 2019
All Rights Reserved

ISBN: 978-1-942956-66-2
Library of Congress Control Number: 2019934165

Cover Photo: ellyn.

Lamar University Literary Press
Beaumont, Texas

This book is in memory of my father
Willie Ellis Duff
who laughed big and told good stories

and for my sister
Nancy Elizabeth Duff McLin
who remembers them all

Other fiction from Lamar University Literary Press

Robert Bonazzi, *Awakened by Surprise*
David Bowles, *Border Lore: Folktales and Legends of South Texas*
Chris Carmona, Rob Johnson, & Chuck Taylor, *The Beatest State in the Union*
Kevin K. Casey, *Four-Peace*
Terry Dalrymple, *Love Stories (Sort of)*
Gerald Duff, *Memphis Mojo*
Britt Haraway, *Early Men*
Michael Howarth, *Fair Weather Ninjas*
Gretchen Johnson, *The Joy of Deception*
Christopher Linforth, *When You Find Us We Will Be Gone,*
Tom Mack & Andrew Geyer, *A Shared Voice*
Moumin Quazi, *Migratory Words*
Harold Raley, *Lost River Anthology*
Harold Raley, *Louisiana Rogue*
Jim Sanderson, *Trashy Behavior*
Jan Seale, *Appearances*
Melvin Sterne, *The Number You Have Reached*
Melvin Sterne, *The Shoeshine Boy*
John Wegner, *Love Is Not a Dirty Word*
Robert Wexelblatt, *The Artist Wears Rough Clothing*

A hunter became lost in the Big Thicket and could not find his village. At the end of his third day of wandering, he was so tired he had to sleep. As he lay on the bare earth, he dreamed he saw a spirit creature sitting high up in a pine tree. The spirit spoke to him: "Do not go the way your head tells you." When the hunter awoke, he took the path his head told him was the wrong one. The spirit had given him true guidance, for the hunter arrived home before the end of his day.

from the Alabama-Coushatta tale
Listening to the Spirit
collected by Howard N. Martin

Prologue

The singing of the tie-snake came in a thin wavery voice, almost too high and faint for Emory Sees the Water to hear against the flow of the stream in Long King Creek. The source of the sound was somewhere ahead and to the right, behind a stand of yaupon and sawvines, and Sees the Water stopped in the middle of the path to listen, his head turned so that he looked down at the beaten earth of the way before him. The path appeared silvery black in the fading light of the end of day.

Again it came, a chant in the language of the Old Ones, four words repeated before a pause and then the same again, growing louder as he listened in the darkness of Long King Trace, the ancient path beside the water.

"Chieftain," the tie-snake, the creature which lives in deep water, sang its invitation, "I have words. I have words for you."

"I will not hear them," Emory Sees the Water answered in the language of the People. "Creature of lies, I will not."

"You must, for the Nation." The tie-snake sang louder, its voice now coming from both sides of the path and from before and behind the place where Sees the Water stood. "You are chief of the Alabamas and Coushattas. You hear for the Nation. You hear for the People."

Now the wood whistled and the drum sounded in the song of the tie-snake and were part of the voice and of what it said. Emory Sees the Water looked above him to the sky at the edge of the tangles of thicket at each border of the trace, but the light was going and he could see no sign of the Old Ones in the coming night. He was alone with the thing which drew him toward the deep pool.

"I do not know you," he said to the singer of darkness. "The people of the Nation want no talk with you."

"Come to the pool in Long King," the tie-snake and the drum and the whistle sang. "Look in my face for the words I have for you. Old man, Old man."

"I do not come to you," the Chief of the Alabama-Coushatta Nation said in a voice clear and strong, but he found himself leaving the brighter way of the path and sinking into the forest between himself and the flow of creek water. He saw his feet move before him and he felt the push of branches and vines against his face and body, and he watched himself kneel beside the dark pool of Long King Creek and lean forward to look into its depth. "I will not come to pass words with you."

The face of the tie-snake was there, the color white mottled under its throat and beside the beak hooked like a hawk's and the blackness, that of the night of no moon, which flowed down the length of the thick body disappearing into the pool. The voice shrill and high now and the drum booming as though it were inside his head and the whistle screaming like the tearing of metal all came together in a place within the throat of Emory Sees the Water and twisted into a knot so close and tight he could not breathe, and he was falling forward toward the mouth of the tie-snake open to show the blackness inside.

"The Nation," Emory Sees the Water tried to say, but the knot was closing and the words of the Old Ones could not come forth to reach the air and be heard. nd the black pit which was the mouth behind the hooked beak of the tie-snake had become all the world and nothing. And the Old Ones in the sky and in the earth and in the thicket of trees did not come forth to save him.

1

Only two of the thirty seniors lined up in rows before him would have finished what he had told them to read. Austin Bullock knew that for a fact, and he knew who the two would be. One was Emma Alice Berryhill, a red-haired girl in the front row so painfully thin he could see the blue flow of blood beneath her pale skin, and the other was Rolando Johnson, the large black kid against the back wall of the room, who at his age had fastened hard on the notion that if he did everything teachers and coaches and bosses told him something was bound to break right for him eventually.

Rolando caught Austin Bullock's eye on him from behind the desk in the front of the room, met his gaze for an instant and then dropped his attention to the back of the head of the person sitting in front of him. That was Bobby Hunts Bear, one of the ten members of Austin Bullock's own people in the American history class, and he, like the rest of the Alabamas and Coushattas in the room, was carefully focused on nothing outside of the two-foot space of air surrounding him.

The tribal bubble, Austin Bullock's ex-wife used to call it, that you people travel around in whenever you're outside the reservation. Impenetrable, invisible, impossible. Don't think about Ellen, Austin reminded himself, not while you're trying to work. Keep that for when you can afford the expense.

"O.K.," he said aloud in the stone-quiet room, two minutes deep into his daily hour with the sixteen and seventeen year-olds before him. "I know you haven't had much chance to think about what might be in chapter seventeen of our book, so I'm going to see if you can't do it right now."

Somebody's foot scraped against the floor, a pencil dropped, and Austin could hear a few deep breaths being drawn in as though the supply of air was being rationed in the classroom.

"It's March," he said. "It's not that hot yet."

Nobody answered.

"It's after the war's officially over," Austin began. "They've stacked their weapons at Appomattox, and started walking home, the ones left, and what do they come back to? What's waiting in Coushatta County, Texas, for example, for a man who's been gone for four years from a farm out close to Soda, halfway between here in Annette and the Indian reservation?"

"Mud," said Billy Murphy and looked around the room for a laugh. He got a small one.

"That's right," Austin Bullock said. "Anything planted in the field?"

"Cotton and potatoes," Billy Murphy tried his luck again.

"Who planted it?" Austin said. "This soldier coming home hasn't been on the place for four years."

"His wife?" Emma Alice Berryhill asked.

"She can't," Austin said. "Mule's dead and she's too sick to lift a hand anyway. And also, Billy, why does a man plant cotton?"

"To sell, I reckon."

"Who's going to buy cotton in 1865 in East Texas? Who wants it?"

"Not nobody," Rolando Johnson said. "There ain't been cotton traded since the war started."

"Why not?"

"The Union army done stopped it."

"You got it," Austin said. "So what does this homecoming soldier see after he's walked over a thousand miles from Virginia to out near the Indian reservation? Was it there, by the way, in 1865? Would this soldier have seen some Alabamas and Coushattas out riding circles around wagon trains?"

"No," half the class said in one voice, and "Yes" the other half answered.

"Got a disagreement," Austin said. "Got to fix it later. What would he have seen on the old home place, this ex-soldier?"

"No cotton," Maria Battise said. "No potatoes, either." She paused for a space and then spoke again. "Hungry people and nothing to eat."

"Anything to sell?" Austin Bullock asked and waited for the voices to say no from all parts of the room. When they came immediately, he felt good enough to stand up and walk to the window to catch a little breeze. The American history class was warming up well on this morning in late March.

Out in the hall thirty minutes later, students flowing past him as though he were a rock in the middle of a creekbed, Austin Bullock stood looking down at a pile of memos from his mailbox and trying to remember whether or not he had lunchroom duty on Monday.

"The once and future chief," someone said from behind him.

"Hey, Phil," Austin said. "You got lunchroom today?"

"No, it's Monday. You're up."

"What I was afraid of. It do come around regular, don't it?"

"She do, she do," Phil Spurgeon said as the two men watched the last of the stray students leave the corridor for the classrooms. "You didn't hear what I called you?"

"You're always calling me names. What, chief? Nothing new about that one, or witty either."

"I guess you haven't heard, then. Or you'd have showed more interest when I used your title."

"Not really my title, Phil," Austin said. "That's just tribal custom."

"Whatever you say, and it's not really funny, but old Chief Emory is no longer with us, from what I hear."

"What?" Austin looked up from the papers he had been shuffling as he talked. "He died?"

"Yeah. You hadn't heard? This morning they said it on the Annette radio. They found him dead in Long King Creek. Drowned, I guess."

"In the creek? In water? That doesn't make sense. He wouldn't be drowned. Not Chief Emory."

"All I know's what I heard. Maybe he went for a little swim in one of the holes and had a heart attack or something. Old man like that."

"No, Phil," Austin Bullock spoke in the tone he would use to a new player on a basketball court. "Why do you think he's named what

13

he is? Was. Emory Sees the Water. His clan claims to know what all manner of danger there can be in water. That bunch, or what's left of them these days, spooked themselves about that stuff always, all the time."

"Like I said, Chief," Phil Spurgeon said, "you know your people and you know your folklore. I just teach English the best I can. Sorry I had to be the one to let you know about your elevation to power, but there it is. Catch you later."

Austin watched Spurgeon until he had disappeared through the third door down the hall, and then he headed for the fieldhouse, hurrying to get there before the morning conditioning session started. After Coach Mellard began that, none of the basketball players would have a chance to think, much less talk, for at least two hours.

"I see you," Thomas Fox Has Him said as Austin Bullock entered the locker room. He stood up and spoke in the language of the Nation. "Abba Bullock."

"Call me coach, Tom," Austin said in English and put out his hand for a white man handshake. "What was the talk you heard this morning before the school bus picked you up?"

The young man stood silent before Austin for a time before answering, his eyes fixed in the space above Austin's head as though he were listening to a sound faint and far off.

"Chief Emory is dead. My father was told this by the one who found him."

"Who was that?"

"Cooper Leaping Deer. He was walking in the early light down Long King Trace. Going home."

"Was Cooper drunk?"

"Only a little, my father said. The night was gone, and Cooper Leaping Deer was almost sober again."

"The radio said the Chief was in the water," Austin said, watching the eyes of Thomas Fox Has Him closely. They narrowed only slightly when he spoke.

"It is so. All his body but his legs was in Long King Creek. The head of Chief Emory was under the water."

14

"He had been swimming in the pool?" Austin asked, knowing the answer. Thomas looked directly at him and said nothing, his gaze expressionless.

"No, of course not," Austin said. "Thank you, Tom. It's time for you to go with the others."

"Abba Bullock," the young man said and nodded once.

"Fox Has Him," Austin answered in the language of the people and began to turn toward the corridor to the field house. Coach Mellard would be outside waiting with the others to start work.

"Do you think Chief Emory was looking into the water?" Tom asked. "Was he seeing what was there?"

"Yes," Austin said. "I think he always saw what was there, what was waiting."

The sounds of the first drill were beginning as Austin Bullock left the locker room, the squeak of rubber on wood, the bright sound of the coach's whistle, the cries and grunts of young men, the echoes in the still air above them.

2

Austin Bullock could see the red light in the answering machine blinking through the door to the bedroom when he walked into the front room of his house. It was well after six, full dark still this early in March, but he didn't bother to flip the light switch before going to see who had called him. Get it over with and then see what there was to eat.

"Daddy," the voice said, speaking as though Laura were actually addressing him in person rather than through acetate and electrical impulse, "I bet you're in that sweaty old gym tormenting some boy about his jump shot or his defense or something major. Just calling to let you know I'm coming home next Friday. I'm getting a ride with a girl down the hall going to Lufkin. She'll drop me off late. So don't wait up for me. And listen, please get that old Spanish medal out for me to see before I get there. I want to use it in a paper I'm doing in an anthro class. Be sweet. Give those kids some room. Bye. Colita signing off."

Oh, God, he thought. She's using the Coushatta name she made up for herself. It's going to be an ethnic damn weekend here in the renthouse for father and daughter. I better brush up on some chants, try to remember a legend or two.

The machine made the noise that meant one call was gone and another was coming. This one began with a silence of several seconds and ended with a reservation voice: slow, careful, and aware there was no human to which it spoke. It knew the machine was stupid and easily fooled, but it was reluctant to have more of the words it spoke frozen and fixed in one unchanging form than was absolutely needful.

"Austin Bullock," the speaker said and paused, and then in the common tongue of the Alabama and Coushatta, went on precisely so the machine could capture in its mindless way the sounds of a man's talk, "you must come to the Nation when the sun rises. Come to the sweatlodge, Abba Bullock."

The machine clicked off, and the tape made its backward hum as it rewound, and Austin lifted his gaze to the darkness of the far corner of the room, closing his eyes and watching the points of false light flare and die and rise again against the inside of his lids. White and red and purple, the changing colors which bled away from the margins of the visions of the Old Ones when a man was granted a flickering portion of such sight.

I cannot do this, he said to himself in the language of the people, and then repeated the thought in words of English out loud. He said them twice in a strong voice, but they sounded lifeless and false in the room of his house on a street identified by a number.

"What I'm going to do," Austin Bullock said," is go out in the kitchen and warm up some bad pizza and drink two bottles of Budweiser beer. And I'm not going to think about a sweatlodge or a three-hundred year old medal from Spain or anything else but grading a set of history exams."

He stood up, walked into the front room, and hit every wall switch he passed on his way to supper. When he finished, the house was ablaze with electric light.

Austin leaned back against the arm of the sofa to rest his eyes after reading the thirteenth student attempt to explain the implications of the Dred Scott decision. He allowed his head to sink deeper into a cushioned corner, and within a minute or two, the examination paper in his hand slipped unnoticed to the floor. He dreamed.

He was at the fall corn dance in the clearing at the center of the Nation. He felt cold, though all those around him seemed not to notice the north wind cutting through the dead leaves of the sycamores. For some reason he knew it was the first night of the festival, but as he looked at the figures in the center of the clearing, he saw that they were dressed in the wrong costumes for the ceremonies of the first night, and there were fewer figures swaying and bobbing in the light from the four fires than were needed for the Crayfish and Buzzard play.

Austin Bullock drew the cloak he was wearing closer about him against the cold, but the material of which it was made was slick and metallic and gave no warmth. He bundled it around himself and walked nearer to the fire burning at the southern point of the clearing. A large crowd of people that he had not noticed before were suddenly between him and the fire. He begged them to allow him nearer the warmth, but none heard. He reached out to touch an old man who stood before him so that he might share the fire, but the old man seemed not to feel the hand on his shoulder. As Austin braced himself to give a strong tug to the old bones beneath the dry skin, the old man was suddenly across the fire from where he stood.

Austin tried to get near the fire burning in the east, and then the one in the west, but at both spots large groups of people suddenly appeared to shut him away from the warmth. The wind blew more fiercely and entered the cloak as though it were made from spider web. Shaking from the cold, Austin turned toward the last fire and saw it roaring with heat and light. One person, wrapped in a long robe, stood facing it, his back to Austin as he approached. When he reached to within a few feet, Austin recognized the figure to be Emory Sees the Water, Chief of the Nation, alone and facing the fire at the northern edge of the clearing. Austin called his name, but Chief Emory continued to stare into the red flames licking up from a huge pile of hickory and oak logs. Austin stretched out his left hand and spoke the

17

name of the Chief again in a louder voice. The head of the old man slowly turned to face Austin, and he smiled as he waited for Emory Sees the Water to see and recognize him. The face of the Chief was hidden in shadows as he began to turn, but as he moved halfway around, the fire flared higher and cast a bright light on what was beneath the gray hairline. The tongue lolled forth from the mouth of the old man, swollen and twisted cruelly with wire so deeply sunk into the flesh that a line of blood defined it. The eyes of the Chief of the Nation were opened wide, as blank and staring as two white stones. They could not see him.

Austin cried out and forced himself awake, sitting up so suddenly from where he lay that everything about him, the papers of his students, his pencil, his reading glasses, the half-empty bottle of beer, tumbled with a crash to the floor.

"Abba Mikko," he said. "Chieftain."

He rose trembling from the sofa, straightened the things scattered about him, and headed for the bedroom, taking several deep breaths to steady himself. Before he undressed and got into bed, he set the alarm for four o'clock, giving himself almost five hours for the roundtrip to the reservation and the sweathouse and the elders who would be waiting there for him. Enough time for him to be back for the first history class of the morning at Annette High School.

Austin Bullock lay down in the still darkness of his room, thinking that he could call Phil Spurgeon to cover in the morning for him and hoping that nothing more would come to him in his sleep before the night ended.

3

The dwarf who called himself Crippled Sparrow moved from one side of the circle of onlookers to the other in a series of quick hops.

As he reached the edge of the cleared space, all the women standing at that spot but one shrank back against those behind them. The little man cackled at their movement and reached with his stubby finger toward the one who had stood firm. She was young, her hair hung past her shoulders, and her feet were bare in the dust and pinestraw of the clearing.

"And a child," he said, reaching up to poke at the elbow of the woman, "shall lead them."

She covered the place on her arm where he had touched with her hand as though nursing where hot grease had popped from a frying pan onto her skin, continuing to rub it as the little man hopped back to the middle of the open space in the stand of loblolly pines.

"You have heard in the stories of your people, the ones the old men of the Alabamas and Coushattas tell, about Rabbit and the Turkeys," he said in a voice so deep and rumbling that it did not seem to belong in a man so small. "Is it not so?"

"Yes," a few of the women said in English to match the language Crippled Sparrow was using. "It is so."

"My people in Oklahoma tell the story, too," he said. "All the native peoples know this tale. We all learn its truth, what it means to us now. Is it so?"

"Yes."

"Turkey fears Rabbit. He knows Rabbit will eat him. He will kill him with the long teeth in front of his mouth. Rabbit wants the sweet meat of Turkey, the white flesh, the dark, the blood on his lips. But Turkey is fast, can fly, can rise up, can sit in trees, can laugh, can stain all below with the waste of his body. Turkey is big, he is strong. Rabbit is weak, must live on the earth, must eat only grass and berries, must search for the sun and air by looking always up, up, never down."

The little man spread his arms as wide as he could reach, threw his head back, staring at the emptiness above him as though he could see what made up the nothing of space. He opened his mouth and showed his teeth, huge in his head and white and pointed more than a man's teeth should be. He closed and opened his jaws slowly three times as though he were chewing a thing he did not want to eat, and then he snapped his mouth shut with a pop loud enough that all the women in the circle around him heard it and flinched.

"Rabbit moved by touching his feet to the earth every step he took, for he could go in the world no other way. Is it so?"

19

"Yes."

"But Rabbit got a bag. A big bag made of cloth sewn together, and he got inside, and he pulled the mouth of the bag closed. He rolled down the highest hill in the Nation, and he laughed as he rolled over and over in the bag. And at the bottom of the hill, he got out and went back to the top with his bag, and he did it again. And again and again. And the rocks he rolled over hurt him through the bag, and the thorns pierced him and he bled from the scratches . But he did not stop. Is it not so?"

"Yes."

"Rabbit did not stop his game until Turkey asked to get inside the cloth bag and roll so he could laugh. And Rabbit allowed the great flying-high thing to enter his bag. And he drew it shut. But did he let Turkey roll down the highest hill in the Nation?"

"No."

"No, my sisters. He took the great flying thing, the thing which was above him always, he took him home to his hole in the earth, and he tore the flesh of this great bird with his teeth, the long sharp ones in front, and he drank the blood and he ate the flesh. And that thing which had been over him was now in his belly and nourished his bones and made his fur sleek and pretty and his teeth longer and more keen. Is it not so, oh women of the Alabamas and Coushattas? Is it not so?"

"Yes," the women said all together, and then one broke into a high-pitched chant of three syllables, repeated over and over, lifting her voice high enough to reach the tops of the pines which stood around the cleared circle.

At this sound, the little man called Crippled Sparrow laughed in his deep voice and began to jig back and forth from one foot to the other, his arms stretched straight up beside his head, so short the tips of the stubbed fingers barely reached above the top of the feathered headdress he wore.

"Rabbit speaks to us, Sisters," he said in English and then added some words in the language of the people he said were his in Oklahoma. "He speaks to us. Tomorrow, tomorrow, I will tell you more of what he says."

Crippled Sparrow said other things in the language which was not of the Nation, but no one understood these words. But they knew the dance he did, and the women standing nearest the little man joined him in the movements he made, and the others after a time did the same. They danced together in the cleared space in the thicket of pine and sawvines behind the house of Myrtle Big Head, and they sang with the dwarf about Rabbit until the sun left the sky and it became too dark to see.

A slow roil of smoke from the fire for heating stones told Austin Bullock where the council had built the sweatlodge. It was not in the old place, but fully two hundred yards deeper into the trees and out of sight of the clearing at the heart of the Nation, and he wondered why they had chosen a different location. Maybe they had moved it simply to get closer to the supply of wood used for the fire, or maybe one of the subchiefs had dreamed a new site for the lodge.

Probably a combination of both, he thought, pulling his car up until it nosed into the edge of the thicket. Somebody got tired of carrying lightwood and oak slabs all the way from the woods to the middle of things and then had a work-saving vision which solved the problem.

Full daylight had come by the time he got out of his car and walked into sight of the sweatlodge, and birds were singing from every direction of the cool morning. Cooper Leaping Deer was maneuvering a shovel beneath one of the stones that had been heating in the glowing core of the fire, and Thomas Two Tongues was returning from the sweatlodge with an empty shovel in his hands.

The three other members of the council of the Nation were standing near the fire, talking quietly and waiting for enough heated stones to be moved into the lodge for the ceremony to work as it should. All of the five old men had removed their outer clothing and were standing in the March chill dressed only in underwear, save for Albert Had Two Mothers who wore nothing as the Old Ones had done when they had entered the sweatlodge in the days before the white man came.

"I see you, Chiefs," Austin Bullock said, reminding himself not to appear to be looking directly at the nakedness of the men before they entered together the darkness and heat of the sweatlodge. "Ho, Alibamu, Kaosati."

"Abba Bullock," said Albert Had Two Mothers, using the term fit only for the chieftain by blood of the Nation. "Ho."

Austin looked away from the men toward the sweatlodge. It was a larger one than he had seen built before, bigger even than the one he had known as a child when his grandfather was head of the council. But that one had been made of a framework of green saplings covered with layers of palmetto fronds from the swamp in the southern part of the reservation. Its door was stitched-together deer hides, made large enough to overlap the opening left in the sweatlodge and thick enough to keep most of the heat from the fired stones within and the light outside.

The sweatlodge before him was different. Austin could see that about half of the framework was made of thin metal rods rather than hickory saplings, the covering was a combination of canvas tarpaulin, black plastic roofing liner, and several worn-out quilts, and that the opening to the lodge was an Operation Desert Storm army blanket which one of the young men of the Nation had probably brought back a few years ago from the Gulf War as part of his booty.

"A few more stones and it is ready," Albert Had Two Mothers said. "Then we leave this world for a time."

Austin nodded and began removing his clothing as the two old men with shovels finished carrying the last few stones from the coals of the fire to the sweatlodge. By the time he had stripped to his shorts, Cooper Leaping Deer had deposited the last of the heated stones in the center of the lodge and had let his shovel drop to the ground.

"Abba Bullock," Thomas Two Tongues said, "you are first to enter the sweatlodge."

"I am not Abba," Austin said and walked to the lodge and threw back the door covering, conscious that the members of the council were all looking up at the sky as if they had not heard him.

Halfway through the opening into the stifling darkness, he remembered to begin the sweatlodge song, and he sang it loudly so that the old men could hear him entering the lodge and leaving the world in the proper way. He kept his right hand in contact with the material of the covering over the frame so that he could find his way to the far side of the enclosed space, his eyes useless against the darkness of the place.

He sat on the ground, his back to the wall, and faced the inner point of the structure's center, waiting until the last of the five men of the council had lifted the blanket to the world outside and entered the lodge. The fifth man was Albert Had Two Mothers, and as he let the blanket fall shut, the lodge stood as the dark place out of the world and at the heart of the governing of the people.

Each man sang the sweatlodge song as he settled himself in the circle around the heated stones at the center of the structure, and then after all were seated, each sang a part of his own song, the one which had come to him in a dream at the time he was a boy becoming a young man of the Nation.

Austin could hear the old men groaning and wheezing in the dry heat of the lodge, their breathing loud in the darkness, but their individual songs filling the space of this small world were outside the large one where men and women lived and worked and ate and drank and watched their bodies grow old and die.

The song which had come to Austin when he was thirteen years old and alone on a dark night in the swamp which touched the edge of the Big Thicket came to him again, and he sang it for the first time in many years. It told of the red bird he had been given to keep by his father in a small cage made of green twigs and raw-hide and of how he had let it escape in a large room in a house of the Nation and of how it had flown away high above him until he could no longer see the flash of its color.

He sang of how he had failed to do the single thing his father had told him and of how he had cried for the bird to return and of how it had not. The song was of his despair and of how he had ceased finally to call for the red bird to return and of how he had fallen to the earth with eyes closed and voice hushed and hope gone. And then he sang of how the bird had returned only at the time when Austin Bullock had lost all strength and purpose. The red bird lit on his shoulder, larger even than it had been before, and it spoke his name in the language of the People and it told him what it must have to eat to live, and he had gone forth to seek the food the red bird needed, and he had thrown away the cage forever, and the bird said it would live with Austin Bullock always from that time.

His song finished, Austin sat silent, feeling the heat of the lodge call forth sweat from all parts of his body, and he thought of nothing but the red bird until the songs of all the old men around him were sung another time to their ending.

For a time all sat unspeaking in the sweatlodge, their bodies open to the heat with which the stones filled the space and their minds empty of the world outside. Austin Bullock sat listening to the breath come and go in his chest and in the chests of the council of the Nation until in a thin wailing voice Albert Had Two Mothers began to sing of the dead chieftain of the Alabama-Coushatta.

"He lives with us no more," he chanted. "Our chief has gone to stay with Abba Mikko forever. All his clothing is white. The beads upon it are many, and each is in its place. His shoes are unbroken. He hunts in that day with no ending in the meadow filled with deer that do not die. He leads his people no more. Emory Sees the Water has left the Nation so another may lead."

"He has gone," the other members of the council chanted. "It is so."

Austin Bullock remained silent, knowing what must come next and willing himself to proper conduct in the sweatlodge until the ceremony had come to its end.

"Who will lead us, the people? Who will be our first chief?" asked Albert Had Two Mothers.

"He who is with us," Thomas Two Tongues answered in the next breath. "He who is made clean in the sweatlodge with us."

"He who is purified for the task before him," Cooper Leaping Deer sang. "He who shares blood with Sees the Water."

"He whose grandfather's grandfather led the people," Had Two Mothers chanted. "He who goes back in his bones."

Austin sang nothing in return, and no one of the old men chanted further, and all waited together for a long time in the heat of

24

the sweatlodge until the second chief of the Nation rose finally and lifted the barrier to the world outside and stepped through it.

Outside, as the six men breathed in the cool air of the morning and put on the clothes of the white man again, Albert Had Two Mothers spoke quietly to Austin.

"Did you eat before you came from town?"

"No. I drank only water."

"That's good," the old man said in a pleased tone, "you remembered how to do. Come to the house and eat breakfast now. My wife will have it for us."

When Austin and Had Two Mothers drove up into the yard of the old man's house, smoke was rising from the stove pipe on the roof, and the screen door to the front room was open.

"Who has the basketball goal?" Austin asked, nodding toward the hoop on a pole near the side of the dwelling. The earth in front of the pole was beaten flat and shiny from use.

"My great-grandson," Albert Had Two Mothers said. "He puts it up all day long."

"I don't know him. How old is he?"

"He is ten. You will know him soon. He is a pure shooter. No defense."

Inside at the table eating biscuits and fried pork, Austin looked up at the old man across from him and began to speak carefully.

"Sees the Water did not drown."

"No, the sheriff wants to say he did, but he did not. It would make it easy if he had died of water, but Emory did not go that way."

"What killed him?"

"I do not think it was the dwarf, but some people want to believe it was. You want some more meat?"

"No, Abba," Austin said. "I've had enough. Who is the dwarf?"

"You don't visit much any more, do you, Austin? I'm surprised you haven't heard of him."

"I stay busy this time of year, you know. Annette is in the playoffs, and I must always teach my classes."

"Oh, yes," said the old man. "You have reasons. He is from Oklahoma. He has come to teach the young people in the pageant how to do the old dances. He calls himself a consultant from the Choctaw."

"You mean in the festival, this Beyond the Sundown?"

"Tourists love this stuff, the people from Houston tell us. All the Nations in the west put on festivals. They say it's a money-maker."

"Money is good," Austin said. "You've got to have it."

"Tell me about it," Albert Had Two Mothers said. "He says his Choctaw name is Crippled Sparrow, this dwarf consultant."

"Whoa," Austin said and reached for his coffee cup. "That name wouldn't be very politically correct with the white teachers where I work."

"What does that mean?"

"You don't want to know. It takes a long time to explain it. I'll tell you sometime when you've got a day to listen. Why would some people believe this Crippled Sparrow drowned Emory?"

"He wasn't drowned," the old man said. "Somebody choked our chief from behind. Some say this poppoyom or maybe a Big Man-Eater did it."

"Choked him?"

"With a string or a wire."

"I hadn't heard that."

"The sheriff's people don't want to get into that is why you haven't heard it. But I know, and I'm going to make them know it, too. And the reason why some people believe Crippled Sparrow did it is just flat-out superstition."

"How do you know Abba Emory was choked with a wire?"

"The best way to know," Albert Had Two Mothers said. "I dreamed it."

"You know, Second Chief," Austin said, looking at the cloudy eyes of the old man, "last night I had a dream about wire and Chief Emory. It was wrapped around his tongue."

"There you go," Had Two Mothers said, lifting both hands up before him and looking back and forth from one to the other. "What did I tell you? We both dreamed it, and it is so."

"That's not superstition," Austin said, "but thinking the dwarf from Oklahoma is a poppoyom, now that is."

"Sure, being a dwarf, that comes from parents. You know, what it says on the television. Genes and inheritance."

"But the poppoyom are in the old stories. The little men who live in the forest and drive the people of the Nation crazy when they run into them."

"You don't have to tell me about the stories," Had Two Mothers said. "But I know the difference between folklore and the truth and so do you, Abba Bullock."

"About that, Albert," Austin said, "you know I can't function as the first chief of the Nation, no matter who my grandfather was. I just came out here to talk to you and the council and to hear what you know about Chief Emory. I'm a teacher and a coach, and I've got a job in town. That's where my life is."

The old man leaned back in his chair and looked up at the ceiling above him. "To tell you the truth, I don't see much wiggle room for you, Abba Bullock," he said. "You study on it, and let me know when your mind is right."

Austin sat for a moment and said nothing in reply, listening to the sound of Albert's wife in the front room and to the bouncing of a basketball on the earth in front of the goal outside.

"Will you talk to the sheriff again?" he finally asked.

"Oh, yes."

"I will visit him in town. When will they do the funeral for Chief Emory?"

"White man's funeral tomorrow at church. Alabama-Coushatta at new moon. Next Tuesday."

"I'll see you then," Austin said and rose to leave. "He starts early every morning, your great-grandson."

"He wants to get in an hour before the bus comes. Look at his jump-shot when you leave. Tell me whose move that looks like."

On his way to the car, Austin stopped and watched the young boy working in front of the goal. The basketball was a fairly new one, stamped with the logo of the Annette Independent School District, and Austin wondered how the boy had sneaked it out of the equipment room. It was probably a late night raid well planned in advance, plenty of honor for all the young warriors involved.

"Let me see your set-shot," Austin said, and the boy promptly sank two in a row from the right side of the earthen court and then moved to the left to launch a couple from that point.

"Good enough," Austin said and moved toward his car. "I'll be seeing you in a couple of years, I expect."

"Thank you, Abba Bullock," the boy replied and drove the basket for a lay-up.

By tomorrow, Austin thought, the council will have trained every kid, every dog and every bird on the reservation to call me that. It is a nonstop struggle to find one name I can be allowed to live with on my own.

The highway back to Annette was empty, and he drove fast enough between the banks of pines and the fields plowed for planting to be in the parking lot well before the bell rang for the first period of the day. Let's do some reconstruction this morning, he said to himself as he walked into the classroom, let's get Rutherford B. Hayes elected one more time.

4

The squirrels that had told him someone else was in the swamp were still barking as Charlie Sun-Singer eased through a tangle of yaupon and palmetto fronds toward the sounds of water ahead. He was eleven years old, and the squirrels were still his brothers. Thus, they spoke to him when he left the clearings and entered the thickets and marshlands of the Nation, letting him know where to look and how to listen and when to move and when to stay still.

Charlie Sun-Singer stood silent, his mouth open to hear better and stared intently at the source of the sounds of movement and activity beyond the screen of vegetation. The chirk of the squirrels came loudly again, and the boy took several slow steps forward, careful not to lift his feet so high that water would splash and mud would suck at them. Two more and he could see through the branches of a downed sweetgum tree the bulk of two men with their backs to him.

Blank eyes, both of them in khaki shirts, pants and rubber boots up to their knees. One of them pointed to a spot near where they stood, and Charlie Sun-Singer strained to see what was indicated, but all he could make out was the surface of swamp water, no different there from the place where he knelt hidden behind the sweetgum.

The other man lifted a long silvery rod with a wire attached to one of its ends and shoved it into the earth beneath the water, not stopping until only a few inches remained visible. He uncoiled some of the wire from a reel on his back and then moved ahead to another spot where the other man stood waiting, pushing another rod and wire deep into the floor of the marsh.

The squirrels in the water oak above fussed a few more times at the white men and then scampered to the highest branch of the tree and leapt to another, vanishing somewhere deeper into the swamp in a few seconds. Charlie Sun-Singer watched the two men work until they seemed to have run out of silver rods, and he began to ease himself backward to leave until he noticed that the first man, the one who pointed to the places where the rods belonged, was beginning to attach all the wire ends to something that looked like a big radio or a tape player.

After he had finished, he turned some dials and knobs, staring closely at the instrument in his hands and then he pressed one button among the others before him. He looked at the other man and spoke for the first time since Charlie Sun-Singer had been watching.

"Is she here or not?" he said. "What do you bet?"

A thin high whine began to come from the instrument, and it was the other man who pointed this time, his hand held out toward the pattern of silver rods and wires planted in the water land of the Nation. A small rumble, like that of far-away thunder somewhere deep in the Big Thicket, came from beneath the water of the marsh, and the man holding the instrument tapped three times with a fingernail on the face of one of the dials.

"If that's not a seismic echo off metal," he said, "I don't know my grandmother. It's in this quadrant, Earl, and we got something to show the man in Houston."

By the time Charlie Sun-Singer had gotten out of the swamp and run the two miles to the place on the highway where the schoolbus stopped to pick up the Alabamas and Coushattas for the daily trip to Annette, his pants were almost dry but the signs of mud and clay were heavy upon them.

"Where have you been?" his brother Milton said. "Playing in the damn woods again? You almost missed the bus."

"I just watched two blank eyes looking for something in the swamp," Charlie Sun-Singer answered, dodging the careless swipe Milton took at him. "They stuck wires in it and made the water blow up. It sounded like the swamp was coughing."

"Quit making up stories and knock some of that dirt off your britches," Milton said. "That bus is full of girls. You fixing to make me look bad."

"They sure look bad, don't they?" Jim Mellard said, the expression on his face that of a man who had just bitten into something hard and felt a breakage somewhere in his mouth. He was afraid to touch his tongue to it to see what it was, but he knew he had to eventually. "Piss-poor bad."

Austin Bullock grunted and when the head coach looked toward him for more comment, he added some words. "They always look bad in practice," he said. "Especially my folks. You know how they act when it's not real to them."

"I've got used to that," Mellard said. "I remember twenty-five years ago how you always scared the punk out of me. But, hell, no matter how much they dog it in practice, they generally hitting their shots."

"Well, yeah," Austin said, "generally."

He watched a fifteen-year old sophomore guard, pressed a little by a defender, suddenly sling the ball up from beyond three point range toward the goal. It hit the backboard like a brick and bounced all the way off court into the third row of bleachers.

"See yonder," Mellard said in a hurt tone and began pulling at the front of his T shirt as though he needed more space to draw a breath. "You heard any cotton since you been out here this afternoon?"

"No," Austin admitted, "not much."

"Tell you what I been hearing," Mellard said. "Metal, metal, metal."

While someone scrambled to retrieve the basketball from where it had ended up in the bleachers, the Annette High starters stood panting and bent over on the court, a few of them cutting their eyes at the two men watching from the half-court line.

"Don't you be looking over here," Coach Mellard called out. "I can't help you from acting like a bunch of junior high kids. It ain't nothing me and the Chief can do for you."

"Slow it down," Austin said, and walked toward the boy who had just thrown the ball as if it were a rock. "When he starts to press you like that, you plant and rotate and look to pass. See."

He gestured for the ball and when it was thrown to him, he demonstrated to the sophomore what he had just told him. "And it's the responsibility of the off-guard and the forward on this side to know when you're in trouble and come to help. Wait on them."

The sophomore, a slight Coushatta youth named Byron Dips Weevil, took the ball and dribbled it and practice began again in the Annette High School Bulldog fieldhouse.

"You wouldn't think it, just looking at them, that that sorry bunch would be playing in the regionals come Friday week, would you?" Jim Mellard said. "I flat guarantee you that Sweetwater bunch ain't acting like this in practice."

"Can't ever tell," Austin said. "They might look worse than we do."

"Huh," said Mellard. "And this here's my last go-round. I would purely love to go out a winner in my last year, the way I come in in my first."

"I bet you will, Coach," Austin said. "More than likely, I imagine."

"I'd like for you to come in as head coach with that state win under your belt, too, Austin," Mellard said. "You are thinking about that, ain't you?"

Austin waited until the next shot went up from the practice floor before he answered. It was a nice jumpshot from about ten feet by Felder Ferguson, and it popped the net as it went through.

"I haven't changed my mind. I really don't want the job, Coach."

"Good lick," Mellard yelled at the players. "That's the time, boys."

He looked at Austin. "Why the hell not? You ain't talking sense now. You know what I think about that way of doing."

31

"I want to keep on teaching as much as I am now. I like it. And I don't want the responsibility of having to deal with these folks in town about the team and the prospects and all that stuff day in and day out."

"You never was afraid to take the big shot when it come right down to it on the court, though, was you?" Mellard said. "Remember that second overtime in the state game with Milby? One point behind, you brought it down with that Mexican kid all over you like a damn blanket and hit that twenty footer at the buzzer. Ever think about that?"

"I was a kid then," Austin said. "I didn't know any better than not to be paralyzed."

"Well, goddamn it," Mellard said, "you ain't stung with a whole nest of wasps now, are you?"

"Sometimes I feel like it," Austin said. "Sometimes I do." He pointed at the flow of play on the court. "Looky there. They've perked right up."

5

The supper crowd was small at the White Station Cafe, so Austin Bullock saw where Walker Lewis was sitting as soon as he walked past the cashier's counter. He was in the next to last booth near the kitchen, and he was looking suspiciously at something stuck in the tines of his fork when Austin slipped into the seat across from him.

"What you got there, Sheriff?" Austin said. "A piece of fried fish?"

"This here's the fisherman's platter they call it, and it's supposed to be a piece of fish, but damned if it don't look like an oyster to me." He pried what was concerning him off the fork with his bread knife and let it drop on the edge of the plate. "I bet that's what it is."

"Nuh uh, Walker. White Station's not going to spring for nothing high-dollar like an oyster on the fisherman's platter. Closest thing you'd find to an oyster in here is a catfish eye."

"Damn, Austin, I'm trying to eat what I got to pay for here," the Sheriff said, attacking a different area of his plate.

"You know about Chief Emory, I reckon," he went on. "I bet you already been out there, huh?"

"Yeah, I have," Austin said and turned to speak to the waitress approaching the table. "The vegetable plate, ma'am. Iced tea, no rolls, just cornbread."

"They's marks on his neck, all right," Sheriff Lewis said. "And the medical examiner from Lufkin is looking and is going to tell us something soon as he figures it out. You don't have to worry. I know what they've been telling you out yonder, but put your mind at ease."

"I know. I never doubted you'd do everything you was supposed to, Walker. But the thing is, Sees the Water never would have been in that hole in Long King Creek on his own."

"Bad medicine, you mean," Lewis said. "Against his religion."

"Something like that," Austin said and watched the waitress put a glass of water and a bigger one of iced tea in front of him. "I just don't believe he'd place himself near what he thought was deep water."

"Yeah, but in a murder, see, you got to have a reason for it to happen. Something's got to be at stake for somebody to kill somebody else. Got to be a motive. The man that does the killing's got to believe it's something in it for him. Hell, even a crazy man think's it's an advantage to him for the one he's killing to be dead. Understand what I'm saying, Austin?"

"Yeah," Austin said. "It's subject to the same laws as history. Like everything else is."

"Whatever you'd say about that history stuff's fine with me. You the one that went to Rice University, not me. But I do know one thing I've learned about killings: The craziest, sorriest, most no-account bastard that ever did one thinks he had a reason to want somebody dead. At least at the time, that is."

"Oh, I'm agreeing with you," Austin said, stirring his tea and watching the progress of the woman carrying his supper to him from across the dining room of the White Station Cafe. "Don't get me wrong."

"You tell me then anybody on the reservation that'd see a reason to kill Chief Emory, or anybody from outside that'd be out there trying to rob that old man that just looking at him you could tell never had a damn dime in his pocket or anywhere else neither. Just name me one."

Sheriff Lewis pointed down at his plate with his fork before he cut off a bite to raise to his mouth. "This here piece is catfish, I can tell."

"I think everything you've been saying is right," Austin said. "All we got to do now is just put it to work."

"Yeah," the Sheriff said, chewing his catfish nugget. "That's right." He reached for another portion and then looked up at Austin. "What do you mean?"

"Like you said," Austin answered him and began to heap crowder peas on his fork. "Act like an historian. Find that cause for the effect."

"Effect?"

"Yeah, the effect is a dead old man who was the Stated Chief of the Alabamas and Coushattas. The cause is what'll tell us who wanted him that way."

"Yeah, that's right," Walker Lewis said. "You know this platter ain't bad once you get past the oysters. It'll eat."

Most of the light had faded from the sky as Austin drove home, and he could tell from the way the air smelled that the rain which had held off all day was impatient to get started. The old beavers in the sky would soon begin pounding their flat tails against the pond, he thought to himself, remembering the way his mother had given him the Alabama-Coushatta explanation for a thunderstorm. Then the people would hear the booming of the beavers at work and the water they splashed from the great pond just beyond the edge of the sky would begin to come down in great drops for a long time, falling with great force because of the long distance they fell.

Or it could just be a cold front moving through Coushatta County, he thought, headed for the Gulf, and he pulled the Honda into the driveway.

He flipped on the television and watched the local news out of Houston for as long as he could stand it and switched channels to a documentary on the failing fishing industry in the Pacific Northwest. Twenty minutes of that, and then an hour reading a new handbook on student evaluation of teachers which Principal Prongle had assigned him to present for discussion to his fellow instructors at Annette High School left Austin tired enough to try for some sleep before Laura would arrive in the middle of the night.

Sleep would be fitful, he knew. When his daughter was out of sight and unscheduled for an appearance at home, he never worried a second about her, though he realized that in fact she might be roaming the streets of Houston with her friends at all hours, full of beer and God knew what else, looking for something dangerous. But that was all right and had no psychic cost. What rattled the nerves was waiting for her to show up at some announced hour, a situation which reconverted him automatically into the anxious father with his daughter away at locations unknown.

It all made for double-mindedness and a few rough hours trying to coax some dreamless sleep out of the supply of soft fibers from the heart of the thistles kept by Abba Mikko in his large house to be granted to those people of the Nation deserving of true rest.

That image in mind, he told himself he would try to work his way into a memory of one of the tales told to children of the Alabama-Coushatta people, lead his mind into playing with a story of animals which talked with men and women who listened and heard them. Leave the instruments of evaluation constructed by committees safely contained in the drawer of some mass-produced desk and slip away into the world where every object was itself and like nothing else around it.

Maybe that'll do the trick, he thought, lying on his back on his bed and feeling the first hint of a drift of disconnection beginning behind his closed eyes. He breathed deeply, slowly, and sensed the gap becoming wider, deeper, possible. How turtle got his red eyes, he announced to himself in the language of the Nation, that's a good story to think about. There's water in it, and a slow journey, and a long way to go before everybody gets to where they're headed.

Two hours later, Austin sat up straight in bed wondering if the water he heard dripping was in his dream or in the world outside. The room was dark but for the red glow on his answering machine, and as he held his breath to listen, the only sound was the slow rain in the gutters of his house.

Something in the tail end of a dream tugged at him, and he closed his eyes to try to remember, but the only thing that rose up for him to see was the outline of a man's head, featureless as though the sun was directly behind it and all that was visible was silhouette. He knew, though, who it was by the shape and the way the long hair was plastered to the skull by water—Emory, Chief of the Nation, who could not breathe and could not speak.

"Abba Emory," Austin said aloud, knowing what he spoke would be of no use to anyone, "lie down in your new clean house and rest with the Old Ones."

He went to the kitchen and got a pot of coffee going, and he was drinking the second cup when he heard the key turn in the front door.

"Did I keep you up past your bedtime?" his daughter asked, dragging a duffel bag through the door. "We got away late, but I didn't want to waste time stopping to call. God, the traffic in Houston."

"Yeah," Austin said, walking to the door to embrace her, "it is a sight, isn't it?"

6

Laura was still asleep the next morning when Austin left early for the reservation, and she would probably still be that way at noon, the time he intended to be back home. She liked to say she didn't need as much sleep as her middle-aged father, but the fact was that she just took her rest on a different schedule. She was like her mother had been, up all hours in the middle of the night and then unconscious half the next day.

Or at least the way Ellen had been until things reached the final stage with her, Austin thought as he backed the car into the street and turned in the direction of Texas 190. Then every prediction had become wrong and every guess as good as the next one. Knowing what his wife would do and when she would do it was as certain to Austin at that time as judging which crow would fly up first when a boy threw a stone into a flock of them.

But don't they call it a congress of crows, he asked himself as he waited to turn left at the traffic light on the highway. Even worse, even stranger.

That's what you get, Gemar Round Head had told him one of those late nights Austin had sought him out to talk about what was happening with the woman he had married. What did you expect, hooking up with a berdache and a blank eyes at that?

I never thought, Austin had said, I never thought at all. I didn't know you were supposed to think when what you were doing was feeling. There you go then, Gemar had said, sipping at his whiskey, see?

The sun was well above the tree-line when Austin drove across the cattle-guard marking the entrance to the Alabama-Coushatta Nation, its rays turning the pines into a dark outline on the horizon. Up ahead on the ribbon of asphalt stretching toward the heart of the reservation, Austin could see a sheet of water crossing the road, but he knew that was a mirage, early for this time of year. Such an unseasonal appearance would mean something to some of the oldest people of the Nation, but what it forecast Austin didn't know. He made a mental note not to mention the phenomenon to the people he would talk to today. Otherwise he would have to listen politely to fifteen minutes of interpretation, and he didn't feel up to it this morning.

Particularly, he wouldn't mention anything to Laura about that or anything associated when he got back home. He had enough to tell her about Chief Emory without having to be a scholarly informant to his own daughter about her Native-American roots, as she had begun to call her father's side of her heritage. She had always as a child wanted to listened to stories, but since she had gone to Rice and fallen into that den of anthropologists and folklorists she wore him out.

Austin guessed that was a healthier response than what had been the prevalent one with the youth of the Nation when he was Laura's age. He could remember times when he was away from the reservation, on out-of-town basketball trips, say, or expeditions to Beaumont or Houston when he and his companions would tell any lie to avoid being labeled as Indian by the white people they encountered. They would call themselves Mexicans, Hindus, Peruvians. Once even he remembered Frank Shoes swearing to a white girl in a honky-tonk in Galveston that he and the other two Alabamas with him were the sons of Arabian sheiks in Texas to buy quarterhorses to improve the breed back home.

"I passed for white," Austin said aloud as he turned off the highway and headed the car down a thin dirt road pointing south. "I've been outside a lot in the sun, see. My family on both sides have all got brown eyes."

In about a half-mile he came to a clearing in the pine thicket with three shotgun houses lined up in a row so precise they looked as though they had been placed on a drawing board. He drove to the last one in the series and pulled up about fifty feet from the front porch and killed the Honda's engine. To the left of the structure was a large satellite dish which someone had decorated with red Christmas tree bunting wound through the mesh and what looked like circular pieces of aluminum foil the size of saucers placed randomly around the edge of the metal structure.

As Austin studied the effect, he heard the spring on the screen-door squeal as someone pushed it open.

"Ho, Delbert Sees the Water," Austin said and walked toward the house, his hand out to the man stepping down off the porch. "Is it too early for me to see you?"

"The time is good to see you," Delbert said in the greeting formula of the Nation. "In the sun or the shadows."

Delbert had gained much weight, Austin noticed, filling his clothing until it stretched tight around him, the pants cinched beneath the belly and the white T shirt riding above it.

"Cousin," Austin said, shaking Delbert's hand, "I have not seen you in a long time. You've been eating well."

"Yes," Delbert said. "And you shake hands just like a white man."

They both smiled and then walked together to the edge of the porch and sat down, looking across the road toward the stand of loblolly pine, sawvines, and yaupon facing the house.

"I wanted to see you before the funeral for Abba Emory," Austin said, "so we can talk."

"There is much talk now about many things," Delbert Sees the Water said. "Many people want to say a lot, but the right one does not speak."

"Who is this right one?"

"No one knows but the red bird maybe or the fox."

"Or the snake who lives in Long King Creek."

"He knows," Delbert agreed. "But he does not use the language of the People to help us understand. He has never done that."

"He will not," Austin said. "Never did he in the stories of the Old Ones."

Both men fell silent and watched three crows in the top of a pin oak tree across the road hop from branch to branch until finally one, then the other two flew off in the direction of the sunrise. After the birds had become black dots growing smaller and smaller in the distance, Austin spoke again, this time in English.

"What was your father doing by himself near that hole in Long King Creek?"

"Hell, I don't know, Austin. It wasn't like him. Everybody knows that. Other than getting himself killed, I don't know what to say."

"Had anything been on his mind? Was he worried about something?"

"He was always worried about stuff. He took the job seriously, you know, more than he should have. He thought being the stated chief had all the old obligations. Speaker for the People, part of the circle, all that stuff they used to tell about the chief of the Nation when we was kids. You know the drill."

"Yeah, too damn well, I think sometimes," Austin said. "Did you see him that afternoon?"

"Naw, I been hauling pulp wood all last week, sun-up to sun-down." Delbert gestured toward the green GMC truck parked in the front yard, its hood propped open with a length of two-by-four. "I done ran that thing until the water pump give out on me here the day it happened."

"I see what you mean," Austin said looking at the truck. "Had Chief Emory talked to you about anything in particular in the last week or two? I mean, you know, anything on his mind he was concerned about?"

"Well, fact is, and I hate to admit it now, but I had got to where I didn't listen real close to him these last few years. You know how it is when your folks get old and want to talk about stuff that happened fifty years ago."

"Right," Austin said. "Or four hundred years ago. Or more."

"But I will say this," Delbert said, leaning forward to look at the earth beneath the eaves of the house where rainwater had worn a trough in the sand, "my father was sure to God worried about the swamp these last few weeks."

"The Big Thicket Swamp?"

"That's right. Something had happened or was going to happen down yonder that was bothering him. He was on it all the time. Wouldn't let it alone."

"What was it ? Did he say?"

"It's hard to sort it out from whatever else he was talking about. You know how he always mixed everything up that's happening now with all them old stories and dreams and songs and stuff. Like all the rest of the old folks do, you know. Everything all connected up and strung together, now and then, what they see and what they believe they see. Today and yesterday and tomorrow all in a wad."

"Uh huh," Austin said and waited for Delbert Sees the Water to go on.

"But this swamp business that was on his mind had something to do with the water." Delbert turned his head and looked at Austin.

"You mean the springs and creeks that feed into it down there?"

"No, I don't think so. The Chief kept talking about water underneath the ground. The big river under the swamp he said. He said the blank eyes wanted what's in it."

"You don't suppose he meant oil, do you?"

"No, I asked him if that's what was worrying him, and he said it wasn't. He said that drilling that B and E did way up close to the village was already over and everybody knows that didn't amount to nothing."

"Caused a little flurry here a few years back," Austin said. "We all thought we were going to be as rich as the Choctaws. Everybody driving a Cadillac."

"Right," Delbert said and looked at his GMC pulpwood truck. "And the little dab they did get out of them holes wasn't enough to keep that thing greased up, much less buy me a new one."

"And that's all he said to you, then?"

"Yep. I can't figure it any better than that. And I still don't know who'd want to kill that poor old man. All I do is think about it."

"I think Sheriff Lewis will come up with something. He's serious about it."

"I hope so," Delbert said and eased himself off the edge of the porch. "I got to get that truck to running."

"I'll see you, cousin," Austin said, "at the funeral."

After he got into the Honda and started it, he spoke out the window to Delbert Sees the Water, who was leaning over to look into the guts of his GMC. "You suppose it would be all right to try to talk to your mother?"

"Sure," Delbert said. "But she ain't going to say anything you'd be able to understand."

"I imagine so," Austin said and put the car in gear.

"Hey," Delbert said. "You going to do it ? Be the man?"

"What'd you mean? Go see her?"

"You know what I'm talking about," Delbert Sees the Water said. "Abba Bullock."

"I can't do that," Austin said and waved. "I got to get my own truck running."

By the time he reached the first turn in the road, Austin could see through his rearview mirror that Delbert had returned to staring into his engine as though by looking long enough he could heal what was gone wrong in the works.

Wait and see, be patient, see what'll turn up. A part of the mindset of the Alabama-Coushatta people that had always given

Austin the most trouble in getting on with his life in the world away from the reservation. The way people had acted when the first B and E oil strike came in was an example.

Now the oil and money would flow, everybody thought, and life would become a redman version of the old Dallas television show. The white man would cheat them, sure, but there would be enough left over after the J. R. Ewings of the world had taken their cut for the Alabamas and Coushattas to share the wealth, get credit, buy cars and bass boats and new clothes for all the family.

A lot of the people who had jobs quit them and sat on their front porches, waiting for the rigs to punch holes that would bubble black crude and bring the world outside up to the doorstep. But only two wells had come in, Austin remembered as he maneuvered the car over a washed-out place in the road as big as a washtub, and those ended up producing only a little over ten barrels a day after steady pumping. The rest were dry holes into which children of the Nation had dropped chunk stones to listen to the echoes until the sides of the excavations had fallen in on themselves.

But poor people lived on hope and patience, no matter their color, and maybe something else would show up down the road, bright and shining like the sunlight falling on a flock of egrets floating above the Big Thicket's swamps.

Until then, keep the water pumps fixed and the pulpwood trucks running and wait for something to happen, someday, amen.

Smoke was rising thinly from the flue pipe over the kitchen of the house in which Chief Emory had lived and where his widow now sat in the backroom alone. When Austin Bullock stepped up on the porch and looked through the screendoor, he could see Noma get up from her chair and move toward him. He addressed her through the door.

"Mother of my cousins, wife of my uncle," he said, "how is it with you now?"

"I cook for those who come to my house," the old woman said, repeating the words she had learned when she first became a wife. "Do you want to eat?"

42

"No, my aunt. I am not hungry," Austin said as the formula for his first response to the offer would have him do.

"You want nothing?"

"Only a drink of water."

After the woman had brought him a cup from the bucket on the shelf in the kitchen, Austin drank its contents in one long swallow and handed it back to her.

"No one is here but you, Aunt," he said.

"Many want to come sit with me and talk, but I told them to wait until after the middle of the day."

Noma was wearing a brown dress with an arrangement of artificial cherries pinned to the front, probably the outfit she used when she walked to the Presbyterian Mission Church each Sunday, Austin thought, noting that she had let her hair hang untended and lank. It reached to the middle of her back, gray and uncombed and undecorated, and it would be that way until her dead husband was buried according to the way of the Nation.

"I am sorry I have come at the time you wanted to be in your house alone," he said. "I will return when it is right."

"No, it is for the others, not for you. I would speak with you in the house of your uncle, Abba Bullock. Sit and talk."

"For a time, then, Aunt," Austin said and reached to touch the hand of the old woman.

"I saw my cousin this morning. Delbert told me about Chief Emory on that day when the bad thing happened."

"Before he went out the door the last time," Noma said, "when he was leaving this little house in the world, Abba Emory showed me a thing to give to you. He said it was a thing you must understand."

She walked across the room to a table against the far wall and removed the lid from a pinestraw and reed basket woven in a pattern of lightning and clouds and dyed deep yellow and blue. What she brought back was small enough that it was almost hidden in her hand until she dropped it into his outstretched palm. It was a metal disk, a dark golden color and heavy for its size, and Austin recognized it to be identical to the Spanish medal he had been given as a child as emblem of the chieftain's heritage of the blood of his grandfathers. It had been

43

a gift to an Alabama chief from a king across the water in the time before the People came to Texas, and it was handed down to each leader before his time was come.

"I do not understand, my Aunt," Austin said, turning the medal in his hand to see the stampings on it. "Chief Emory told me when he gave me the king's medal that it was the only one and that there had never been another."

"Yet you see it," the woman said. "It did not talk to him. Abba Emory said, this other one. He said you would know the way to ask it the right questions. You would make it speak."

"Where did my uncle find this?"

"In the Big Thicket swamp on the morning of that day. It is of the water, he said."

"Did he find it in Long King Creek? Or in the swamp water itself? Did Chief Emory say?"

"He said," Noma answered, her eyes closed as she spoke each word slowly, "that it is not of the water on the earth, but of the water beneath."

"The water beneath," Austin repeated.

"Yes, the big water underground. The water the blank eyes know."

"My Aunt, thank you for this medal my uncle sends to me. I will try to understand it," Austin said and slipped the disk into his shirt pocket, feeling its weight tug coldly at the cloth, heavier than it ought to be.

"Can you tell me if Abba Emory was afraid that day? Did he think a bad thing was waiting for him?"

"No. He did not speak of such to me. Now I do not want to talk of my husband on that day any more. I do not want to think of the time he was on the earth in this house. The place I will see him again, that is where I want to point my eyes."

The old woman bowed her head, crossed her arms over her breast and fell silent. She would have nothing else to say until after the Nation's funeral for her husband, Austin knew, and he began to walk toward the door, trying to think of the proper words to offer in farewell to her. They had something to do with the feast her husband would have prepared for her when she came to be with him in the great meadow after her life in the world had ended, and they would have to include the naming of things there to eat.

"My Aunt," Austin Bullock said, pausing halfway through the door, "you will eat the food Abba Emory will have waiting. Corn, beans, squash, many berries and wild peaches." Was that all, he asked himself as he stepped onto the porch, have I left out the one she needs to hear? Is there something else I should have named to comfort her?

The old woman alone in her house remained silent, and Austin hurried to the car to leave her where she wanted to be. As he closed the door and reached to turn the ignition key, he thought he could hear her begin to chant in a high quaver, but the sound of the engine soon covered that. He hoped he was right.

As he backed the car around to head down the road, he thought suddenly of huckleberries, blue-black against the green of the leaves behind them, huckleberries in a low dark part of the underbrush of one of the thickets of the Nation. He should have called them by name, he remembered, seeing the deep contrast of colors in his mind, he should have called each thing by its rightful name.

Laura was up when Austin walked through the door of his house a few minutes before noon. She had found some dry cereal left over from her last visit home nearly a month ago, and she was eating that from the package and chasing it with diet-cola.

"Hey," she said, looking up from a book on the kitchen, "back from the reservation already. How can you stand to drink this old off-brand coke, Daddy?"

"It's not coke," Austin said. "It's Mr. Sam's Diet-Cola. I can't afford the high-priced stuff and support a daughter at Rice at the same time. I tell you what, though. I do look forward to the time when I can go into the big store and pay cash for a six-pack of Classic Coke."

"I bet this stuff lasts you for a while all right. Plus it might take a few pounds off your tum-tum, too."

"Girl, you're looking at a man with a washboard belly. Totally ripped," Austin said, opening the refrigerator. "How'd you know I've been at the reservation?"

45

"Your eyes, your mouth. You had on your Native-American look when you came in the door."

"What look is that? I always look the same as far as I know."

"Oh, yeah? Well, it's not the same look you have when you're teaching a class or sitting on the bench at a basketball game."

"You're just seeing things, child. You read too many anthropology books. I'm the same man, here and there, day and night. I thought I had some orange juice in here."

"I drank it," Laura said. "Drink some Uncle Sam's."

"Mr. Sam's."

"All I know is when you come back from the Nation or any other time you're thinking about things out there, your eyes go flat as stones and you crawl in behind them where nobody can see you."

Austin grunted and popped open a can of cola. "Oh, yeah? And what about when my eyes look human? What then?"

"I didn't mean you don't look human when you're being an Alabama-Coushatta," Laura said. "It's just a different dispensation that takes over. You just look a lot realer than when you're being a history teacher or a basketball coach for the blank eyes."

"Blank eyes," Austin said, sitting down across the table from his daughter. "I can tell what dispensation's been working for you this morning, anthro-major. You're half blank eyes yourself, remember."

"Takes one to know one…"

"Yeah, but we're not talking psyche here. We're talking blood, we're talking genetic inheritance, child."

"You think I don't know it, Daddy?" Laura said, her mouth pinching suddenly at the corners. "You think I don't know that everyday of my life? You think I don't feel it all the time?"

"Hey," Austin said, reaching to touch her hand, "I don't know what I just stirred up here, but I'm sorry. I was just playing, and I thought you were, too. What's wrong?"

"I know, I know. It's nothing for you to worry about. I've just been thinking a lot about her lately, and it seems like everything I do at school, papers and listening to lectures and reading, all leads back to the same thing."

"What's that, sweetheart?"

"Oh, me. Just me. I don't know who I am any more, if I ever did. And I seem to know less the more I learn about things."

"Nobody ever knows that," Austin said, "who they are, for sure. It changes all the time."

"The people in the Nation do. They don't even have to think about it. It just comes with the territory. They're just who they are, and they accept it."

"It's not that simple," Austin said. "I wish it was. Every Alabama and Coushatta on the reservation wonders all the time where they are and how they got there and where they're going next. They're as scared as I am all the time."

"Only because of the blank eyes," Laura said, keeping her head down and refusing to look at him directly, "only because of the damage the white patriarchal structure has caused and continues to cause. Only because they're people of color."

"I see," Austin said, leaning back from the table. "I see. That's where you're coming from."

"That's where I am," Laura said, now looking up at him, "and that's where you are, too, if you'd only admit it."

"I admit all kinds of things all the time," he said, "every minute of my life."

"Let me ask you something, Daddy," she said, "one thing. Why didn't we move back to the reservation after my mother left us? Why didn't you let me grow up there with our people?"

"I have spent my entire life trying to get off that reservation," Austin replied, feeling the blood rise up hot in his throat and face, "and I would be damned if I was going to slide back into it and make you start where I had to. You were born outside it, and I'd never put you in the situation I've spent my whole life working my way out of."

"Daddy, don't you know I've never been out of your situation and that I never will be? Can't you accept that? I know it more and more everyday. And I want to do something about it . Don't you?"

Austin took a sip of cola. It tasted flat and metallic. "What do you mean? Do what about what? What am I supposed to do other than what I'm doing? I go to work everyday and get to bed late and try my best to keep everything headed in the same direction."

"I'm not talking about you in your role as care provider," Laura said. "Nobody could fault you about that, about living up to your responsibilities. It's something else, something more fundamental you keep closing your eyes to. I mean letting yourself accept your identity. Letting yourself, I don't know, feel you're a part of the Great Circle. That's what I'm trying to do."

"I think I get you," Austin said. "I see where you're going. You want to go native, huh? Move to the reservation, maybe marry some sit-on-the-porch and raise a bunch of little red brothers and sisters. Cook on a wood stove and think about corn-dance ritual."

"I can't believe you're saying these things to me. You won't accord me any intellectual respect." Laura's voice broke on the last word, and she lifted both hands to her face.

"I'm sorry," Austin said. "Yes, I do. I've got a lot on my mind, and it's all just boiled over on me. Don't pay any attention to what I said."

"It's all right," Laura said after a minute. "It's just that you're always so earnest. You believe in the Western myth so much, and you don't want to listen to any challenge to it."

"The western myth? You mean Horace Greeley or Clint Eastwood?"

"You know what I mean. Perfectibility, faith in change, self-improvement."

"Well," Austin said in a careful voice, "not to argue any more, but I only know what I read."

"That's not what I'm talking about. You know a lot more than that, but you won't let yourself admit it." Laura paused and looked at Austin with the eyes that always put him in mind of her mother's. It had never seemed fair for both of them to gang up on him like that.

"How's the classwork going?" he asked. "Are you keeping up with your assignments?"

"Fine. Everything's clicking right along. Can I say one more thing, and then I'll leave you alone?"

"Why not? But you've got to promise to let up on the old man."

"Do you know how the whites in Annette look at you?"

"You mean as a group? No, I just try to take people one at the time, white or red or black or yellow or in-between."

"I'm not talking about individuals," his daughter said. "I want to stay beyond that. The power structure likes you. You fill a quota at the high school, and you have great symbolic value in their social construct. And when you were a basketball player for the Bulldogs, you won the state championship for the town. But you know what?"

"No, what? You tell me."

"They never really see you as anything but as an Indian off the reservation and out of place."

"I think that'll about do it for this session," Austin said and walked to the sink to pour the rest of his cola down the drain. "I've got to go downtown to talk to the sheriff about Chief Emory, but I'm going to walk to do it. I'll leave you the car to use the rest of the day."

"O.K. Thanks."

"Right. I'll see you at suppertime," Austin said and walked toward the front of the house.

"I love you," Laura called after him. "Abba Bullock."

7

"You know what I don't like about Houston?" Martin Utz said, looking through the wide expanse of shaded glass of the room on the top floor of the Galleria Hotel just off I-695.

"Nothing to eat?" the other man in the room, Clarence Denver, said. He was standing over a table against the wall by the door to the other bedroom of the suite, moving a plastic ruler down a computer print-out filled with columns of figures, his head pivoting back and forth as though he were watching volleys in a women's tennis match.

"No, I expected that," Utz said. "Besides it's got a lot better in the last three or four years. You can get something, you know where to look. There is a place. Two places. One on Richmond and the other way out LaBranch. You know, by that rainforest place."

"Rainforest?" the other man said, not missing a stroke as he chased the numbers back and forth across the green paper.

"Not a real rainforest. Just a humongous plastic balloon some genius set up, full of weeds and water and birds and shit."

"A balloon?"

"Yeah, for kids to sweat in. Educational like. You know, learn how the frogs and snakes live, all them things that like hot water to crawl around in."

"I got you."

"No," Utz went on, "what I don't like about Houston, the main thing, is right out this fucking window. Come here and I'll show you."

"What? I'm busy."

"Learn something. Come over here for a minute."

Denver laid his ruler carefully down and adjusted its angle until it suited him and joined Martin Utz at the window, blinking his eyes behind the lenses of his glasses. He rubbed his temples and leaned forward to peer into the glare which the deeply tinted gray glass couldn't quite conquer.

"What do you see out there?" Utz gestured.

"Cars, trees, highways, I don't know."

"No, way out there," Utz said, pointing to the horizon wavering in the heat.

"A bunch of buildings sticking up."

"That's right," Utz said in a disgusted tone. "Now over there." He pointed to the right. "And there." This time to the left with the other hand.

"Same thing. A bunch of tall ones in the middle and on both sides."

"That's right," Utz said. "And you know what? Not a damn one of them's downtown. You ain't gonna find a fucking downtown anywhere in Harris County."

50

"And that's what bothers you?" the other man said, starting back toward the stack of computer sheets.

"Fuck yes, that's what bothers me. You can't go downtown in Houston, walk around on the street, look into some windows, buy some cigarettes, have a drink, get a paper, read the scores. It ain't possible."

"People do all that stuff here," Denver said. "You can spend some money."

"Yeah," Utz said, "right. But you got to drive a car and park the fucker eighteen times to do it. There ain't even any sidewalks in this place. Just one parking place after another one, all of them full up all the fucking time."

"I see what you mean," the other man said and straightened up from the table to look back at Utz by the tinted window. "But you know something? There's no parking lots in East Texas, up there in the woods. Just those trees and creeks and rocks and sand." He pushed his glasses up the bridge of his nose and smiled. "Nature," he said.

"Yeah, and we got to go wade around in it," Martin Utz said and pointed toward the table. "That seismology report from Earl Stroup says it's out there underwater somewhere. If I had my way, I'd turn every fucking swamp in East Texas into desert."

"Don't go questioning nature's plan now," Clarence Denver said and turned back to his printouts. "She won't like it."

The sheriff of Coushatta County had been out when Austin arrived at the office in the courthouse, his shirt sweated through in back by the walk from his house to downtown Annette. Two people had stopped their cars and offered him rides along the way, but he had waved them on, claiming the need for exercise. Both of them, one a high school kid he recognized but couldn't name and the other a nurse on her way to her shift in Coushatta County Memorial Hospital, had looked at him strangely. I know it's weird, he said to himself as he watched the kid pull away in his pickup, a man on foot. Funny looking. Not right. Plumb un-Texan.

A deputy at the desk by the door had explained that Sheriff Lewis was out poking around somewhere, probably on county business.

"I bet I know where," Austin said. "In that bass-boat on Lake Leggett."

"I imagine," the deputy had said, "but he didn't tell me that, and I didn't say it. You want me to tell him you come by?"

"You could. But I'll catch him later on."

"Them boys gonna take Sweetwater next Friday? Go on to the State?"

"I hope so," Austin said, giving his stock answer to basketball questions. "It'd sure make my life a lot easier if they do."

"Go Bulldogs," the deputy said. "Get some."

"You bet."

Out in the street, Austin decided to go by the grocery store on the way home and pick up some chicken breasts and greens for salad. Vegetarian though she claimed to be, Laura could be persuaded to eat chicken if he stir-fried it with enough chopped-up vegetables to make it seem Oriental. Things hadn't changed that much. When she was a child, he had at times coaxed her into eating by making up tribal stories about the dishes he prepared. Now what it took was to present food in the light of the multi cultural, and his daughter would still eat his cooking.

He could see that his car was gone from the driveway as soon as he turned the corner at Peachtree Street, three blocks away, the plastic bag of groceries heavy in his hand. Laura was probably out looking for Amy Stonecipher or Elizabeth Hubbard or one of the others of the bunch she had run with in high school, Austin thought, trying to scare up her up some nostalgia at age twenty, reminisce about the days of old eighteen months ago.

But after he had reached the house, put the chicken and vegetables away, and drunk two glasses of water, he discovered a note she had left stuck under an empty Mr. Sam's can on the kitchen table.

"Sorry about my lecturing this morning. I'm going to the reservation to visit people and look at things. Back by dark. Love, Colita."

It's going to be that kind of weekend, Austin thought, and lifted his eyes to the window over the sink. He could see that the forsythia along the back fence of the yard were near full bloom in the noonday sun, bright yellow against the gray branches. Ethnic renewal all day long, sun-up to sun-down, and get out of the way if you don't want to get with the agenda. Why couldn't she have been a computer freak or a pre-med major? Better yet a budding capitalist?

By seven o'clock, the sky completely dark and the carrots and broccoli and onion and garlic all chopped and ready under plastic wrap and all Austin's papers for junior class American history graded and bunched together with a rubber band, Laura was still not home. I will give her thirty minutes more, he told himself, and then call Grandma Bullock out there and see where she is.

At exactly half-past the hour, Austin called and the old woman answered on the first ring. "Is it the radio station?" she said in English. "KCOU Dial a Dollar?"

"No, my grandmother," he answered, "it is only Austin who speaks to you."

"Oh," Grandmother Bullock said, lapsing into the language of the Nation, disappointment obvious in her tone. "The blank eyes calls this time each day to give money to the one with the right words. The whip-poor-will told me this morning that they might call me. I was ready."

"They will call one time soon, I hope, and you will know what to tell them. But it is not this day. I am sorry."

"Better luck next time," she said, throwing in the white man's phrase. "What do you want, grandson?"

"Did your great-granddaughter visit you today, old mother? She drove my car to come to the Nation and has not returned."

"Colita was here to talk to me today. A grown woman now, but not married still."

"She goes to the college in Houston to read and study first."

"She said the things she ought to say to her grandmother. She remembers the words she learned as a child."

"Thank you, old mother. Do you know where she is now?"

53

"She is with her cousins, Nelda and Lawanda. They are married and have young ones now, although they have fewer years than Colita."

Austin remained quiet, waiting for the old woman to continue, knowing that any word from him would likely lead her in another direction.

"They have gone to the sing," she went on. "With the others."

"There is a sing in this month? I did not know this. Is it the Corn Dance?"

"No, that's in April. Don't you remember how the year goes? Are you too busy out there to know when seeds are planted?"

"No, old mother. I remember."

"It's another sing. For the young women only. It is a sing the little man will do for them."

"When does it end? Do you know when? Who is the little man?"

"I know I need to listen to my telephone to see if it will ring," Grandmother Bullock said. "The whip-poor-will this morning told me to wait for the Dial-a-Dollar."

"Yes, old mother. If Laura comes again to your house, ask her to call me."

"If I am not talking to the telephone, I will tell Colita."

Austin listened to her hang up and then spoke into the dead mouthpiece. "Good luck with KCOU," he said. "Dial those dollars, old mother."

Austin poured himself two fingers of gin over ice, flipped on the TV and prepared to watch as much of a documentary on ozone depletion as he could stand. It wasn't like Laura not to call when she was going to be late, but there was no telephone handy at the places in the Nation where sings were typically held, and he told himself to put her out of his mind as much as he could and concentrate instead on what he had heard today about Chief Emory's last few hours alive.

Not much, really, that he was able to make any sense of, except that the old man had been convinced something was going on with the water in the Big Thicket area of the reservation, something was wrong about it, something that had to do with the old Spanish medal his wife had passed along to Austin. He still had it in his shirt pocket, and he took it out to examine again.

54

It still made no sense, he thought, turning it over in his hand in the light of the lamp on the table by the sofa. The important thing about the Spanish medal he already had, the mate to this one and emblem of the true line of the chieftainship of the Alabama-Coushatta, had always been that it was the only one, the sole gift of one king to another and therefore precious beyond measure. And here's another one. Where would the old man have found it, and what would it have to do with water underground?

The voice on the television was speaking in a hushed, confidential tone about fluorocarbons, and Austin flipped the silver medal before him as though it were a coin to be used to make a decision, yes or no, heads or tails, your ball or mine. It flashed brightly in the light, up and down, over and over, a king's head on one side and the image of a crown on the other, no help to anybody waiting to start the game.

Austin started to replace the disk in his pocket, thought better of it, and opened the small drawer in the table and stuck it with the other Spanish medal under a stack of papers there. The thing to do now was to drink his gin, try to get into the program flickering before him on the screen, and not think about waiting for the telephone to ring. It never would if he did.

He lay back, closed his eyes, and in a few minutes he could feel himself beginning to drift, the taps of a small drum, accompanied by a faint chant in the language of the People, starting up far away somewhere near the edge of his mind. He let himself listen, and the sound of the TV faded gradually and was gone.

He wore the clothing of a hunter, and he had looked for game all day with no success. The sky was darkening, and he was far from the village and he had forgotten the way to turn toward home. In the dense forest each path looked the same, and the night was upon him. He lay down the weapons he had been carrying, the bow and the three arrows tipped with red points and the leather pouch of chunk stones. He built a fire and looked for the meat he had placed in his pouch to be cooked, but the container was empty and he lay down hungry to sleep and to wait for the light of morning to show him a way out of the place where he was lost.

Sometime in the middle of the night he heard a voice shouting in the distance, and he knew that someone was searching for him. The noise came closer, and it was no longer human, but the howls of a beast, and he was afraid in the darkness and he wanted to get nearer the fire, but he knew he should not.

He moved away from the heat and light and lay in a field of stones, and in his dream he fell asleep, twice in that sleep removed from the world and he knew that, even though unconscious of where he was. He woke from a dream of a dream in the morning and searched all day for the village, wandering paths that led back to where they had started and following streams of water that ran in both directions and joined no other ones and found no relief.

He camped again, clad in the dress of a hunter, where he had spent his first night lost in the forest, and animals he did not know came to look at him as he lay outside the circle of fire, their eyes projecting a strange light in the darkness.

In the morning when he woke, a great tree stood where his fire had been, reaching so high above the tops of others that he could not see its branches no matter how far he leaned back to look and how hard he rubbed at his eyes to clear them of the mist that hung in the clearing. He drank water from the stream before him, but he could not quench his thirst, and it wasn't until he had pulled leaves from the lower branches of the great tree and eaten them that he felt refreshed and able to look at the day again with hope.

On the third night as he sat with his back against the bole of the tree, now so large around that it felt flat against him, a voice spoke from the darkness above, somewhere hidden in the branches and foliage, and called his name.

"Abba Bullock," it said in a tone so deep it sounded of thunder far away beyond the horizon, "the place you seek is in the direction your head lies."

"How do I know which path to follow?" he said in a tone pleading and weak in his own ears. "I am not lying down. There is nothing above me to which my head is directed."

"Lie down," the voice grumbled in the manner of a storm moving away out of hearing, "lie down and wait."

Austin could hear himself groaning loud enough to rouse him where he lay on the sofa, and he rose up so abruptly that he banged his hand and arm against the side table, knocking it against the wall and overturning the glass with its dregs of gin and melted ice. He caught the lamp as it teetered and fell, swinging his body into a sitting position on the edge of the sofa.

The telephone was ringing in the kitchen and he went to answer it, thinking that if he told one of the old men of the Nation's council of his dream he would provide enough material for a half-day's interpretation. He hadn't had dreams that elaborate since his vision of the red bird at age twelve during the manhood ritual. Add that one to the nightmare he had had after learning of Chief Emory's death earlier in the week, and he could provide substance for two Coushatta shamans and a whole seminar of Freudian psychologists. Not to mention Karl Jung or Oprah Winfrey, he thought, and picked up the phone.

"Coach Bullock," a female voice said, "this is Nelda Battise. I'm calling for Colita."

"Where is she? Is anything wrong?"

"No," Nelda said and paused. "She's fine. She said to tell you not to worry. She's going to stay on the reservation until Chief Emory's funeral. She'll see you then, on Tuesday."

"She can't," Austin said. "She's got to go back to Houston. She'll miss some classes."

"Only one, she said to tell you. No big deal, she said, just one in English she's way ahead in."

"Is she there? Let me talk to her, Nelda. Put her on the phone."

"She's dancing. She'll see you on Tuesday. That's all I know."

"Wait a minute," Austin said. "I'm coming out to the reservation tomorrow." He looked at his watch. "It's almost three o'clock in the morning. What's going on? What do you mean dancing?"

"Good bye, Abba Bullock," Nelda said, and the telephone clicked off.

"Bullshit," Austin said. "Bullshit." He looked at the dead telephone in his hand. He could hear thunder in his silent house, faint in the distance, somewhere in the west toward the reaches of the

Trinity River. He listened until it faded away completely and the only sound he could hear was the clicking of the refrigerator beside him in the little house on Peachtree Street.

8

Alton Pritchard's wife's car badly needed a tune-up, misfiring steadily at idle speed and perking up only when it was pushed above fifty miles per hour. The problem with maintaining that speed had to do with the vibration which set up in the right front wheel at anything past forty-five. Alton had warned him about it.

"It'll feel like that wheel is trying to come slap off," he had said. "But it ain't yet. I'd let you use the Buick, but we're going to go to Corrigan after church, and Libby wants to ride in the good car when we make that trip."

"I appreciate your letting me use this one," Austin had said, revving the engine to keep it from dying. "I'll take care of it."

"I wish you wouldn't," Alton had told him. "I kinda hope it'll fly all to pieces, so I can have the excuse to buy me a Toyota pickup. And then just let her have the Buick."

"Right," Austin said, easing the clutch out and heading for the highway to the reservation.

By the time he arrived at the dwelling place of Bobby Crow Fly, the Chevrolet was running much better, having benefitted from the seventeen miles of highway driving, but the front wheel was no better, and Austin was glad to be able to bring the machine to a stop.

Bobby was sitting on the front porch, drinking coffee from a large blue cup, when Austin cut the engine and stepped out of Pritchard's Chevrolet. Bobby lifted his cup in greeting.

"Why you driving that thing?" he said, "Where's your Japanese car?"

58

"Laura's got it, and I'm the next thing to being on foot. Is she here? You seen her?"

"No, but Nelda has, I reckon." Bobby sipped at his cup. "You want some coffee?"

"Yeah, I'll take some, if it's not too much trouble. Is Nelda in the house?"

"Uh huh. I'll tell her you're here. And get you some coffee." He went into his house, and Austin looked about him at the collection of motor parts, bathtubs, and ruined bicycles in the Crow Fly front yard. It was a typical display for a house-place on the Alabama-Coushatta reservation except for the bathtubs and the sole china commode up near the steps. Bobby Crow Fly had attempted plumbing as a sideline for a time, and these bathroom fixtures were testament from then.

His business had not prospered, Austin thought, walking over to look more closely at the largest of the tubs, an old fashioned one with claw feet, like most of the ventures of people on the reservation into commerce. Bobby Crow Fly had made himself the king of old bathtubs, at one point though, even if all this one contained now was a foot of dirty rainwater.

The front door opened, and Nelda Crow Fly stepped out on the porch, a three-year-old child riding one hip and a younger one close behind her with a firm grip on the tail of her dress. He was rubbing his eyes with the other hand.

"Good morning," Austin said. "Thanks for your call last night. I appreciate your giving me the message from Laura."

Nelda nodded and set down the child she was carrying and picked up the other one. The same age as Laura, Austin thought, and Nelda had been a good student in the freshman social studies course she had taken from him before she had stopped coming to Annette High School. She had two little ones on the porch, and judging from the looks of her, another one coming in a few months. Austin gave her a big smile.

"Do you know where Laura is now?" he said.

"I left the sing before she did," she said and watched her father head for Austin with a cup of coffee in each hand. "She was going to stay for all of it and the dancing too, she told me."

"Uh huh. Do you know where she would have spent the night after the dancing was over?"

"I guess Lawanda's, where she lives with her husband," Nelda said, "over to the other side of Long King Creek."

"Is that the old Felder Sylestine place? There by the three big sycamores?"

"No, further down the creek. Lawanda and Tommy have a new house. Four rooms in it. A bathroom inside."

"Government issue," Bobby Crow Fly said. "They building some more of them now if you can get on the list."

"Gustin's going to get us one," Nelda said in a quick voice. "As soon as he can get the paperwork started."

"Right," her father said. "You keep watching for it. Wish for it in one hand, do you know what in the other one. See which one fills up first."

Both of Nelda's children began crying at once as though on cue. The three adults watched them for a minute without saying anything.

"You've got pretty babies, Nelda," Austin remarked finally and set his coffee cup on the edge of the porch. "I bet the next one will be too."

"You can't miss Lawanda and Tommy's house," she said. "The little man's RV is parked in the front yard. He pays them money to let it stay there. It's silver color all over."

"Thanks," Austin said and started for the Chevrolet. "Tell Gustin I'm sorry I missed him. Tell him I hope he comes to the game next Friday. Say I wish I had him at point guard still."

Bobby Crow Fly was pouring the untasted coffee in Austin's cup into his blue one as Austin pulled away in the backfiring Nova, conducting the operation as though he were transferring gold dust between the containers.

Austin could see his Honda pulled up close to Lawanda and Tommy's government-built house when he arrived thirty minutes later. The house was covered with white vinyl siding, and small bits and pieces of that material along with shards of plywood and short

60

lengths of two-by-fours used in the construction were gathered into a large pile for burning in the side yard. A twenty-foot Air Stream vehicle took up most of the front yard, two plastic hoses running from it, one to a water faucet near the house and the other one in the opposite direction to a pit in the earth that had been dug by a backhoe. The ridge of dirt surrounding it was waist-high to a tall man.

An industrial-sized electrical cord led from a plug on the side of the silver vehicle across the yard, up the porch, and vanished into a front window of the house. The Oklahoma vanity plate on the polished rear of the Air Stream read SHAMAN.

"Well, kiss my red ass," Austin said out loud and cut the engine. The only sound in the clearing was the hammer of a woodpecker high in a sweetgum somewhere in the stand of trees behind the house. Austin listened to him work for a space before opening the door and stepping out into the sandy clay of the yard. Get that grub, Brother Woodpecker, Austin thought to himself. Uncover him and eat him up.

There was no sign of life in the new government dwelling, and after Austin had knocked on the screen door twice to no response, he decided to sit in one of the two new lawn chairs on the front porch and wait. More than likely, Laura and Lawanda and Tommy had gone looking for somebody or something and would return in a few minutes. Maybe. In the meantime he would admire the side view of the Air Stream and try to plan what calm and reasoned words he would say to his daughter when the chance came.

The RV had two doors on the side facing the house, he noticed, one to the passenger's seat in front and the other in the middle of the vehicle opening to the living area. A design in red and yellow had been painted in the center of the second door, something that looked to Austin from where he sat in the lawn chair like a stylized bullfrog or a large toad surrounded by the rays of a setting sun. Leaning forward, he could see that the rays were depicted as originating in the mouth of the creature and that balanced on the upturned front feet were identical blood-red balls.

The aerodynamically sleek cooling unit on top of the vehicle suddenly kicked on with an abrupt jolt and whine, drowning out the distant taps of the woodpecker behind the house, and the door Austin had been studying rattled and slowly swung open. Two metal steps pivoted down to ground level, and a small spotted animal with a large head and a body that looked as round as a soccer ball descended with mincing steps from inside. It walked as though its feet hurt over to the mound of dirt surrounding the waste pit and began rooting at a clump of Johnson grass, its head jerking in a regular feeding motion.

"She is a pot-bellied pig," a voice said from the door of the vehicle, "from Vietnam."

The man speaking was three or four inches short of four feet, Austin judged as he watched him come down the metal steps, but the voice was that of a much larger person, deep and resonant as though it were coming from a television anchorman or an announcer at a University of Texas football game. He was dressed in a sky-blue jumpsuit embroidered across the chest with elaborate red and gold swirls, moons and stars, and his pants legs were stuffed into the tops of black cowboy boots with lightning bolts worked in white snakeskin on the sides, across the insteps and ending at the points of the toes. These were tipped with silver, winking brightly in the sunlight.

"She's cleaner than a house cat," the man announced in that voice. "She'll use a litter box only once and then somebody has to change it."

"That particular, huh?" Austin said, looking at the shining braids of black hair descending from the man's temples, each finished off with tiny bows of rawhide wound with scarlet ribbons.

"Exquisitely so," he said, pausing at the bottom of the steps. "But what I value most about her, and what's most remarkable about her kind, is the display of affection. Unstinting and unafraid to be dependent. And willing—this is the thing I want to emphasize—willing, I say, to demonstrate that dependence."

He looked at Austin with a gaze as serious as that of a surgeon, gestured broadly with one hand and began to walk toward the house. "What other creature," he said as he proceeded in small, hopping steps, "will do as much? What other creature, human or animal, will admit such trust?"

Not waiting for a response, he reached the porch, stuck out his hand toward Austin and spoke again. "I am Crippled Sparrow, as translated from the Choctaw. The name on the birth certificate in Tulsa, however, is Roy Blending."

Austin started to rise from the lawn chair, thought better of towering over the man before him from his position on the porch, and stuck out his hand from where he sat. Crippled Sparrow's fingers were short, but his hand was broad and powerful, and he leaned into the shake with all he had.

"You, sir, are the new chief of your Nation," he told Austin. "I don't know the name you were given in darkness, but the blank eyes know you as Austin Bullock."

"That's what everybody who knows me calls me," Austin said. "And my status as Chief of the Alabama-Coushatta is much exaggerated."

"Your people and mine had healthy disagreements in the days before the white man stole everything. The Choctaws and the Alabamas in the old time, I mean."

"That's what I understand," Austin said. "Back before the People came to Texas."

"One of the best stories of your people concerns one of our small flare-ups," the little man said, leaning forward to flick at a spot of dried mud his right boot had picked up in his journey across the yard. "Do you know it? The tale of the Alabama man with horns who put the wolf head on a pole to detect Choctaw warriors on the move against your Nation?"

"I seem to remember McKinley Big Eyes telling us kids that one," Austin said. "But it was a long time ago."

"Yes," Crippled Sparrow said in a syllable so loud and heated that the pot-bellied pig working on the Johnson grass jumped and spun about to look toward the two men at the house. "It was all a long time ago. The stories, the songs, the animosity between the Nations of the native peoples of this continent. Vanished, gone. But what remains is holy. Our brotherhood and sisterhood with all the people of our blood. We are united now, we face the common foe together, we look in the same direction. The same wind blows at our back, and we feel it and are moved."

The small volleyball-shaped pig turned to a new clump of Johnson grass, and Austin focused his gaze on the jewelry of the man before him, the three rings on his left hand and the four on the right, the heavy bracelets on each wrist—silver set with blue and green stones.

"I'm here looking for my wandering daughter," he said. "She left me my car this time, but she's still out of pocket somewhere."

"Not to worry, Abba Bullock," Crippled Sparrow said. "Colita is with the other young ones on a trek in Lost Man Marsh."

"That's a new one for Laura. Walking through a nasty swamp. So she came to your sing last night, did she?"

"They all come, the young ones, more and more of them. They are hungry for the center of the world. They are famished for the food of the spirit which grows in that middle where nothing is lost in a straight line."

"Circles and straight lines," Austin said. "You're working all this up for the pageant, I understand. Beyond the Sundown. Getting things ready for the tourist trade."

"It's a bear," the little man said with a deep sigh, "like any new production. So much to do all at once, so much synergy to get established before it gets up on its feet and begins to walk for itself. Do this, do that, be practical, but don't lose the dream. You know what it's like? Let me put it to you in terms you can understand."

"Please do." Austin said. "I'd be real grateful." In the yard the pig continued to root away, but the sounds of the woodpecker tapping at the sweetgum had ceased. Gone on to greener pastures, Austin thought, or deader trees.

"It's like a basketball game," said Crippled Sparrow. "And you've got the job of getting all these parts to realize they're a whole thing together and nothing alone. You understand me, Abba Bullock?" He looked up at Austin, his eyes glowing as he stared deeply into the taller man's face. "Got me?"

"Got you," Austin said. "Don't call me that, please."

"What? You mean the words which recognize what you are? You did not seek it, Abba Bullock. You must not feel guilty for taking on the old man's job. He is gone; you are here. Rejoice in yourself."

"I don't quite see it that way," Austin said in a measured tone, "and I really don't want to talk about new jobs of any kind. My plate's full up."

"I understand. Believe me, brother," Crippled Sparrow said, shaking his head back and forth until the tips of his shining braids described identical circles. "The death of Chief Emory is causing me problems in my mission here, too."

He looked to the left over Austin's shoulder as though he were focusing his gaze on a scene of great sorrow and loss over which he had no control, but to which he offered a boundless reservoir of sympathy.

"Many of your people have had over the years of oppression by the blank eyes much suspicion bred into them. They fear what they should welcome." He stepped back and pointed the fingers of both hands at the embroidered material covering his chest. "You will find this astonishing, Abba Bullock, but I must tell you in sorrow that some of the Alabama-Coushatta Nation think I played a part in the death of their Chieftain."

Austin stared at the little man's pointing fingers, shook his head and said nothing.

"I speak not in anger, but in deep sadness. Some say Crippled Sparrow raised his hand against a red brother, and this with no evidence of foul play."

"I understand the case is still under investigation. Maybe the sheriff of Coushatta County won't agree with what you just said about no foul play."

"Of course not. Why would the blank eyes want the truth? They just see it as a chance to destroy two of us for the price of one. They'd indict the whole Nation if they thought they could get away with it."

"Walker Lewis is a fair man," Austin said, "careful too. I've known him a long time."

"Do you know what I heard one of his deputies call me two days ago? Not to my face, for he fears me by instinct, but to another one of the blank eyes."

"No, I don't."

"A little red nigger. And you know what part of his insult bothered me?"

"What part?"

"Not the little part and not the nigger part. One I have dealt with, and the other is nonsense. It's the word red I find telling. Who is the blank eye to judge colors? We are the original color. All else is departure from us. My skin," he said, patting the backs of his forearms, "and your skin set the standard. Anything else is a mongrel, a thing that is not all there, a half-breed."

He said these last words in a voice that filled the yard, bouncing off the trees surrounding the house clearing, and mounted up toward the sky above where he stood facing Austin Bullock.

"I heard that," Austin said, "look yonder. I think you might have spooked your little spotted hog. She's running up the road like something's after her."

The animal's ears were laid back, its snout was leaned forward low to the ground, and its feet were lost in a blur of motion as it headed south down the gravel road. It had reached a sharp bend and was tilted into a slant to avoid spinout by the time Crippled Sparrow took up the chase, churning toward the road like a man trying to beat out a bunt.

"Honey-Suckle," he called, as he kept up the pace of his gait and neared the bend around which the pig had vanished, the heels of his snakeskin boots pounding the red clay of the Nation. "You come back here. You come back here right now."

"The shaman is going to ruin his shoeshine," Austin said to himself, "and if his little pot-bellied pig's not lucky something in the bushes is going to grab it for lunch."

He walked over to the Honda. It was unlocked, no key in the ignition, and the only sign that Laura had been driving it was an empty soft-drink cup from Wendy's stuck down between the bucket seats. Austin popped the lever to release the lid to the trunk and was walking around to look inside when he heard a car coming up the road. It pulled in beside the Honda and stopped. He closed the trunk.

"Lawanda," Austin said. "Tommy. I like your new house. The front porch sits real well."

"Coach Bullock," Tommy said, stepping out from behind the wheel. "You got to come inside and look at it. It's got a bathroom."

"I heard it did. Makes it real nice, doesn't it?"

Tommy and Lawanda Bear-Killer were both wearing cut-off bluejeans, running shoes and T shirts with slogans. Just Do It said

Tommy's, but Lawanda's was too faded for Austin to read without staring.

"Colita's not with us," Lawanda said.

"I noticed."

"She wanted to walk further than we did, and she said she wanted time to be by herself in the woods. But she'll be back before dark."

"If I didn't know better, I'd think my daughter's trying to avoid her old man. I'm beginning to wonder what I did to make her mad at me."

"It's not that," Lawanda said.

"Nuh uh," Tommy added. "No way."

"Well, she's a big girl," Austin said. "I expect she'll call me, if you give her the message for me."

"Right, sure. She plans to see you at Chief Emory's funeral day after tomorrow," Lawanda said. "She knows you have to teach and all tomorrow. Colita just wants a little break from school."

"College must be hard, huh, Coach?" Tommy Bear-Killer said. "Rice University, hooee." He shook his head twice and pursed his lips. "She told me the subjects she's taking. I don't even know what they mean, the names of them."

"Not as bad as it all sounds, Tommy. You could have done it. Still could, too."

"I doubt that, Coach Bullock. I don't know where I'd be if I wasn't right here."

"Did you meet Crippled Sparrow?" Lawanda said, touching her husband on the hand and nodding toward the silver vehicle before them.

"Yes, I did," Austin answered. "He's chasing his little hog down the road the last thing I saw of him."

"He loves that little pot-bellied pig," Lawanda said. "Honey-Suckle. She's so cute."

"Is Mr. Blending a good tenant, living here in front of your new house?"

"He's a wonderful man," Lawanda said. "Isn't he, Tommy? He tells us stories and songs. He's so deep, what he knows about the

67

People and all. He's studied everything. He helps us understand things."

Austin glanced at Tommy. The young man was staring impassively across the house clearing toward the thicket of pines and yaupon and picking at the sleeve of his Just Do It T shirt. He looked half asleep.

"Nothing wrong with understanding things. I believe in that," Austin said. "Tell Laura to call me sometime today, no matter how late she gets back. I need to talk to her."

"Yes, Abba Bullock," Tommy said, roused from his reverie. "Good luck to the Bulldogs on Friday."

"Thanks," Austin said and headed for Pritchard's old Chevrolet. "I hope the little philosopher catches his hog before something eats it."

"Who?" Tommy asked.

"He means Crippled Sparrow," Lawanda said, pulling at her husband's hand. "Let's go in the house."

9

The next morning just before walking into his first class of the day, Austin realized that he would have to walk to the courthouse at noon or get somebody to drop him off. It wasn't like Laura to leave him on foot for more than a few hours, and the fact that she still hadn't called home from the reservation despite all his messages was a puzzle. Maybe she was just increasing the pressure for wheels of her own, or maybe she was so deep into her ethnic weekend she couldn't be bothered to pick up a telephone. Or maybe she was just being twenty years old.

Austin walked into the classroom, loaded with books and papers to return, and by the silence and averted eyes he encountered in the rows of desks before him, he could tell he must have his

Alabama-Coushatta face on. Your eyes, his wife used to tell him back in the early days, look just like pecans. Nobody can see into them. Everything bounces off.

He caught Rolando Johnson chancing a look at him from the back of the room, and he tried to smile. "Good morning, young historians," Austin said, "it's not all that bad, is it?" His students began shifting in their seats, and the teaching started up again.

"I'm glad you came in today," Sheriff Walker Lewis said and walked around his desk toward Austin, fiddling with his belt as he came closer. "I was going to give you a call when I got the chance. Sit down. Better yet, let's go get something to eat."

"I'd like to, but I haven't got the time, Walker. I got to be back to the high school by ten after one."

"Yeah, right, right," the sheriff said and closed the door behind Austin. "Busy time, ain't it?" He walked back to his desk and leaned on the edge of it, crossing one boot over the other.

"Thing of it is, see," he went on, "is we got the official verdict on the cause of death on Emory Sees the Water, and I wanted to let you know the good news."

"Good news?"

"That's a bad way to put it, of course. There ain't nothing good about it, I mean, The old man dead and all. That wasn't what I meant. No, what I meant to say is it was natural, the death was. No sign of violence, just a plain old infarction. Heart attack."

"No violence," Austin said. "A heart attack in the creek."

"He must have fell in when it hit him. Hardly any water in the upper respiratory system. Maybe the old fellow drawed in a breath or two before he went, but that wasn't what killed him."

"But what about the marks on his throat? That shows an external cause, doesn't it?"

"No sign of ligature, Austin. Oh, he had a couple of scratches, but more than likely that's from rocks or brush or something there in Long King Creek. That's all."

"That's hard to believe, that version of what happened to Chief Emory. He felt like something was a threat to him. He told his wife and he told her to let me know he was worried."

"I know it's hard to believe, Austin. I understand what you and the people out yonder are thinking. But I've seen upwards of a thousand deaths, and people just have always have a real hard time accepting the simple explanation. But you know what? That's generally the right one. The simplest one is the true one, nine times out of ten. It doesn't take much to die, but people don't want to believe that for some reason."

"So the investigation is over?" Austin said. "That's what you're telling me?"

"Well, if there ain't no crime, there ain't no reason to look any further into it. That's the way it works. You see that, don't you?"

"I guess I do. I guess I'm beginning to see how it works, Walker, right down to the bone."

"I just wanted to set your mind at ease," the sheriff said. "I know it's a period of mourning for you and everybody else on the reservation, and I was hoping that getting the word out would help."

"Can I talk to the medical examiner? You said he was in Lufkin, didn't you?"

"Yeah, he's in Lufkin, all right, but I don't see what good that would do you. You can talk to anybody you want to, Austin. I never kept lids on nothing and don't plan on starting at this age. You know that."

"I do, and I appreciate your telling me."

"Well, it's hard, I know. You got a lot on you right now. I hope the ballteam takes Sweetwater when the time comes. That'd be a relief, wouldn't it?"

"Yeah, the basketball game. One more magic tip-off to set things right. Get everybody's mind pointed in the right direction."

"Yeah," the sheriff said. "Now you're talking."

Austin moved toward the door and stopped before opening it. "I almost forgot. Chief Emory passed along something that I wanted to tell you about. But I guess it won't make any difference now."

"What? Something another he said?"

"No," Austin said, reaching into his pocket. "It's a Spanish medal, an old one from way back when half of this country belonged to them. The Spanish used to give them to the native people's chiefs as a sign of favor from the king of Spain. The Alabama-Coushatta have always had one of them, going way back to the seventeenth century, and we hand it down, you know, from chief to chief. And now here's a matching one."

"I'll be. Reckon where he got that? You say it's supposed to be just one of them, huh?"

Austin nodded and held the medal out toward the sheriff. "That's all I know about, and I would have been told if there was another one like it kicking around on the reservation."

"Big medicine, huh? It must be worth some money," Walker Lewis said, leaning forward to peer at the gold disk. "You want me to keep it in the file? Won't be no trouble."

"No, I'll just save it for a keepsake. Put it in the house with the rest of my junk."

"All right. I hope you get you a chance to get in a little R and R once this ball season's over with."

"I'm looking for some R and R," Austin said, slipping Chief Emory's emblem back in his pocket. "I need me some relief as soon as I can find it."

The Nation's funeral for Abba Emory began at dusk of the fifth day after he had died. The white man ceremony in the Presbyterian Mission Church had been earlier in the day, an hour before noon, and Austin had stood in the rear of the building, watching Lawrence Spotted Horse at the raised altar, preaching about everlasting life and a race well-run. He had worn a dark robe and a white collar, and he had read from the Bible and the prayer book loudly at great length.

Bobby Hunts Bear had sung two hymns, solo, "Amazing Grace" and "The Old Rugged Cross," and the Alabama-Coushatta Native-American Ladies' Choir, which sang special programs in white churches all over East Texas, had performed three of its best numbers. The dead chief of the Nation lay in an open coffin at the foot of the altar, and after a last prayer was given by Lawrence Spotted Horse, people had stood up from their benches and filed by for a last look at the body of the man who had lived so long among them. Austin had not joined the viewers, slipping out the door instead to walk toward the graveyard between the church and the stand of pines to the west.

Somebody had removed the discarded anvil that had been fastened to the cable to keep the gate to the graveyard pulled shut, and the barrier hung partly open, its bottom board propped up on a reddish stone. Austin threw that aside and looked for the anvil, hoping that it hadn't been carried off to serve a function somebody else thought more important than keeping the gate to the graveyard of the Alabama-Coushatta Nation shut against the world outside. He found it half concealed under a thornbush down the fence-line and carried it back to the gate. The wire holding it to the cable had rusted through, but he was able to refasten it with what was left, and when he pushed the gate open, the weight pulled it closed again against the pin-oak post.

The stones marking the graves of his mother and father were a hundred feet or so from the gate, and he could see as he approached them that the favorite blue china plate on his mother's mound was still in the same position and that his father's shaving mug with the old safety razor inside was where it always had been. There was a little rainwater in the bottom from a recent shower, and he started to pour it out on the sand and pebbles marking the grave site, but then thought better of it and left the mug as it was.

The little yellow flowers around the edge of his mother's china plate were faded more than the last time he had seen them, and Austin judged that a couple of more years in the sun and rain would obliterate them completely. Maybe not, he told himself, maybe not. They could hold at some point and last forever.

All around him, wherever he looked, he could see household utensils and keepsakes marking the graves of the people gone before: here a coffee pot upended so that its stained bottom shone in the sun, beyond that two water glasses in matching pattern propped against a headstone, there on a child's grave a doll cracked and broken by the elements and sinking into the sandy soil. The wooden stock of a shotgun was shoved into the mound of one grave up to the point where the right hand of its owner once grasped it to aim. The combat medals and campaign ribbons of an Alabama who had served in the Pacific over fifty years ago now lay arranged in a precise line across the foot of his mound of earth.

The sun shines and the rain falls, Austin told himself, and the only ones of the People with nothing on their graves to mark their time in the world are those who have been here the longest and those who are just arrived.

The place for Chief Emory Sees the Water was across the graveyard near the back fence, a raw hole dug by a backhoe which was parked about twenty yards from the site, ready to be cranked up for the refilling. The crew from Pace's Funeral Home had covered the mound of earth removed from the hole with a large swatch of green plastic grass that looked like artificial turf carted in from a football stadium.

Sitting on top of the green mound was an old man in blue overalls and a khaki shirt beneath, wearing a black Stetson. He had his back turned, and he was gazing across the fence toward the woods beyond, but Austin could tell who he was by the time he had taken two steps in the man's direction.

"Hola," Austin said, picking his way among the graves between himself and the old man on the green mound. "Albert Had Two Mothers. I see you in this place."

"Abba Bullock," the old man said before turning to look over his shoulder, "he told me you would come, and now you are here."

"I am here," Austin said and watched the old man turn slowly around on the hillock of earth to face him. The lower half of the face of Albert Had Two Mothers was painted white, and a stripe of black ran across the width of his forehead and the bridge of his nose. The white was caked unevenly in the wrinkles around his mouth and in the deep lines of his throat, and seeing that made a sad knot rise up in Austin's chest.

"Who told you I would come to the graveyard?" he asked.

"Your father," Had Two Mothers said simply and nodded in the direction of the graves of Austin's parents. "He said I would be able to talk to you alone here before the burying of the dead Chief."

"When did he say this thing? Did you dream it?"

"No," the old man said in a patient tone. "He told me in this world when I came to see him and your mother while the women were singing together in the church. His woman, your mother, did not speak to me, though. She was thinking of something else, I reckon. Maybe she was walking in Abba Mikko's meadow to see the new flowers come up."

"What did my father say to you when you visited the place he is buried?"

"Oh, we talked of several things. Some stories that happened before you were born, things which are not the business of a man's children. You know, from the time when we were young together, Toman Bullock and I and a few others. I was glad your mother wasn't there listening."

"What did my father say to you that you can tell me, my elder?"

"Toman told me that you would do the right thing when you had to, Austin Bullock. You would be reluctant, you would want to think too much about a thing as always. You would stand away from the fire to avoid the hot sparks that jump out at a man. You would do this, even though you were freezing in the winter wind. But that finally you would stand close to Fire with the People and be warmed."

The old man lifted both hands to his face and patted his cheeks in a delicate gesture. "Do you like the white paint I use to show my mourning for Sees the Water? I looked in the glass to put it on my face."

"It is a good job you did," Austin said, "as in the old stories."

"There is a picture that a blank eyes made many years ago of the People at a funeral dance. You have seen this photograph in the trunk of McKinley Big Eye?"

"Yes, he showed it to me when I was a boy," Austin said, remembering himself and Delbert Sees the Water sitting in a crouch before the old man as he drew forth his treasures, one by one, from the great wooden box he kept wrapped in a bearskin. Where was it now, he wondered, lost, burned, or somewhere in a storage room of a university?

"Now do I look like those Alabamas in the picture?" Albert Had Two Mothers asked.

"Yes, just as they were in the blank eye's picture. You are just as our fathers were, my elder. One could not tell you apart."

"Well, it's not the same kind of paint," the old man said, looking at a smear of white he had gotten on a finger tip. "I had to use

74

what I could find in my granddaughter's makeup kit. But it looks all right."

Both men fell silent for a space, the only sounds that of a crow cawing far away and a puff of wind rattling some artificial flowers on a grave near the parked backhoe. People were leaving the church in small groups and walking toward their cars, pickups and pulpwood trucks across the road. Three small boys wearing white shirts and ties were trotting together ahead of the rest, jostling each other as they ran. A woman called to them something Austin couldn't hear.

"What is this thing my father told you I would finally do?" he asked.

"The thing the Chief of the People does, of course," the old man said. "The thing required, Abba Bullock. That is what will warm you."

"How will I do this?" Austin asked, knowing the answer he would hear.

"You will talk with the Council, and you will decide," Albert Had Two Mothers said. "It is the way of the Nation. It is how you will let yourself know. The path will show itself to you, and you will walk before us in the direction we must go."

"You see things in me that I do not believe are there, my elder. This task is not mine."

"That's the white man talking in you," the old man said, brushing the air before his face as if gnats were bothering him. "What they put in your mind in all those schools. You will see clear enough when the time comes. Your eyes will be sharp again. They will be the hawk's."

Austin shook his head and stared down at the green plastic grass covering the earth of Emory Sees the Water's grave. No sense in arguing with an old man who paints half his face white, he told himself, and who holds conversations with people who've been dead for over twenty years.

"Trust me on this thing," Albert Had Two Mothers said in a kind voice, holding out his right hand. "Help me climb down off this little hill. An old man's bones are brittle."

At dusk, Austin stood at the edge of a crowd of people surrounding the clearing at the center of the Nation. A few were talking in small family groups, and the shrill voices of children rose at scattered points in the mass of onlookers as the people of the Alabama-Coushatta waited for the players in the middle of the circle to begin the ceremony which would allow Abba Emory to be put into the earth.

The coffin rested on three sawhorses positioned at the northern point of the cleared circle, just beyond the limit of the beaten area where the dances of the Nation took place. As the sky darkened, the patterns of light from the fire flickered across the surface of the coffin, picking up reflections from the metal braces and handles and highlighting the near side of the casket containing the body of the dead chief. The flower arrangements which had earlier decorated the scene in the Presbyterian Mission Church were now gone, and in their place was a single pine sapling cut earlier in the day by one of the players in the story to be presented and topped with two feathers, one from the wing of a crow and the other from the tail of a wild turkey.

The tap of a drum began in a slow-paced rhythm somewhere in the gathering darkness beyond the circle of people, and a single voice began to chant one of the songs of the Nation, a simple one taught to children, Austin recognized, and the sound grew stronger as the singer approached the clearing at the heart of the dance ground. The crowd opened a way for the singer to enter and closed behind him as he worked his way forward.

People could see the large clay pot worked with designs in black and white he was carrying, and by that they knew the story to be told for the placing of Chief Emory in the earth would be the tale about Why Sickness Still Exists. Murmurs arose as the singer carried the pot toward the dance ground and died away as he placed it upright to the south of the central fire.

"Here is a container," he sang in a clear ringing voice, "large enough to hold in one place all the sickness and all the trouble sickness brings."

Jimmy Black Fox, Austin recognized, a long way from the Annette High School choir behind that reed mask he's wearing, but he hasn't forgot how to project from the diaphragm.

"I have made the pot and drawn the magic lines on its sides," Black Fox sang in the language of the Nation. "Nothing put inside can

76

escape. Now who will take the pot into the sky and leave it open so that sickness will creep inside?"

No answer came, and the singer asked the question twice more, moving slowly around the clay pot in short dance steps as he made his song. The long reeds hanging from his mask made a rustling sound in the silence, and his steps on the earth matched the tapping of the drum beyond the circle of light.

At the end of his third circle around the clay pot, the singer stopped suddenly and looked to the west side of the clearing where an opening in the crowd of spectators was appearing. Through it, a person in a dress of many feathers moved in a birdlike dance of sudden stops and hesitations, his feet pointing first to one side, then the other as he came.

"Snipe," a child somewhere in the audience called, and someone immediately hushed him.

"I will take sickness into the sky so far it can never return to the Nation," the bird dancer sang. "Watch me fly. See how well I can carry sickness away."

The dance he did was filled with swooping movements which carried him from one far point of the clearing to the other, and his feathers rustled and shone in the firelight as he imitated the flight of the Snipe. Sounds of approval and appreciation rose from the audience as Snipe danced the proof of his ability to remove the plague of sickness from the Alabama and Coushatta forever.

The chief saw his skill and believed it, and he took the clay pot from the earth and handed it to Snipe so that he could trap sickness where he dwelled in the sky. Snipe took the pot of black and white markings and ran toward the eastern side of the clearing with such speed that when he jumped to begin his flight into the sky, many in the audience cried out in wonder. Like a spark from the fire Snipe was gone, and on his vanishing the masked singer began a song which the Alabama and Coushatta joined as they stood in the great circle around the center of the Nation where the body of Abba Emory lay.

Austin Bullock sang in a low voice with the others the chant of celebration and thanks, and as he stood watching the singer in the middle of the circle, he felt someone touch his arm. When he looked down he saw his daughter standing beside him, wearing a deerskin dress decorated with embroidery and beadwork. Her hair was tied back with a snakeskin band worked with copper wire, and she wore the white paint of mourning on her face.

"Laura," he said. "Finally."

"Abba Bullock," she said, grasping his arm and nodding toward the firelit circle, "watch for Snipe to fly back."

As she spoke, an avenue in the crowd opened to the east, and the chanting of the people died away as they waited for the bird dancer to reappear, back from his journey to the sky with the clay pot filled with sickness.

He came with a great flitting movement of his feathered arms, juggling the clay pot from one hand to the other, chanting his song of triumph as he danced nearer and nearer the center of the circle. The masked dancer waiting for Snipe lifted both arms toward him in welcome, and as the bird dancer moved to present the clay pot to the Chief of the Nation, one hand slipped and the other faltered, and the great container which had captured sickness flew up into the air, turning once in the firelight, and then tumbled to the earth where it broke into many pieces.

The crowd uttered a shuddering cry, the shrill voices of children and women floating above the deeper groans of men, and once again sickness was free to bring its sorrow to the Alabama and Coushatta people.

"To live in the world is to suffer," the actors sang together, "to live in the world one must be strong."

"Look," Austin muttered under his breath to Laura and nodded toward the sky above the dancers' heads. "There goes tuberculosis and asthma. Isn't that cancer I just saw fly up out of the pot?"

"It was beautiful," Laura said, "like all the myths. You shouldn't make jokes about your own people when they're trying to cope with loss, Daddy. These mechanisms are your own."

"Lighten up, girl," Austin said, stepping back to let a group move past him as the crowd began to follow the pallbearers carrying Emory Sees the Water's coffin toward the church and the graveyard surrounding it. "For God's sake, leave the playacting to folks who don't know anything else."

"You know too much," she said, looking into his face with an expression he had been observing since she was a two-year old.

Patience, it said. Just listen to reason, father, it said. Pay attention, and I'll explain it in words even you can understand.

"I don't blame you," she went on. "You intend well for me and you always have. But the conspiracy has always worked to take you in, and you've allowed it to do so without even realizing what's happening to you and the Nation."

"The conspiracy. What are you talking about?"

"The Western intellectual conspiracy to close avenues, to exclude, to shut down, to narrow everything into one focus."

"Avenues," Austin said in a voice which sounded stupid to his own ears. "Avenues," he repeated.

"The avenues of perception," his daughter told him, "the ways of knowing without knowing. What the people of the Nation do in their stories and songs and the dances and rituals."

"Anthropology," Austin said as he walked beside Laura toward the grave site, "what sins are committed in thy name."

"It's not anthropology. It's learning to listen to darkness. What the people know without knowing they know it."

"You need to go sit down and write a term paper," he said. "Get this out of your system, and let some Ph.D. put a grade on it."

Up ahead the procession had reached the hole in the ground the backhoe had dug for Chief Emory, and the people following were clustering around the spot to get a view in the darkness as the coffin was lowered into its final place. There was no pause for words now or for any ceremony which would delay the bearers from immediately putting the dead man in the box into the ground.

No time could be wasted before covering the coffin with the dirt mounded beside the opening into the earth, and no opportunity for a berdache, a half-human witch, to toss a charm or a magic sabia bead into the grave could be allowed. Only the bearers, who had been cleansed for the task earlier in the day, would be allowed to handle the loose earth as it was shoveled into the hole to cover the dead man.

People were nervous, looking about them as the shovelfuls of earth hit the coffin of Chief Emory with a hollow final sound like a fist on a broken drum. Night was total now, and it was hard to see in the pale beams of a couple of flashlights someone had brought along, and everyone knew from the old stories that the man or woman or child

79

standing next to him might have been seized for riding by a witch for a way to get near the grave of the dead chief.

The one carrying the witch would not know of his rider, but his eyes would reveal the truth if they could be seen. Hiding somewhere deep in his head, peering out through his eyelids, would be the witch, biding time until the chance came to place the object which held sickness and loss into the resting place of the dead man. It could be a thorn, a small polished stone, a seed from the paw paw fruit, a coin of the white man treated in a special way to blind the head stamped on it, anything the witch had tainted to accompany the dead on the journey to the land beyond the sky. If the witch was successful in hiding the black charm in the dead man's grave, the one so cursed would stand forever in the wood at the edge of the Great Meadow, forbidden to enter and unable to return to the living world of the Nation. The pain in his head as he gazed within would mirror that of the poisoned arrows of the people who lived by the big water of the Gulf, and that pain would last for all time.

The Alabamas and Coushattas who had given their hearts to Jesus had been taught better, Austin considered as he stood at the edge of the gathering and listened to the rapid thrusts and grunts of the shovellers, but you couldn't tell so by the way everyone in the crowd clustered more closely around the grave of Abba Emory Sees the Water. Even Lawrence Spotted Horse, ordained in the Presbyterian Church, U.S.A., a graduate of the Duke University Divinity School, and just come from preaching the Christian burial of the old man in the coffin, had moved in tightly among the guardians around the grave, twisting his head from side to side, searching for any glimpse of a witch peeping from the face of one of his parishioners.

"I always feel cold at one of these things," someone said in Austin's ear, "no matter what time of year it is. It feels like a norther's blowing right through me, I don't care if it's the middle of August."

"I know the feeling, Delbert," Austin said to his cousin. "It's always a chilly time at a burying."

"Hello, young lady," Delbert Sees the Water said to Laura. "You look like a girl in one of them pictures from the old days the way you're all dressed up."

She nodded once and moved a step closer to the knot of people around the grave, now filled enough so that the sound of shovelling was dirt on dirt.

80

"You think he's here, Austin," Delbert said, "watching?"

"The witch?" Austin said. "You know what I think about that kind of thing, Delbert. Maybe somebody thinks he's a witch. Maybe somebody with a white beard thinks he's Santa Claus. That doesn't make it so."

"No, no. I mean the one that did it. The son of a bitch that killed my daddy."

"Well, if somebody did. Walker Lewis tells me that the medical examiner has ruled out violent death."

Ahead at the focus of the circle of Alabamas and Coushattas, the grunts of the shovellers came in rhythm, the beams from the flashlights jerked about erratically, and the grave filled steadily with earth. Austin watched Laura move even closer, putting two people between herself and where he stood.

"I knew it," Delbert said. "I knew what they'd say. They don't give a damn about a dead old reservation Indian. Never did, never will."

"Walker mentioned," Austin said carefully, "that there's no sign of ligature damage on Chief Emory's throat. But there's clear evidence of a heart attack."

"Shit," Delbert said in English and then continued in the language of the Nation, "what do you think, Abba Bullock? What killed the leader of our people? Where do you stand?"

"Delbert, it's not a question of where anybody stands. It's a question of trying to find out the truth. You know that as well as I do."

"There's truth, and then there's the blank eyes' truth. And a lot of times there ain't much overlap. What I want to know is which one you're buying, Cousin Austin?"

"I'm not a policeman, Delbert. Goddamn it, I just teach history at the high school and watch kids bounce basketballs off the wall. How can I know anything about Chief Emory except what the sheriff tells me?"

A woman standing in front of Austin turned to look over her shoulder at him, all of her face but the eyes hidden by a scarf wrapped around her head as protection against the berdache. She looked like someone he should know, but he couldn't place her. I know fewer people all the time, he thought, here in the Nation or in town at work. I'm forgetting everybody. At this rate I won't even be able to recognize myself some morning when I look into the mirror to shave. And everybody I do know is beginning to look strange to me.

He spoke again in a lower voice to Delbert. "You live here day in and day out," he said. "Why do you expect me to know more than you do about what happened to your father? Can you give me an answer to that?"

"All I know is what the People know," Delbert said, "and they know when the Chief of the Nation is dead Abba Mikko gives us our next one. At least He always has up to now."

The four men shovelling earth into the grave had now thrown in enough to reach the level of the ground, and as they did so, the single voice of an old woman somewhere near the front of the crowd rose in a chant immediately joined by most of the people around her. "Now he is buried," they sang together, "now he can leave this life. Now he can journey to the place where the sky meets the world. Now he can slip through the opening Abba Mikko has made for him."

"It's time," Delbert said into Austin's ear close enough that he could feel the warmth of the man's breath on his face, "to show the colors. It's time, Abba Bullock, to suit up for the big game."

Austin stepped forward, bumping against the back of the woman in front of him as he looked over her head toward where he had last seen Laura. Asking the woman's pardon, he slipped past her and caught sight of his daughter moving through the crowd of people to the left. He called to her, conscious that Delbert Sees the Water was close behind him as he walked in her direction.

He called her name. She stopped, and as Austin neared where she waited, the crowd parted and he could see a child standing near Laura, his back turned. Before he reached her the figure made a small hopping motion to one side, and Austin recognized the head, even in the poor light.

"Father," Laura said, "you've met Crippled Sparrow, I know."

"Abba Bullock," the little man said, extending his arm in a wide gesture of greeting, "the Chief of the Alabama-Coushatta. It's your big night."

82

"Compared to what?" Austin said. Crippled Sparrow was wearing a black leather coat which brushed the ground, and he held a gourd rattle worked with beads and feathers in his left hand. It hissed brightly with his every move.

"Pretty nice ceremony of burial," he said. "Deteriorated, of course, from what it must have been in the prelapsarian days, but there's still some power in it, to a small degree, don't you think?"

"I wouldn't know," Austin said, looking at his daughter who was gazing down at Crippled Sparrow as though he were a particularly well-marked artifact. "I don't know any others."

"Oh, you should see what the Navajos do, especially the Wind River people," Crippled Sparrow said. "I've seen shamans summon up real weather changes at a burial scene. I mean spectacular lightning displays and gale-force winds. Scare the bejabbers out of you, even the blank eyes and the non-believers. I remember seeing Ph.D.'s down on the ground crying and praying. People that thought they were educated just begging for relief."

"It must have been quite a show," Austin said to the little man and then addressed his daughter.

"It's getting on toward late, and we've got two cars to get back to town, Laura. Have you said hello to everybody you need to?"

"I'm not going back just yet. A great thing has happened. They're going to let me stay and watch the grave all night with the three guardians."

"What?"

"Yes, you know, to be sure no earth-eaters come to disturb the burying place. Don't tell me you've forgotten the stories Grandmother used to tell about the witches who eat the earth, Daddy."

"I haven't forgotten any stories, Laura," Austin said. "I remember more of them than I want to, in fact, but you don't need to stay up all night out here when you've got classes to get back to."

"The thing about your people I appreciate," said Crippled Sparrow, "is that they still have fear, fallen as they are. And that's been lost almost everywhere, even in belief-communities a lot less depraved than the Alabama-Coushatta Nation."

"Depraved?" Austin said. "What the hell are you talking about, Mr. Blending?"

"You remembered my white man name," the little man said in a happy tone. "That's impressive. No, what I'm talking about when I mention depravity has to do with the present state of the ritual life of the Nation. It's impoverished, almost irreproducible, on the verge of winking out like a crushed firefly." He stopped speaking and lifted both hands before him as though he were waiting for someone to place gloves on them. "But what you do have here is fear. You've got unthinking, blind fear, and that, pardner, is something you can't buy in a store or learn from a book. It should make you very happy, Abba Bullock. That fear could make your time as stated chief a really smooth slide, if you handle it right."

"I'm the first woman ever asked to guard against earth-eaters," Laura said, "and that's at the grave of a dead chief of the Nation. I can't pass it up, Daddy. I owe it to myself and to everything I represent to be here until morning. I am obligated."

"What about school?" Austin asked. "What about your obligations at Rice University? What about getting behind in your studies?"

"I'll learn more here in one night at a grave-watch than I would in a semester of seminars at school. I'll learn what can't be taught."

"She'll come to no harm, Abba Bullock," Crippled Sparrow said. "She will be with the People and the Old Ones. At one with meaning."

Austin looked down into the face of the little man staring up at him and wondered how far he could throw him if he buttoned up the scaled-down black leather coat first. He imagined himself seizing Roy Blending, getting a good running start and launching him from the spot where Snipe had hopped into space. He could see the little man twisting like a fired bullet as he vanished into the dark sky above the treeline, his befeathered and beaded goard rattling alongside.

Austin opened his mouth to speak, thought better of it, and gestured to Laura to follow him to a spot away from where Crippled Sparrow was standing. "I'd like to talk to you alone for a minute," he said and moved past a clump of people discussing the burying ceremony just completed.

He stopped and looked back for his daughter a few feet behind him. Crippled Sparrow had already begun talking to three women of the Nation, rocking back and forth on the heels of his boots as he spoke up at them clustered around him. Wherever the little bastard stops, he creates a circle, Austin thought, just like a dead sparrow lying next to a bed of ants. Here's something to eat, or at least to try a bite of. Jump on.

"Girl," he said to Laura, "don't you think you're pushing this ethnic weekend a little far? You've been out here on the reservation for almost three days, just having a hell of a time. Trying new hairdos and new makeup and dressing like the Indians and learning all kinds of new chants and folkways. Isn't it time to call it a day and get back to work?"

"I knew you'd be like this," she said, rubbing at the white paint on her chin. "You're just floating out there, aren't you, Daddy? You're like a balloon that some little boy has lost the string to, and you aren't connected to anything at all anymore."

"Where'd you learn that one? In a book of fairy tales or on television? Let me remind you that the subject is not me, but you, and the fact that you've got to get back to school tomorrow morning."

"Are you telling me that I can't stand watch at Chief Emory's grave against the earth-eaters tonight, Daddy? Is that what you're telling me? After I've been honored by being the first woman of the People allowed to do it?"

"That's about the size of it," Austin said. "I couldn't have put it better myself."

"Are you speaking to me as the stated chief of the Alabama-Coushatta Nation?"

"No, hell no. I'm speaking to you as your father, as the man who pays the tuition at Rice University and who expects you to do your part."

"If that's the case then, I can't accept your request. I will not honor what you say about it. I'm staying to help guard the grave against earth-eaters."

"Does this have anything to do with what that little windbag runt has been preaching to you?"

"I act on my own," Laura said, "as Colita, a woman of the Nation, and you're going to have to learn to deal with that."

She turned and began walking toward the gravesite, settling her leather bag on her shoulder as she moved away, her head thrust up at an angle.

"I'm taking the Honda," Austin called after his daughter. "And I expect you home tomorrow."

"Go ahead," Laura said over her shoulder. "I don't like the white man's machines anyway."

"Hondas are made by Japanese," Austin said. "The ones with narrow eyes, not blank ones, remember. Don't let your categories get all confused."

10

The moon was riding high over the tops of the pinoaks and the loblolly pines, and Charlie Sun-Singer could see the shadows of their branches and of the new leaves on the dogwoods in the water of Lost Man Marsh. He squatted quietly behind a clump of palmetto fronds and held his breath to listen for the sounds of his brother and Sam Shoes and President Polk as they searched for him. He had hidden himself well, he knew, and the head start they had given him was longer than usual because they thought him a child still, unable to elude and outsmart trackers as old as they.

They were wrong. He was small, but he ran quickly, and his wind never gave out, and he had spent so much time in the marsh at the edge of the Big Thicket that he knew places to hide that not even those who had already had their manhood dream had ever discovered. Charlie Sun-Singer had followed squirrels, birds, raccoons, and armadillos to their homes deep in the marsh. Once he had spent all day tracing the track of a bobcat in the mud of the swamp and the fallen leaves of the forest until he had found the den where the animal lived. He had listened to the cries of the young cats inside as they waited for their mother to return to nurse them, and he had looked inside the den and seen their eyes glowing in the darkness, five pairs of them burning at him as they smelled his strange scent.

The others would not find him before the moon rode his horse to the end of the sky and hid behind it, and that would signal the end of the game, and Charlie Sun-Singer would have beaten the older boys who laughed among themselves and treated him as a child of the village, not as the young man of the forest and marsh he really was.

Touching the small leather pouch which hung around his neck on a rawhide string, he let himself sink a little lower into the moss and creepers behind the palmetto, careful to make no noise, and watched the clear white face of the moon hanging in the sky like a stone. "Takahasi," he said in his mind, "Night Father, look at me."

From somewhere deep in the thicket came the cry of a rabbit pursued by a fox or a lynx, and Charlie Sun-Singer held his breath to listen, hoping to be able to hear the end of the hunt when it came, but nothing else followed. Rabbit has fooled Lynx again, he told himself, maybe by jumping into the swamp to swim away or maybe he has found a hole so deep the cat cannot reach him. He has used his big eyes and long ears so well that not even the sharp claws and needle teeth of Lynx could win this time.

Behind him and to the right fifty feet or so away, someone stepped on a dead stick on the forest floor, and it popped with the sound the first kernel of corn makes in a pan held over a fire. President Polk looking for me, Charlie Sun-Singer thought, most likely it is he and not Sam Shoes or Brother. He is older, but he is big and clumsy, and he does not look before he steps, and when his feet come down they break what they fall on. He is strong, and his weight is greater than mine, but President Polk cannot track, and he could never catch me by himself.

His thought made Charlie Sun-Singer so happy that he ventured to hoot softly twice like a hunting owl in the shadow of the palmetto fronds. Later when the game was done, and none of the three older ones had been able to find him, he would ask President Polk if he had heard the owl's cry, and when he said yes, Charlie would tell him the true source of the call. The others would laugh at President Polk, fooled in the darkness by a young Alabama small and quick like Rabbit, and Charlie Sun-Singer would make his face still and smooth like the surface of a deep pool in Long King Creek, and no one would be able to tell by looking that he too was laughing beneath. But all would know it, no matter how quietly Rabbit hid in his den.

Something rustled in the cane reeds, nearer this time than the place where President Polk had made the popping sound before, and Charlie Sun-Singer closed his eyes so that the world would be brighter when he opened them again, a trick old Alfred Two Hearts had taught him and the other young men who would listen to his stories. It was what the old warriors of the Nation had done in their raids against the Karankawa by the Big Water, and Charlie Sun-Singer knew it worked, for he had tried it many times in the nights he wandered the swamps and forests of the reservation.

So when he opened his eyes to detect President Polk searching for him in the hiding game, he could see clearly the bulk of the Big Man-Eater looming over the fronds of the palmetto behind which Charlie crouched. The beast was dressed in a robe of reeds and deerskins, his hair rose up against the moon like moss floating in water, his eyes were hidden by a shiny material that glittered as the head moved forward like a striking rattlesnake, and the hands as they reached through the palmetto were fingerless flippers with thumbs the size of gourds.

Charlie Sun-Singer had time to move only his head and shoulders before Big Man-Eater was on him, and the single cry he gave was that of Rabbit as Lynx bites through the neck at the base of the skull to make sure of no further struggle.

Sam Shoes and Norman Sun-Singer and President Polk searched Lost Man Marsh throughout the night, and they ventured places deep in the swamp they had never gone before and they did not find Charlie Sun-Singer until the moon had ridden his horse to the end of the sky to hide there during all the day to come.

Pritchard's old Chevrolet was parked at the curb in front of his house when Austin Bullock drove home at lunch, so at least Laura had come back after standing guard at Emory Sees the Water's grave all night. He felt a mixture of relief and anger kick up just beneath his breastbone as he pulled into the driveway, and he determined he was going to hold these emotions in balance when he talked to her. There was no way to win in an argument with her if he didn't remain above the fray and maintain a fatherly detachment. But goddamn, it was going to be hard to do. "Earth-eaters," he said under his breath as he stepped through the front door, "Jesus Christ."

The door to Laura's room was closed, but she had left a yellow stickit note in the middle of the top panel. "Wake me," it read in her tiny handwriting, "when you get in. Terrible news."

Austin knocked twice and opened the door a crack. "What's the matter?" he said. "You didn't catch your witch?"

Laura sat up immediately in her bed, shaking her head and blinking against the light from the open door. "Has anybody called you yet?" she said. "Have you heard?"

"No, what?"

"Charlie Sun-Singer is dead."

"Clement Sun-Singer's boy? The little one? What happened to him?"

"I don't know his father's name. Something killed Charlie." Laura lifted both hands to her face and began to cry with no sound, tears sliding down her cheeks.

"Was it a car wreck?"

"No," she said. "No, it happened in the swamp. Somebody killed him. Oh, Daddy, they choked him and they broke his neck. Oh, God, they hurt that little boy until he was dead."

"Was it a bear? There's not supposed to be any bear left in the Big Thicket these days. Could it have been a wolf? Maybe a pack of wild dogs?"

"His brother and some other boys found him. They'd been playing, you know, like the kids do out there when they sneak off at night."

"Did the boys see what did it? Was there animal sign around him?"

"No," Laura said, "not according to Sam Shoes and the other Sun-Singer boy. Some of the men were going to look this morning when it got light. I don't know anything else about it."

"Somebody's called Walker Lewis, haven't they? They did notify the sheriff, right?"

"Oh, yes, they're all out there. I should have called you at school, but I just wanted to go to bed and sleep. I didn't want to stay awake any more now, at all, at all. I just wanted to pass out."

"Look," Austin said, "why don't you try to go back to sleep for a couple of hours while I do some calling? I'll try to get back here as early as I can from work. Don't leave until I show up."

"I won't," she said. "Why did it happen, Daddy? Who could have done such a thing to that little boy?"

"I don't know. Terrible things happen all the time. It's just the way the world is." Austin put his hand out toward his daughter and watched it stroke her shoulder. He could feel the small bones beneath the flesh, and he imagined being able to pass strength, comfort, something from himself through to her.

"Well, I hate the way the world is," she said and lay back on the bed, pulling the quilt up to the level of her eyes, "when it's like this."

"I know, I know. I'll be back as soon as I can. Try to go to sleep."

The telephone rang at least eight times before someone at the home of Albert Had Two Mothers picked it up. No one spoke until Austin broke the silence.

"Hola," he said in the language of the Nation, "it is Austin Bullock who talks. Can Had Two Mothers talk back to me?"

"Abba Bullock," an old man's voice said, "is it you on this wire?"

"Yes. I have heard about the son of Clement Sun-Singer, how he is dead this day."

"They kill the children now, not just an old man almost ready for his last journey anyway."

"From what Laura told me, maybe it could have been a wolf or a wild dog, maybe a bear no one knew about in the Thicket. Is this true, my elder?"

"I have seen the sign in the earth where the water touches it. It was an animal who wears shoes. He leaves a track a baby could follow."

"The sheriff has seen this sign?"

"Oh, yes. He comes with his helpers. They make copies with a white powder with water like cement. They pick up all the footprints and put them in plastic bags and take them away in a box."

"That's good," Austin said. "Maybe they will find the one who did this killing."

"No, I don't think so. These things are interesting to see the blank eyes do, but they can't catch a Man-Eater."

"Well," Austin began, thinking to start a new direction for the conversation, "I will talk to Clement Sun-Singer later today."

"No," Albert Had Two Mothers went on, "that kind of footprint stealer won't do it. The blank eyes' machines and the laboratory workings they do. These things are nice, and I respect them, all these inventions. Like this telephone in my hand. Do you have a pushbutton, Austin Bullock, in your house?"

"Yes, I do."

"So do I," the old man said, "with big numbers to make it easy to see. It's nice. Especially the redial button. But the Big Man-Eater won't be caught by these things. You know that."

Austin didn't answer, waiting for what he knew would come next. Press one, he thought, if you want to hear folk remedies. Press two, if you want to hear who people think you are.

"It is the Chief of the Nation," Had Two Mothers said, "who must find this thing. And you know what he must do then."

"What, my elder?"

"Kill it," the old man said. "That's all."

The redneck driving the blue pickup ahead sped up when he realized Martin Utz was trying to move around him to get to the next lane in time to make the exit off the loop to 59 north. A puff of blue smoke came from the tailpipe just under the Don't Mess with Texas bumper sticker as the driver punched the accelerator, and Martin pointed through the exhaust as he spoke to the man in the front passenger seat.

"Look at this asshole," he said. "A big Texan, see. He doesn't want me to pass him just because I happen to be the car behind him. Car ahead he don't worry about."

"Far as he knows you might be trying to lap him in this big circle we're all going around in."

"They think this is traffic, see, all these other fuckers," Martin said and moved his index finger in a twirling motion. "They got six lanes going in the same direction for a few miles, and they think it's Boston on 128 there. They don't think they got to cooperate, don't got to yield, see."

Martin let the rented Lincoln Towncar have a little more gas until the bumper was less than two feet from the rear of the Chevrolet pickup ahead. The vehicle sped up, but Martin adjusted, keeping the Lincoln spaced behind at the same distance as though it were nailed to a connecting bar.

"You missed your exit," the other man said, twisting in his seat to look over his shoulder at the rear of the sign growing smaller behind them. "There it goes, 59 north."

"It's worth it," Martin Utz said. "Uh oh. What do I see in the truck ahead? Our cowboy friend is looking in the rearview mirror. Give him a howdy, Clarence. I believe he thinks he knows us."

The other man obediently raised a hand in greeting, and Martin let the Continental gain six more inches on the truck ahead. "He's leaning forward in the seat now," the man called Clarence said, "you can see his hair under the edge of his cap. It looks like he dips it in mayonnaise."

"Looking for more rpm's," Martin said, "but he ain't gonna find them in that Chevrolet. Watch this, Clarence."

With that, Martin tapped the rear bumper of the blue pickup with the Continental once, twice, and then dropped back about a car-length. The driver twisted around to look directly through the rear window, his mouth working and his eyes popped.

"I knew it, I knew it," Martin said. "Look at that shitty little beard he's trying to grow." He laughed and bounced both hands on the leather-padded steering wheel of the rental car. "Look at that pitiful foliage. It looks like an old man's legs with all the hair rubbed off."

"He doesn't know the meaning of the word trim," Clarence said.

"Hello," Martin said, "here we go," and slammed into the rear of the pickup with enough force to make its tires screech and the yellow gimme cap of the driver fly off as the man's head jerked back.

"His brake light's come on," Clarence said. "Think he wants to stop and look for damage? Maybe exchange insurance agents? Whip your ass in the bargain?"

"I wish. No, he's putting the pedal to the metal again, see. Cowboy thinks we're a Lincoln full of soul brothers going to carjack his ass. Mess with his Texas all over the fucking road."

"Another exit coming up," the other man said, "you want to take it and get back on the right highway."

"Yeah," Martin said, "if I didn't have work to do, I'd follow that cowboy all the way home. See if I couldn't get his attention."

"Fun's fun, no doubt."

"Right. That's what I say," Martin said, pushing the Lincoln across two lanes of traffic to get to the exit. "You got to lighten things up when you can, you know. See a chance to give a little instruction, help a asshole learn some manners, you do it."

"Go left," Clarence said, "hook up with it again on the rebound."

"What time did he say up there in the woods, this county seat fucker, Mr. Big Big?"

"Eleven."

93

Martin made the sound of a man trying to dislodge something adhesive from the back of his throat. "We'll be there when we get there," he said. "He'll wait."

"These people are good at that," the other man said. "That's all they know how to do. They've had lots of practice."

"You know, Clarence," Martin said, steering the maroon Lincoln back up onto the loop, "that's what I like about you. You can sum a bunch of dumb fucks up real good. Put the right word on them."

"I do a lot of simulations," the other man said. "You can make it just like life, but better. It's all in the software."

The office was just off the square in a small white house with a screen of evergreen shrubs and magnolia trees in front, and Martin Utz had to circle the courthouse twice before he spotted it. On the second circuit, he had caught sight of the statue of a soldier on the courthouse lawn and had pointed it out to Clarence.

"Wo ho, looks like we're in Mississippi. Every little dipshit town in that state's got one of them old boys up by the government building looking to stick his bayonet up somebody's ass. I didn't know they had them in Texas, too."

"Oh, yeah," Clarence said, "this is about as far west as the infection reached. Starts in DC and ends where the pine barrens run out. I think it has something to do with sunlight getting to the ground. It changes the pH in the soil."

"Say it do? I love it when you talk dirty," Martin said. "There it is. The little white house in the weeds."

He nosed the rental car into a parking place at the curb and cut the engine.

"What's it say on the sign by the door?"

"Three names," Clarence said, "as always. Interchangeable. One of them's his, I bet."

"A little after 11:30," Martin said, "just on schedule, central redneck time. Let's go see our man."

As the two walked around the car to the sidewalk, Clarence pointed to its grill. "You put a pucker in its lip, didn't you?"

94

"That kind of ding is supposed to pop out of the bumper," Martin said. "No quality in nothing no more. Everything's turning to shit."

A black woman looked up from a computer terminal as they walked through the door, late twenties Martin judged from her looks, but she was dressed for success in a gray suit and a miniature man's tie and that ruined the effect for him, definitely.

"Gentlemen," she said, rising from her chair and half-turning toward the door behind her. "Are you the party from Houston that Mr. Blatchford's been expecting?"

"We better be or else we're not here yet," Martin said, making a production of staring at the place on the woman's suitcoat where the tie bulged.

The door opened, and a man in a dark suit, a yellow tie and black dress cowboy boots stepped through. He had half-glasses perched on the end of his nose, and his silver hair was combed in a great pompadour that swooped two-thirds of the way down his forehead. "Truman Blatchford," he said. "Welcome to Annette."

"No," Martin said. "I'm Utz and this is Clarence. You must be Blatchford."

"Uh, yeah," the man said in a puzzled tone, "come in," and then with a well-manufactured laugh, "I got you, Mr. Utz. A different way of saying things, right? Lakisha, bring us some coffee, would you, honey?"

"Nor for me or Clarence," Martin said, stepping through the door into the inner office, "but, hey, suit yourself, Truman."

The room took up the rest of the house and was furnished with a leather sofa and chairs and a desk made of a large polished cross section of a dark-wooded tree trunk. A metal cast of a life-sized armadillo sat on one side, and a single piece of paper lay in the center of the desk. The walls of the room were filled with photographs of football players holding helmets and of middle-aged beefy men in blazers staring directly into the camera lens.

"That desk is made from a single cypress log," Blatchford said, watching Martin look about the room, "and these old boys on the walls I imagine you recognize if you follow A&M football any."

95

"You're kidding me," Martin said, nodding toward the largest of the framed photographs in the middle of the wall behind the desk. "Who's that there looks like he just bit into a bad oyster?"

"Coach Bryant," Truman Blatchford said in a reverent tone without having to look to see where Martin was directing his attention. "The Bear himself. Nineteen fifty six, the hell camp."

"Clarence," Martin said to his companion, "can you believe that?"

"Easy," Clarence said.

"I was there," Blatchford said, "I don't mind telling you I suffered. But I survived it I'm here to tell you."

"Not right now," Clarence said in a soft voice, "if you don't mind."

"Yeah," Martin said, "we need to have you tell us how to talk to Indians at this particular time. How to make a deal with the noble redman. What it takes to do business with the Native American."

"Like I said when we talked before on the phone," Truman Blatchford said, "you have come to the right man. I can help you with that project. See, you got the federal government, you got the Department of the Interior, you got the state of Texas, you got the tribal council, you got what they call their stated chief. On and on. It's a complicated situation with the Alabama-Coushatta."

"No doubt," Clarence said, leaning forward to look closely at the metal armadillo on the polished slab of cypress.

"We just want to do these fellow Americans some good," Martin Utz said, "in the name of equality and diversity and what have you."

"We can all do each other some good," Blatchford said. "That's what this country's about the last time I looked it up."

"Amen," Martin said, "Allah Akbar and shalom, Mr. Truman Blatchford. Amen and hallelujah and all that good stuff."

12

"I know it sounds unpatriotic and self-serving," Ruella Petry was saying, "but at this time of the semester I find it hard enough to keep the attention of the students. Now with all the hysteria of the basketball play-off, I find it well-nigh impossible."

She looked away from the face of the man to whom she'd been addressing her comments, Mr. R.P. Prongle, principal of Annette High School, and swept her gaze around the group of teachers seated in the first two rows of the school auditorium. Trying to judge the effect of that well-nigh, Austin Bullock thought. Ms. Ruella is proud of that turn of phrase. She's probably been planning since September a way to work that into one of her statements at a faculty meeting. Now she's launched it, feels all giddy, and hopes it finds a happy home.

"What are you proposing, Ruella?" the principal asked, obviously struck by the comment. Dick Peter, Austin thought, the only man in Texas educational circles, according to Coach Mellard, all of whose three names mean prick.

"I just want to know what measures the coaching staff is taking to insure that Annette High School remains an institution of secondary education instead of a basketball factory. That's all," Ms Petry answered and sank back into her seat, well-satisfied.

"As you all know, we have among us a teacher who also coaches basketball," Dick Peter said, smiling under the thin sprinkling of black hair on his upper lip and looking toward Austin. "Perhaps Austin Bullock in his bi-faceted role can respond to your question."

Putting on a large smile, Austin turned in his seat to speak, remembering another thing Coach Mellard had said about Dick Peter, "His little bitty mustache looks like he can't quite get that last part of that mouse swallowed."

"I agree with Ruella completely," Austin said, "and so does the rest of the coaching staff. Our constant effort is to keep before our students the fact that their primary allegiance is to their studies always. That's well-nigh paramount."

Right back at you, Ruella, he said to himself, here's your well-nigh and a primary allegiance and a paramount to boot. Maybe that'll buy me some space to think during the rest of this hour and a half.

The triple shot seemed to work. After a few concluding noises by Ms Ruella Petry on the subject, the attention of discussion shifted to other topics, and Austin was able to tune out and focus on what he was going to say to the tribal council the next day at dawn.

Sheriff Lewis had agreed to meet with the elders then and to tell them all he could about his findings so far in the death of Charlie Sun-Singer. The session would be a hard one, and it would not satisfy any member of the Nation present, and Austin dreaded what the council would expect of him in the process.

First of all, the old men of the council and most of the people in the Nation they represented would be certain the young boy had been killed by a hanka, a Big Man-Eater, the creature who lived in the swamps and marshes of the Big Thicket and had done so since Crawfish first brought mud from the bottom of the deep water to create the world. It would not matter if the footprints left at the scene were those of running shoes manufactured by Nike or if when apprehended the killer was found to be a resident of the Nation or someone who lived in the world outside the pines and sawgrass and yaupons of the reservation's limits.

All Alabamas and Coushattas knew from the old stories that a Big Man-Eater could take the form of any human it was able to fool into eating the fruit of the chokeberry bush and that the only evidence of the death of a Big Man-Eater were the huge skeletons of stone sometimes unearthed by those digging in the soil of the Nation. So to point out to a believer of the old ways that no one had ever seen a Big Man-Eater or found any strange sign identifying one was of no weight. As old McKinley Big Eyes had explained to Austin when he listened on the long evenings of his youth along with other young men of the Nation, "the only man or woman or child who ever sees a Big Man-Eater in his true form as a beast with floating hair and yellow fangs and no fingers on his hands is the one who can never tell."

"Why, my elder?" Gemar Long Arms had asked, knowing the answer, but giving the response he knew the old man expected.

"Because," McKinley Big Eye had answered, "this unfortunate one of our people is the one bitten to death by the Big Man-Eater. He can speak only through his wounds and his death marks."

The council would also know the identity of the proper person to seek out and destroy the Big Man-Eater who had killed one of the people, and they would know that Austin Bullock would share the knowledge, protest though he might and want to reject the notion though he would. It would be the stated Chief of the Nation, Abba Whoever it Was, solely fitted for battle with the death creature, and Austin groaned aloud in the Annette High School faculty meeting at the vision that rose before him of the gaze the old men of the council would fix upon him as they beheld the man they considered the Abba in succession to old Emory Sees the Water: Abba Bullock, slayer of monsters.

"Are you ill?" Jennifer Brady whispered in his ear from the seat next to his in the auditorium.

"That's not the word for it, Jennie. I am sick at heart."

"These pissant meetings do the same thing to me," she said out of the corner of her mouth, "every single damn time."

The meeting finally ended, and people began to pick their way down the aisles and out into the hallway, freed from one cycle and in place for a new one to begin.

At the door to the auditorium, Austin turned away from the familiar grumble of the groups of teachers dribbling out into the hall and headed for the gymnasium for basketball practice, hoping he would be able to concentrate enough to do some good. It was one of the last opportunities to work with the players before the regional game on Friday, and Mellard would be needing all the help he could get.

The head coach would be wired and roaring, as desperate as a condemned man the night before his scheduled execution, and the players on Annette's team, particularly the blacks and the Alabama-Coushatta, would be looking to Austin for something a little quieter than a full-bore scream.

If I can provide it, Austin said to himself as he reached the locker room, in the middle of raking over the things that were happening on the reservation and of trying to keep Laura from reverting to the nineteenth century and setting up housekeeping in a mud hut. The way she's been going ethnic, the next thing will be her sitting crosslegged in the dirt chewing on a deerskin to soften it up for clothes.

"Austin," Coach Mellard said from the door of the locker room which opened onto the corridor to the basketball court, "man, I have been waiting for you."

"Here I am. Directly from the faculty meeting."

"Yeah, I knew you were somewhere. Listen, I need you to talk to Tom. Something's wrong with him all of a sudden."

"Thomas Fox Has Him? Is he sick?"

"Naw. I don't think it's that. It's his damn head that's all screwed up. He got suited up, but he won't take part in the drills. He's just sitting there."

"Where is he ? Out on the court?"

"Sitting in the stands," Mellard said. "With an attitude. He won't say a word back to me when I talk to him, and damn if I did anything to make him sull up like that. He's out yonder."

Mellard pointed toward the wall behind him like a man giving firefighters directions to his burning house. There, he was saying, there, there, run out of your boots and save my homestead.

"I'll go talk to him," Austin said. "See what's bothering Tom."

"He's got to get his mind right before Friday. I can't do it without my point guard, goddamn it. I told him that straight out."

"Why don't you just get the other kids working on something," Austin said. "I'll see to Tom."

"All right, all right, he's in your hands, Austin. You got to get him to pick up a basketball like he's supposed to. Get that head focused in the right direction. Get them priorities straight."

Thomas Fox Has Him was sitting two rows up in the spectator's seats, staring before him as though his eyes were fixed on some object far away only he could see. He was suited up in a practice uniform as Mellard had said, but Austin noticed that the laces of his shoes were

100

not tied, a sign that the road he saw before him was not one he wanted to take. He said nothing to acknowledge Austin's appearance, but his eyes flickered as the older man climbed the row of seats and sat down beside him.

"I see you, Thomas Fox Has Him," Austin said in the language of the Nation, and after a few seconds the young Alabama answered him.

"I see you, Abba Bullock."

"Coach Mellard puts much store in the drills of practice," Austin said.

"All the blank eyes do, even the teachers in the high school."

"They are not always a bad thing, the drills. They help to make movements..." Austin paused to think of a way to put his thought in the language of the people, couldn't find a combination of words that would match up, and finally used the English, "Automatic," he said. "There is no need to think what to do if the muscles have learned their lesson on their own."

"I have heard the coach say this many times. It makes his mind easier to see us do the drills."

"You have always done the drills before and pleased your coach and your teachers," Austin said. "That is not why you are sitting here with your feet not ready for the journey you, is it?"

"No, Abba Bullock," the young man said, taking a deep breath and letting his head drop so that his eyes were no longer fixed on whatever he had been studying in the distance before. "It is not the drills. I do what I have to do to get along with the blank eyes. Just like you always do."

Zinger, Austin thought and looked down at his fingers, waiting for Fox Has Him to go on. His skin looked darker than usual to him against the white sweat pants he was wearing.

"It is the killing of my cousin, Charlie Sun-Singer, that I am thinking about," Fox Has Him said, "that, and what did it."

"You know it was not what the old people say, a Big Man-Eater, but something much worse, a human being, who did this thing."

"I know that, yes. I believed the old stories when I was a child, and I have tried to believe as much as I can since I have become a man, but I know better than what the people like to say still. I am not afraid of spirits and witches."

"You grieve for your young cousin," Austin said, "like all of us."

"Yes, I do. Charlie was a funny kid. No one knew the woods and swamps like he did so young. He learned how all the animals lived; he went everywhere by himself. He found things no one else knew were there."

"That is a good thing to hear. Something to remember about him always."

"Yes," Fox Has Him said, and Austin could hear a break in his voice for the first time. "I will not forget that about him. It's why they killed him, I think."

"Because of something he found?"

"He kept it in the medicine pouch he wore on a string around his neck. When his brother and the other boys found him, it was gone."

"What was it," Austin asked in a careful voice, "this thing in the pouch?"

"I don't know. A coin, maybe. He showed it to me, but I couldn't tell what it was. A disk of metal, gold color, heavy to the touch. A man's head on one side, on the other a design, a crown, maybe. Bigger than a silver dollar."

"Have you told anyone else what Charlie showed you?"

"No, my elder."

"Do not. Not even your father or mother." Austin paused, then spoke again. "Not the sheriff, either. Not yet."

"I will not, Abba Bullock."

Before them on the court, Coach Mellard had two sets of teams working on bringing in the ball against a press. A badgered player jiggled back and forth, trying to see somebody open for a pass while two other boys flailed their arms in his face.

"I believe I will go take the ball in from out of bounds," Thomas Fox Has Him said. "Jerry McNeil always gets nervous doing that." He leaned forward to tie his shoes.

"Go show him how," Austin said and touched the young man on the arm. "That would be useful."

Now there are three, Austin said to himself as he walked toward the center of the court where Mellard was standing. Three golden gifts from one king to another, and where had an old man and a young boy come up with the two nobody had ever heard of before? What would two of them be doing somewhere in the swamplands at the edge of the Big Thicket that backs up to the reservation? Are there more of them? How many could there have been in the first place, back when the king of Spain was peddling his likeness to savages in exchange for everything they owned?

They couldn't be worth that much, not even as artifacts, surely not enough to kill two people over. No surprise that Emory Sees the Water and Charlie Sun-Singer would have thought such objects found in the swamp to be strange and significant enough to be kept and treated as talismans. Everything had been some kind of medicine to the old chief, from a feather from a blue jay's wing to a pebble in Long King Creek that looked to be out of the ordinary in color or shape or way of having been encountered or picked up. Everything meant something, and a new match for the old medal passed from chief to chief for generations would have seemed magical to him.

Once, Austin remembered from a time in his childhood, the old man had showed him and several other young boys a tiny pencil that had come in the mail in a package addressed to him from Newsweek Magazine. Even then Austin had known it was an advertising gimmick designed to make it easy for the recipient to check the yes box on a form for subscription to the magazine, but Chief Emory had declared it an instrument of writing which disclosed by its size the true nature of the people in New York who had sent it. "Their hands are tiny," he had said, "but quick, and they write their messages in marks so small only Mole with his little eyes can read what they say."

The old man had retrieved the red pencil after the young men of the Nation had passed it from one to the other for examination, careful not to let their chief know what they were really thinking, and had placed it in the wooden box in which he kept his sabia beads and the blue stone he had found in the stomach of a deer. More than likely it's still there, Austin told himself, part of the old chief's legacy to his people, one tiny red pencil out of the ten million mailed.

As for Charlie Sun-Singer, the dead boy who had taught himself the forests and swamps of the reservation at an age so early not one of his peers could match him, he had all the promise of a shaman of his people in the making. Surely the golden medal he had found somewhere in his searching of the world he saw as magical would have spoken powerfully to him in its strangeness, in the imprint of the head of a king on one side and his crown on the other.

But the medal in Charlie Sun-Singer's medicine pouch had been taken, according to Thomas Fox Has Him, and the one found by Chief Emory was in the drawer of a lamp stand in Austin's living room.

I should take it to Rice, to the anthropology people, he thought to himself, and see if they can tell me anything about its history.

"Thanks, Coach," Mellard said from his post in the center of the tip-off circle, gesturing toward the clot of players across the way attempting to prevent Thomas Fox Has Him from passing a basketball in from out of bounds. "That was a hell of a job of motivation you just gave him."

"He wanted to do it himself," Austin said, watching Fox Has Him bounce a pass safely over the line to Billy Manry. "I just let him talk himself into it."

"No matter how you got it done, he's doing what he ought to be doing, and that's all I care about."

"I know," Austin said. "I know."

13

"Remember when Lodge Boy made all them arrows while his father was away on a hunt?"

Albert Had Two Mothers was the one who asked the question, and the five other men sitting with him in the circle around the small lightwood fire seemed to be looking at the same spot in the roil of smoke before them as they pondered an answer. In a minute or so, Thomas Two Tongues spoke, looking at Austin Bullock who was sitting back away from the heat as he did so. Austin kept his gaze fixed steadily ahead.

"This is the one about the two boys, right? It's two of them in this."

The other members of the council muttered in agreement, nodding at the smoky fire before them and waiting for Albert Had Two Mothers to go on.

"Later on," he said, "but not right at first. See, it was at least two hunts the father went on while Lodge Boy stayed home to make arrows, and he didn't find out at first how all them arrows was showing up."

"It was three times he went on a hunt," Two Tongues said. "Things always happen three times in the old stories."

"Sometimes two," Cooper Leaping Deer said, "but mainly three like you said just then."

"On the third hunt the father came home early," Had Two Mothers announced in his story-telling voice, "because his luck was not good, and that's when he found out how Lodge Boy was making all them arrows so fast."

"The other boy," somebody said. "He was helping out."

"Another boy had been helping Lodge Boy," Had Two Mothers went on, ignoring the comment. "He was Woods Boy who lived by himself, afraid of grown people, in the forest. He had been coming in while Lodge Boy's old man was gone to give him a hand in making all them arrows."

"He was an orphan," Cooper said. "No mama, no daddy."

"When the father saw the way Lodge Boy was making all them arrows he wasn't mad, not when he thought about it. And he asked Woods Boy to come stay with him and his son there in the house."

"He took in the orphan," Two Tongues said, "like a Coushatta would do."

"Everything rocked along, rocked along, rocked along," Albert Had Two Mothers said in a singsong voice, "for a good long time. Plenty of arrows to shoot, see, and no need to worry about wasting them, so the father got plenty of game on his hunts."

"Everybody eating high on the hog," one of the old men said. "Big fires and beaucoup meat."

"Until one day when the boys' father was hunting deep in the swamp over yonder to where Batson, Texas, is now, something happened back at the lodge."

Albert Had Two Mothers paused and looked around at the four men sitting with him in the circle and then craned his neck to see Austin Bullock a little way behind him.

"The rest of you don't tell," he said. "Abba Bullock, do you remember what comes next?"

"Yes, my elder. The old man of the swamp came into the house clearing."

"He was wearing weeds," Albert said, "water lillies all over him like a cloak. He had a hat made of them little vines that grow in the bottom of still-water ponds. All over he was dripping water. He called himself Wet Man, that's what he told Lodge Boy and Woods Boy his name was. Wet Man."

Albert Had Two Mothers was well into his story now, and no one else offered comment as he went on with it. Instead they looked deep into the patterns of smoke rising from the fire at the center of the circle, a couple of them rocking back and forth in a small steady motion as they listened to what the retelling of the Lodge Boy story might say to them this time through.

"Wet Man spoke soft words to the boys, and though they were afraid at first of him and the way he looked with all them weeds and that water dripping off of him, they quick got used to the way he looked. He offered to show them his canoe, a real big one he told them it was, and he said he would give them a ride on the river where they had never been before. Back home before dark, he told them, before their father returned with the meat he had killed with all them arrows they had been making for him.

"And so they did. Went with him for a ride on the river, what the blank eyes call the Trinity River now, saw all kinds of birds they never seen before, an alligator somewhere in it too, maybe they fished some, I don't remember. And sure enough, Wet Man got them back home before their father had returned.

"But when the two boys got out of the canoe to get on the bank of the river, Woods Boy was the second one out, and just as his foot touched the ground, Wet Man jumped on his back and held on. And they couldn't get him off, no matter how they tried. He was all slick with them water lillies and bottom vines, and he had got a good grip and they couldn't break it. Them boys they both tried hard.

"When the father come up with the meat he had killed, he saw what was going on with Wet Man there fastened on Woods Boy's back. So he heated up some water real hot in a big kettle, and he throwed it all over Wet Man."

Albert Had Two Mothers stopped talking and looked deeply into the smoke for fully a minute before he went on to finish the story for the men of the council and Austin Bullock.

"Wet Man let loose of his hold when that hot water hit him, and squalled real loud and ran under the house. Woods Boy was saved from the old liar, but the bad thing is, see, that Wet Man is still under the house, waiting to jump on somebody when he thinks he can. You can hear him at night."

Had Two Mothers fell silent again, and Austin waited, thinking to himself now comes the moral application and I know who it's going to be directed toward, and I'm not going to look up until I hear my name called.

"Moaning up under there," Cooper Leaping Deer said. "My old meemaw she claimed she could hear him late on winter nights, cold and hurting you know with them burns still on him. What do you think, Abba Bullock?"

"I'm sure your grandmother thought she heard Wet Man," Austin said, "when she was the only one awake late at night in her house in the winter."

"The old stories tell us things," Albert Had Two Mothers said. "They're not just fun to listen to. You hear them right and you learn something. You can see how to do now, not just how the people did in the Old Time."

Here it comes, Austin thought, instruction for the young and reluctant. Let me see if I can't speed things up and make it a little easier for the teacher.

"You speak true things, my elder," he said. "And it is good to hear you tell of Lodge Boy and Woods Boy again and of how Wet Man fooled them for a time. What do you think the old story says to the people of the Nation now, Abba Albert?"

"Well, it's not one to one, you understand," Albert Had Two Mothers said, staring deeply again into the smoke of the small fire. "It ain't that simple."

"No," a couple of the other council members said in unison.

"It's not an equation," Cooper Leaping Deer, whose son had gone to college for many years, added. "I wouldn't claim that."

"Here's what we can get from the story of Lodge Boy and Woods Boy and Wet Man," Had Two Mothers began, "without reading too much into it. See, Abba Bullock, you got this family of Alabamas, getting along fine, helping each other, taking in a boy on his own without a mama or daddy, and he helps out, too. Then you got this creature that looks like a man, for the most part, and acts like one the same as a man."

"Always wet, though," Thomas Two Tongues said, "and wears weeds for clothes."

"Right," said Had Two Mothers. "That tells you something, if you look hard enough at it and think about it. And this outsider fools the family and tries to kill it, picking on the one he thinks is the weakest.

"But it doesn't work, and the reason why is the father comes back from the hunt and knows what to do when he sees the damn thing up on that boy's back. He does something. And it works."

"Not all the way, though," Cooper Leaping Deer said.

"No," Had Two Mothers agreed. "Wet Man's still up under the house, and that's the way it always is in this world. You can scare off these bad things for a while, but you can't make it permanent unless you kill them."

"That's a hard thing to do," Thomas Two Tongues said. "Just a dose of hot water won't do it."

"You got that right," Leaping Deer said.

"But when these creatures pop up," Albert went on, "the father has to see what needs to be done and then do it. That's all."

"I think I read you," Austin said, looking first at Had Two Mothers and then at the other old men of the council. "But I have a question. Who is Wet Man today? You can't tell him by his clothes, like in the old story, and there's sure not anybody standing around dripping water any more."

"That's what you got to figure out," Albert Had Two Mothers said, "and then know what to do, Abba Bullock."

"It's like looking into the smoke off a fire and seeing things," Thomas Two Tongues said, "but they're always changing shape when they're twisting and rising up into the sky."

"It's a booger to keep them in your mind and not forget," Cooper Leaping Deer said. "I'm glad it ain't my job."

"I hear you," Austin said. "I hear you, my elders."

Later, after the fire had died down and the five old men of the Nation's council had crawled up from the damp ground on which they had been sitting, moving stiffly as they helped each other rise, Albert Had Two Mothers gave Austin a signal that he wanted to speak to him alone before he left the reservation for town.

They walked over to Austin's car together as the four other men began to pick their way up the path toward the village center.

"That was a good talk we had," Albert said, watching the rest of the council depart. "I think we got something done."

"You told a good story," Austin offered. "I haven't heard that one in a long time."

"It's not one of the mainstream ones, but I think it can tell you something if you let it, Austin. We talked enough about that situation, though. Let it work on its own."

The old man looked at Austin, looked away at the backs of the other men, smaller now in the distance, and then began to speak again with the air of a man who had made up his mind to say what was bothering him with no more postponement. Here comes the hard sell, Austin thought, to hell with indirection.

"You think this sheriff will call this young boy's death a killing or not, Abba Bullock?"

"There's no way he can't. That's clear from the way they've been investigating. You can rest your mind on that."

"Because we need to get it cleared up," Had Two Mothers said. "Got to catch the one who did it and when we do, we'll be catching the one that killed Chief Emory, too."

"Maybe so," Austin agreed. "But they don't want to call that an unnatural death, Chief Emory's."

"It makes no difference what the blank eyes say about that. We'll know what the truth is about Chief Emory enough to satisfy us. Once we get the one who killed the little boy, we'll know what's what."

"That's a good way of looking at it. Meanwhile, I want to go talk to Walker Lewis and see what he'll tell me about the little boy and what they're doing about that."

"Another thing is Truman Blatchford. Has he said anything yet to you about the men from Houston?"

"Blatchford? No. I haven't had any dealings with him for years. I see him around town some."

"He knows you're going to be chief, and he understands you got to be in on this thing. You got to be the one to sign us on."

"I wish you wouldn't say stuff like that, Abba Albert. You know what I've been telling you. And what do you mean about signing on? Signing on what?"

"Blatchford can tell you better than me. I don't know much yet because it's not my place. All he's told me is that the Nation can make a big deal with these men from Houston. Bigger than the oil ever was, bigger than the pulpwood."

"That's not saying much."

"Right, that's what I'm telling you. It's some big money he's saying about."

"You know Truman Blatchford, though," Austin said. "Besides, what's the Nation got left to sell? Or give away? There's nothing left, you realize, except tourist trade. And that's never going to be a big draw, situated where we are."

"It's good to hear you say we, Abba Bullock."

"Of course, I say we. But that doesn't mean I live here anymore."

"You'll find out where you live," the old man said. "If you look hard enough, I'm satisfied."

"What's the Blatchford deal you've been talking about?" Austin said, trying to keep to the subject he wanted to discuss. "What would some people in Houston want from the Alabama-Coushatta reservation? What's out here?"

"He said it's back over in Lost Man Marsh, down there by the Big Thicket."

"You mean where Charlie Sun-Singer was killed and close to where Chief Emory died? That the area you're talking about?"

"Generally, I imagine. Yes. But that doesn't have to mean nothing."

"I understand that. All I know is that a part of the reservation that's usually got nothing but a few sparrowhawks and an alligator or two wandering around on it has got awful busy all of a sudden."

"I thought about that," Albert Had Two Mothers said, "for a good long while, and then I just give part of it to our Heavenly Father and the rest to Abba Mikko. We can't sort everything out ourselves."

"What is it Blatchford says is back over there that interests these folks from Houston, then?" Austin sneaked a look at the dashboard clock in the Honda. "Couldn't be oil, like I said."

"No, he just said rights. Mineral rights in general."

"I thought the government let the Nation sell the mineral rights to Arco, back there when we were going to all get richer than the Cherokees."

"Nuh uh," the old man said. "Wrong. You look at the contract. That lady lawyer the feds sent down here limited it to petroleum and to specific lots. She was a smart little thing, worth every dime President Reagan paid her."

"She was?" Austin said, trying to remember if he had met the legal team negotiating for the Nation and the government with Arco. Probably not. He was doing a master's thesis at the time, driving back and forth to Houston, sunk deep into the Treaty of Ghent and trying to read French. "Saved us something, did she?"

"We still got stuff to sell," Had Two Mothers said, "if the price is right."

"I bet it'll be a lot different trying to sell mineral rights off of Department of Interior administered lands now, though," Austin said, "with a different man in the White House and environmentalism and all."

"That's why you got to go to Washington, Abba Bullock," the old man said. "You know how to talk to these kind of blank eyes. You know what's on their minds."

"Wait a minute. I've got a job to do."

"You're telling me," Albert said. "You got to find all them hot buttons."

"Hot buttons?"

"Hot buttons," repeated the chief spokesman of the council of the Alabama-Coushatta Nation, "and where to hit them. You know, what moves a man."

"Where have you been hearing all this stuff, my elder?" Austin asked, reaching for the ignition key. "Who have you been talking to?"

"I try to keep up," the old man said. "It's a changing economy."

14

On the ride back to Annette, Austin tried to think about what Albert Had Two Mothers had told him about Truman Blatchford and the men from Houston with an interest in mineral rights, but his mind kept drifting back to an image of Charlie Sun-Singer dead in Lost Man Marsh. He could see the boy on his back with his arms thrown above his head and nothing in his eyes, his deerskin medicine bag around his neck on a thong as somebody reached to break it free.

The man looming above the fallen boy had the floating hair of Big Man-Eater, and he made the howling sounds described in the stories about the creature as he ripped open the medicine bag to get at the shiny piece of metal inside. The gleam of his teeth, Austin thought, the gleam of his teeth in the moonlight.

He made himself yell aloud as he rode alone in the car, and he bounced both fists off the steering wheel until the horn blasted along with him. Before him the head of the driver in the car in front jerked, and the vehicle, a large beige sedan, sped up in response.

"That's right, lady," he said aloud, "there's a crazy Indian right behind you with a head full of tomahawks and a belly full of legends. And he's coming after you in a kamikaze buggy."

None of that's true, except maybe the crazy part, but at least I've got my mind out of the swamp and back on the highway. If I'm lucky, I'll be able to get in a day's work today at what they pay me for, maybe even forget for a few minutes one or two of the names I'm carrying around, Austin thought to himself.

Up ahead, the beige sedan pulled around a long bend and out of sight, and Austin told himself to take several deep breaths and think about the day ahead of him in one-hour segments. Get through it sixty minutes at a time and don't look any further ahead than the next ring of the bell. First get the car parked. Next walk into American history for juniors. Think about Reconstruction. Talk.

He did that. Kept his head down and his eyes focused, and at noon he drove home for lunch and to make certain Laura had left for Houston and the dens of anthropology at Rice University.

She had left a note stuck in the front door, Austin could see as he got out of the car, but the door itself was standing open three or four inches. Out of here in a hurry, he thought, not even bothering to lock the door. Not like her. She's really shaken by what's happened out there. Probably can't wait to get out of range of the reservation now.

"8:25 a.m.," Austin could read across the top of the yellow paper as he stepped up to the door, "Got a ride with John David Garner back to school. I'll call tonight, Laura."

Laura, he thought, not Colita, worse off than I expected, and then he opened the door to the living room.

They had used a knife on the sofa and the two overstuffed chairs. Chunks of cotton and straw batting littered the floor from the doorsill to the kitchen and from the fake fireplace to the open door to the bedroom. The prints on the walls had been broken from their frames and the glass and backings were all heaped in one area of the floor, where the one with that task had done the work.

The table lamps had been turned upside down to remove their bottoms, and these were tossed randomly aside. Through the opening to the kitchen, Austin could see that the contents of the refrigerator had been dumped on the linoleum along with the cereal and flour and cornmeal from the pantry, and someone had even gone through all the cans of cleanser and the plastic garbage bags under the sink.

He started toward the kitchen and then stopped by the sofa, looking toward the small table which stood at its far end and hoping they had found it before they had gone into the bedroom. They had. The single drawer had been pulled out and dropped with its coupons and paper clips and rubber bands and letters and ballpoints at the far end of the sofa.

Austin squatted and poked at the refuse of the drawer and saw no sign of the golden medal passed on to him from Emory Sees the Water. "Goddamn it," he said out loud. Why hadn't they started with the drawer like somebody with sense rather than slashing and throwing and breaking things as soon as they got into the house? "Trash, nothing but trash."

He rose and walked to the bedroom. Nothing overturned or ransacked there, but somebody had left his sign in the middle of Austin's unmade bed. Holding his breath, he bundled the sheets together and took them out into the backyard and stuffed them into a large green plastic garbage can. He replaced the lid and looked at the sky above the fringe of green buds opening on the pear trees at the back line of his property.

The sun had broken through the March haze, and its noon angle lay down perfect silhouettes of the vegetation he could see around him, bright light from above and the dark shadows cast by everything below, perfect copies with no life of their own and no way to move until the source that cast them down decided.

"Onoolichi," Austin said, uttering the Nation's word for cloud people, those creatures captive and with no will left to them, doomed forever to wait on the intentions of a force not their own. They stood always fixed, according to the stories told about them by the old men of the Nation, their feet frozen to the earth in one place and the muscles of their bodies and the gestures of their hands and the expressions of their faces caught in one moment. "What tortures them most," McKinley Big Eye would say, "these cloud people, is not being paralyzed. No, it's not that, not the fact they can never move on their own. What's the worst is the waiting, what's bad is the expecting to move. See, that's what hurts so bad."

"I understand you now, my elder," Austin Bullock said, staring into the noonday sun of March. "It comes to me today about how the cloud people hurt as they stand and wait."

"You don't think it was just some kids then?" Walker Lewis said from behind the desk to which he had retreated as soon as Austin came into the office. "You know, just a couple of mean boys with nothing better to do than to bust into their teacher's house."

"No," Austin said. "That wasn't who did it."

"Not to quarrel with you, Coach, but how can you be so sure? Hell, you know I've seen kids do all kinds of stuff, especially to a teacher's property. You remember here a few years back when them twin girls of Ted Baker like to drove their English teacher crazy by phoning her all hours of the day and night. They had her scared to go home and scared not to. Remember that?"

"Yeah, I remember all about that. But what happened at my house is in a whole different world from that. These bastards are not from around here, Walker, and they didn't do it because I teach at the high school. They were after something."

"What?" the sheriff said, looking over the top of his glasses at Austin. "Did they find it, whatever it was?"

"I don't know. I hope they did. I can't afford to buy any more furniture. I know that much."

"I'll send some folks out, just as soon as I can. I ain't got anybody to spare right this minute." Walker Lewis looked apologetic. "You understand, what with the investigation of the Sun-Singer boy and all."

"This one was a killing then? You're still persuaded?"

"No doubt about it. You can set your mind at ease about that. Nothing like the business with poor old Emory. Naw, somebody killed that little boy."

"I know you can't tell me much," Austin said. "But everybody on the reservation's going to be all over me about what you're thinking about it. I'd appreciate whatever you can say."

"Well, Austin," the sheriff said and looked out the window at the courthouse square. "What I'm thinking, mind you, just thinking, is maybe it was a ritual gone wrong. You know, these older boys got to playing out some legend or something. Maybe got to believing some of these old tribal stories too much, you see, and things just go too far. They get caught up in the action and everything just gets too real all of a sudden. And then, bingo, you got a dead little boy, and nobody meant to do it."

"Bullshit. Walker, you know better than that."

"All I know is we're picking up them boys that were with Sun-Singer for questioning this afternoon."

"For questioning?" Austin said. "That's all?"

"Well, yeah. At first, that's all. Of course, if we see a reason to charge them with something, well then we will."

"And what would that reason be? What might cause you to charge them?"

"Discrepancies in their stories. If they get to lying about stuff and we catch them at it. Stuff like that."

"Don't do it, Walker," Austin said. "Please think about it first."

"Kids ain't the way they used to be when we was little. They're killing each other all over the country for tennis shoes and shit. Used to, we'd settle an argument with our fists, maybe a little tussle on the ground. Now, these teenagers'll go for a gun the first jump out of the box."

"There's no gunplay involved with this killing. This is not Houston or Washington, D.C. We're talking about a bunch of kids on the Alabama-Coushatta reservation, one of which has been choked to death by a grown man. The other boys aren't in it at all."

"You don't know how mean kids can be these days, Austin. It's something you don't know anything about, pardner."

"Don't talk to me about kids, goddamn it," Austin said. "I work with kids every minute of the day all year round, and I've been doing it since before you ever put on that badge and stepped into a county car."

"All I know is proper police procedure in a murder investigation, Coach Bullock. And it ain't like watching kids play with a basketball, and I'm following the rules right down the line."

"O.K., O.K. I'm not faulting you on that, Walker. I just want to ask you to step back and think about the way people live on the reservation. Just keep that in mind as you go along. Remember how they are. Remember how they think. Just slow it down a little."

"Hell, Austin," the sheriff said, rising from behind his desk, "we're old teammates. You know how I always respected your people. I used to feed you the ball when you was setting all them records. You don't have to worry about me knowing how y'all think. You know that, don't you?"

"Yeah, I do. I do know how you think after all this time."

"Well, that's good then, ain't it? And listen, I'll get Thurman Thomas out to your place to look around in the next hour or so. All right?"

"All right," Austin and turned to leave. "I'll talk to you later today, then."

"Fine. Make it real late."

If I didn't know better, Austin thought to himself on the way to his car, I'd swear that Walker Lewis has got a red man somewhere in the family woodpile, the way he's talking about legends and boys acting out tribal rituals. He's just like me and the cloud people. Something's moving him around, and he doesn't even know it.

15

"The fuck is that thing?" Martin Utz said, pointing toward the corner of the main room of the Airstream RV where the grunting noise was coming from. "Sounds like it's trying to work up a shit, whatever it is."

Martin had taken off his suit coat and loosened his tie, but the sweat was still beading on his forehead and sliding into his eyebrows and making them prickle. "And why is it so goddamn hot in this tin can? Ain't you got air conditioning? Clarence is about to pass out from the heat. Right, Clarence?"

The other man on the sofa was looking closely at a cushion between him and the arm of the piece of furniture on which he sat. He shrugged at Marty's question and poked at the pattern of weave in the fabric. "Earth tones," he said. "Tres tres Santa Fe."

"I'm a fool for it," Crippled Sparrow said from his perch on one of the stools fastened to the floor by the bar dividing the kitchen from the Airstream's main area. "Can't get enough of those desert colors. And the sunset shades, oh my. I swear if you keep your mouth open out there at dusk you can literally taste the russet and sage." He turned his attention to Martin, still focused on the corner of the room.

Martin was patting his forehead with a handkerchief and studying the results as though he hoped to find a message in the pattern of sweat stain on the cloth.

"That little creature is Honey-Suckle," Crippled Sparrow said, "a Vietnamese pot-bellied pig, and she is the reason why I have to keep it so warm in here when she's inside."

"Pre-basting for the barbecue," Clarence said. "Softening up the gristle."

"Perish the thought," Crippled Sparrow said. "I'd sooner go vegan than harm a hair on her chinny-chin-chin."

"Looks like somebody took a bite out of that ear," Martin said, watching the pig stroll toward the bar stool on which her owner sat. "Not much left on that one side of his head."

"Her head," Crippled Sparrow corrected. "I know. It's horrible. Something in the bushes around here grabbed her once when she wandered off and just ruined her looks. She's lucky to be alive, I suppose. I should be grateful for that alone. I'm thinking about reconstruction for her poor ear if I can find a surgeon I can trust."

"Sew a pork rind to it," Clarence said. "You could dye it the right color."

"That's a terrible joke, isn't it, Pretty?" Crippled Sparrow said to the pig and leaned down to pat her head. His hand didn't quite reach, and he had to dismount from the stool to get within range, his purple boots hitting the metal floor with a boom muffled by the carpet. "Don't you listen. The man is just having some fun at your expense."

"Clarence doesn't joke much," Martin said. "You're lucky to hear that one. He's in a mood."

"Nice basketwork," Clarence said, looking at an arrangement on the wall across from the sofa.

"Mimbrosa," the little man on the floor with the pig said. "Snake River clan."

Everyone watched Honey-Suckle root at something Crippled Sparrow held in his hand for a while, and then Martin spoke. "O.K. Enough nice nice. Clarence and I want to get back to some cool air here in a bit, and I expect you got things to do, too."

"Slop the hogs," Clarence said. "Fix the pen so she won't root out."

"Mr. Bloodworth said he had you already working to help us out with this thing we're doing," Martin said. "With these people in these shacks in the woods." He made a gesture with his right hand that included all he perceived around him, the mass of greenery, the narrow roads in the mud, the brown children in T-shirts and jeans, the old men sitting on the porches of the two-room houses they lived in, women and girls walking single-file down paths with sacks and sticks of firewood in their arms, the dead trucks and cars nosed up into the bushes, the entire pit called an Indian reservation.

"All this junk," he said.

"That's what Mr. Bloodworth is paying me for," Crippled Sparrow said, "that and some other services. It's all part of the assignment."

"How is what I want to know," Martin said. "We got this other guy in town there to help us talk to the council, the chief, whatever. What have you done for us already, and what can you do now, Crip? That's the question, see. Hey," he added, "you don't mind me calling you Crip for short, do you? Or do you want the whole thing there, all of it like?"

119

"His whole name is not politically correct," Clarence said. "You should know that, Martin. We should probably call our host Vertically Challenged Feathered Being."

"You can call me Roy," the little man on the bar stool said. "That's my citizen of the United States name. Crippled Sparrow is talismanic. It speaks to the dark side of my double nature."

"Got you," Martin said. "O.K., Person of Color, what's the deal?"

"I have been creating," Crippled Sparrow said, pausing to draw a circle in the air with both hands, "a climate. No, better to call it a resurrection, a new beginning for an old mindset."

"This is good," Clarence said. "Do it, little red brother. Wail."

"Hush up, Clarence," Martin said. "You been drinking? Let Roy here get it out."

"It doesn't bother me," Crippled Sparrow said. "What anybody says. I like a sceptic in the audience. It makes for better bonding, And come to think about it, bonding is what it's all about. What I'm doing with these people, see, is reminding them they used to exist. They were alive once, dead though they are now."

"Yeah? So?"

"It takes a while to get them to wake up. You start with the women first. They understand things in their blood. I don't really know where it comes from. The menstrual cycle, I guess. They know stuff most men could never imagine. It takes a special male to realize what's going on."

"Like you," Martin Utz said.

"Yes, like me. Why do you think I'm a shaman? I see life from both sides, any way you want to define it. Male-female, animal-human, body-spirit, little-big, light-dark, fucking-getting fucked, you name it."

"Oh, the dualties," Clarence said and leaned forward to make a sucking sound at the pig. "Come here, pork-chops."

"You see things that scare you, don't you, Mister Clarence?" Crippled Sparrow said. "That's why you have to distance yourself from the darkness all the time. I sense this in you."

"A climate you're making," Martin said. "So what's that do?"

"These people are so debased that they can't see further than the next allotment check. They drink," Crippled Sparrow stopped to shudder, "vanilla extract, if you can believe it, for the alcohol that's in it. It's a dry county, you may have noticed, and the next closest one is, too."

"I do miss seeing the pretty signs in the liquor stores," Clarence said in the direction of the pig, "especially the Budweiser young folks at play."

"When I got here," Crippled Sparrow said in an exasperated tone, "to get them up to speed for the tourist trade, you know what I discovered?"

Neither Martin nor Clarence responded, and the little man went on. "These people had only one ritual dance left, a little bitty thing they call a corn dance in the fall. You know, a harvest festival, or the remnants of one. I had to start from that." His voice lifted, and the Vietnamese pig looked up at him and began to scratch behind one ear with a hindleg.

"But when I get through," Crippled Sparrow said with conviction, "the Alabama-Coushatta are going to forget about material reality. They'll be in such a state of mind they'll give anything to be able to look into the sun without burning their eyes. These yokels will believe anything I tell them and go any direction I point."

"Yeah, well," Martin said, "do all you can along that line as fast as you can. And we'll carry on with the heavy lifting. Right, Clarence?"

"Yessuh, boss," Clarence said. "We'll give them the beads and the mirrors and the firewater and a good kick in the ass when they need it. Like we've been doing all along."

"I feel good about this thing," Crippled Sparrow said. "You can tell Mr. Bloodworth. We'll bring them around. These flatheads don't have a chance. I've got the circles going. The signs are all here, and they're speaking to me like thunder."

"Kaboom," said Clarence. "Kaboom and crash."

"As long as it all goes down all right with what we're here for, no sweat," Martin said. "Roy, I like your attitude, but I'm just curious, you know. You don't believe all that junk, do you? Legends, stories, shit like that?"

"I believe all kinds of things," the little man said. "These are truths as real as Honey-Suckle sitting down there on the floor of this Airstream. But don't misunderstand me. Anything a present day so-called Indian tells me for a fact I don't put a grain of faith in. Don't worry. I know what not to believe, too."

The pig looked up again at the man on the bar stool and grunted twice deep in its throat.

"Honey-Suckle heard that," Clarence said. "The hog knows."

The telephone rang in the middle of the night, and Austin came out of a deep sleep and reached for it before it could sound again. Laura, he thought and said her name into the receiver when he put it to his ear.

"What's wrong?" he said. looking at the time on the clock radio. "Where are you?"

"It's not Laura," a woman's voice said after a pause. "It's me, Ellen. And I'm in California."

"Oh," Austin said. "All right."

"Why did you think it was Laura? Is she O.K.?"

"She's fine. I was asleep. She's the only one who'd call me at this time of night."

"Sorry I woke you. I forgot about the time difference."

"Right. What do you want, Ellen? Do you want to talk to Laura? She's not here, obviously, but I can give you her number at school."

"No. I don't want to talk to her. I wanted to talk to you."

Austin said nothing. The number eight on the clock radio blinked to a nine.

"Are you there?" Ellen asked. "Austin?"

"Yes."

"I've been thinking a lot lately. I'm into this new therapy thing. It's not really therapy, it's Life Consequence, and part of the program of scaling my personal consequences is having to go back over my life choices and construct a connecting graph. Do you follow?"

"Oh, yeah, sure."

"It sounds complex, but it's not really once you accept the concept of the web of consequence and the thread of decisions. You don't know what that means, Austin, but don't worry. It's just like you and your history books. To a degree, I mean. And I'm really just, you know, summarizing what it actually takes months of consequence tracing when you're seriously into it."

"I see."

"No, you don't, and I hate that tone. It used to drive me crazy when I heard you use it, but not any more. Not since Life Consequences."

"What do you want, Ellen? I've got to teach in the morning."

"Can't you give me ten minutes, Austin?" Her voice rose two notches, and Austin felt his breath come shallower in the way it always did when her levels began to change. "I just want to help myself find where the connections are and where the consequences graph out in my life."

"Ten minutes. I'll spare that."

"I think," Ellen said in the tone of someone trying to recall the steps in a recipe, "it all reached the first consequence, what the program calls Consequence Roman Numeral One, when I would feed her at night when she was still an infant. At first it was only when I wouldn't turn on the light, and then it got to be all the time, even in the daylight when you were at work. You know, back in Houston in college."

"Yes," Austin said as neutrally as he could make the word come out.

"It was her eyes. She would look up at me with those eyes so brown they were black and just stare as she was eating. But it wasn't like eating, it was like feeding. And I couldn't see anything human in her eyes."

"For God's sake, Ellen. She was just a baby. I told you that then."

"Physically, yes. But there was something else behind her eyes. And I couldn't read it, never, ever. That was Consequence Number One."

"One. All right. Fine."

123

"Yes, one. One is she was of another race. Not mine. Yours."

"O.K. That's eight minutes. Two more and the connection gets broken."

"I'm not being racist, Austin," Ellen said. "You know that. Not in a human sense. But that's why I couldn't stay with you and that child. She wasn't in the same species with me, and you put that little thing in my womb. Her with those inhuman eyes that just bored into me."

"Right, Ellen. I did that. Goodbye now and please don't call again."

"Oh, I won't. But I've got to get all my life consequences scaled so I can come out the other side. Without my full pattern, I can't. I'll be in Texas next week."

"Don't," Austin said. "I won't talk to you, Ellen, then or ever."

"I'll be there to complete my graph scale in Life Consequence. Goodbye, Austin."

"Holba," Austin said into the dead telephone, calling the woman who had just hung up the Nation's name for the creature who leads lost hunters far into the deep marshes where a man cannot tell earth from water and where the sun lends no light for the journey home. "Holba."

Austin got up, walked into the living room, and straightened his wrecked house for the rest of the night, picking up the last feather from the slashed throw pillows just at dawn.

16

The crowd had begun arriving early for the regional game against Sweetwater, and by the time Coach Mellard led the Annette High School Bulldog basketball team out the door of the locker room onto the court, the space was filled. Every seat was taken, even the extra rows of folding chairs arranged at each end of the court, and people stood wherever they could find floor space. A great shout arose as they saw the players.

Austin looked across the way at the far end of the stands where he knew the spectators from the reservation would be sitting together in a group and immediately picked them out of the field of white faces surrounding them. He wondered if Charlie Sun-Singer's family would be there and then, remembering that Thomas Fox Has Him was first cousin to the dead boy, knew they would be. Sure enough, high up in the last row the father sat, dressed in a white shirt buttoned to the neck, blue jeans, and a yellow mourning sash tied around his head to hide his hair.

He would not remove the band of cloth until the first full moon after his murdered son had been buried, and if it were fifty years earlier, he would have kept his hair cut as close to his scalp as a sharp knife would have gotten it for twelve months after. His wife would have stayed in the house unseen for the same period.

Austin lifted his hand to the Alabamas and Coushattas seated in the stands, and several of them nodded at him.

"Who you waving at?" Coach Mellard said, looking up from the twelve players warming up on one end of the court before him. "They all here, huh, your folks?"

"Some of them," said Austin. "At least the relatives of the boys on the team."

"Your people clump together worse than the black folks, don't they?" Mellard said. "I swear they do."

"Yeah, they're real used to being together," Austin answered. "I think we shouldn't let the boys go on much longer out there with warm-up."

"Why?" Mellard asked in the tone of a man who had just been told of a suspicious shadow on his X-ray. "You see something? What?"

"They've already broken a sweat, and their heads are going ninety miles an hour. I just think we ought to sit them down for a minute before the tip-off, that's all."

"Yeah, right," Mellard said, reaching for the whistle on the chain around his neck. "We sure got to keep their focus right, Austin. I'm thinking the same thing."

The whistle blew, a bright sharp sound in the crowded gymnasium, and the players dressed in the white and green uniforms let the balls trickle from their hands and headed for where their coaches were standing, one several feet behind the others as they trotted off the court.

It was Thomas Fox Has Him, his head dropped as though he were having to watch for things in the way on the polished wooden floor that might trip him up before he reached the safety of a boundary line. As he arrived last, stepping carefully over the black painted stripe on the floor, Austin spoke his name and called him aside three or four feet from where the other players had clustered around Coach Mellard.

"Abba Bullock," the boy said, lifting his eyes to Austin's.

"Coach," Austin said. "Just coach, that's all."

"Coach."

"Is it a good night for you, Tom?"

"No."

"You think of your cousin."

"Yes, he is not here. My uncle and my aunt, my other cousins, they will not see him again."

"No," Austin said. "Not at the basketball game and not in this world."

"Charlie Sun-Singer knew many things for a boy so young. He was at home wherever he went."

"Yes, you have told me this."

"I want to make it a good night for him," Thomas Fox Has Him said. "For him to see as he goes to a place he does not know."

"You said he was in his home wherever he found himself. He will still be. And if you want to make a good thing for him to see as he travels you will be able to."

"Yes," Fox Has Him said. "I will do that."

Later, just before the tip-off, as the ten players stood in a circle on the court and strained in their waiting for the basketball to be released above them into the air, Mellard asked Austin about his conversation with the young Alabama.

"What was that all about with Tom yonder? Was he worried about something?"

"A little, but not any more," Austin said as the rival centers waited to release into their jumps. "You watch him play tonight and see."

"Wooee," Truman Blatchford said as Austin Bullock walked through the door between the reception area and the main office. "Son! Did y'all eat them up or did you not? I want to know. Tell me about it."

Blatchford was wearing a Saturday outfit: a yellow polo shirt with the emblem of a lamb embroidered in white on the left breast, a maroon pair of sansabelt trousers imprinted randomly with crossed golf clubs, and tasseled loafers in deep burgundy. He came around his desk, extending his hand with the palm facing Austin for a victory slap.

Austin gave him what he wanted, and after their hands had met, Blatchford grabbed him in a bearhug and lifted his feet off the floor. "Hot damn," he said, "remember the last time I did that?"

"No, Truman," Austin said, taking a step back, "I don't."

"I guess you never looked at the front page of the Austin American Statesman the morning after Annette won state our senior year, then. Hell, that picture was everywhere. There's a copy of it in the display case at the high school. You walk by it every day that rolls."

"Oh, yeah. I don't look over there usually."

"Superstitious, huh? Might jinx us, right? Well, that picture of you being lifted up in the air after you hit the shot to win it in the overtime? The lifter's me, man. I just run out of the stands and grabbed you. And you know something?"

"Nuh uh. What?" Austin said, easing himself into the chair in front of Blatchford's desk.

"That was one of the best things I ever did in high school. I'd have given up the class presidency if I had to choose between it and being in that picture with you, Buddy. I flat guarantee it. That photograph of me and you there in that UT fieldhouse has sure served me well."

"Well, that says a lot about you."

"You ain't wrong. And now y'all are taking Annette back to the state playoffs again. Y'all, huh. I should say you, Coach. Mellard's a fine old gentleman, but everybody knows who does the real coaching out there on the court."

"Don't sell Coach Mellard short, Truman," Austin said. "He's a great teacher of Texas schoolboy basketball."

"I knew you'd say that. I'd be disappointed if you didn't. But after that game last night the Fox boy had, there ain't no doubt who fired him up."

"Fox Has Him," Austin said.

"What?"

"That's his name."

"Right," Blatchford said, "and we better all learn how to spell it, huh? He's gonna show them a thing or two in the state tournament."

"We'll see. Truman, I want to thank you for meeting me in your office on a Saturday morning like this. I know it's an imposition."

"No problem, Buddy. And I bet I know what's on your mind. Mineral rights on the reservation. Am I right?"

"That's part of it, Truman. Bottom line, I guess. But I want to ask you about some other stuff, too."

"Shoot," Truman Blatchford said, going around his desk and rearing back in the leather chair behind it. "I'll tell you all I can."

"Albert Had Two Mothers talked to me and told me some, and he asked me to consult with you about the details."

"Idn't he a character?" Blatchford said, smiling fondly. "I wish I could bottle that old fellow's authenticity and sell it for souvenirs. I'd make a fortune. I just love talking to him."

"I'm sure he'd appreciate that. What he tells me about the mineral rights matter is that some outfit out of Houston is interested in those marshes in the southern part of the reservation land."

"That's true, Austin. The gentlemen who've retained me are out of Houston all right, but I don't think they're headquartered there."

"Where are they based?"

"It's an international concern they represent, Austin, and their offices are in some European centers and in other regions as well, I believe."

Blatchford leaned forward in his seat and took a cigar from a drawer on the right side of his desk. "Don't worry," he said. "I'm not going to fire up. Smoking with me's like an old man's sex life. I don't do nothing now but lick on it."

Austin gave Blatchford the chuckle he wanted. "What other regions?"

"Oh, the mideast, I believe. Mainly."

"Not interested in another oil deal, then?"

"I expect Arco's about to pump the last teacup out of that little old pocket on the reservation," Blatchford said. "No, these fellows are after something a lot less exciting than a new oil strike."

"What would that be? What minerals do they think are out there?"

"Oh, stuff to use in industrial processing. Bauxite, maybe some beryllium. Low level stuff like that. I tell you the truth, Austin, it ain't much of a deal. Of course, the old second chief got all excited when I talked to him, but he's just, you know, hopeful beyond reality. I bet he believes in magic, too. You know what I'm saying?"

"Uh huh. I see how you'd think that. What makes these people think it would be worth their time to look for this industrial stuff on reservation land?"

"It's just guesswork, Austin. A bunch of these geologists looking at maps and topographical features and like that. It's what they do for a living, you know, sniff around here and yonder, trying to figure the odds on what they might turn up. It's a crapshoot, you understand, with these boys. They don't know much more than we do. They just keep working at it's all."

"So you don't see much need for excitement, then, Truman? No reason for the tribal council to get all worked up?"

"Naw, naw," Blatchford said, rolling his cigar between his fingers and then licking delicately at each end of it. "Nor the new stated chief, neither. But you know, it's worth a try, best way I can judge it. You know me and the way I always keep an eye out for your people. If I can find a way to shove a little business y'all's direction, why I'm gonna do it, no matter how much time it takes me. I ain't in this deal for the financial end of it, and I never have been. Whatever I get's nominal. Help pay, you know, for the water cooler expenses, maybe buy a box of cheap cigars and a fifth of second-rate bourbon."

"What'll these Houston people think about what's happened on the reservation in the last week or so? Is that a concern to them?"

"You mean poor old Chief Emory getting drowned and that little fellow getting killed by his buddies?"

"Yeah," Austin said. "Those two events."

"Well, they sympathize, of course. They think it's a shame, and like me, they figure if they can be a part of something to bring some good news to you people, that'd be just real gratifying to them."

"A real Christian attitude."

"Yeah, that's right. That's what I think, too, Austin. Look, can I set up a meeting with you and the council and Mr. Utz to talk about possibilities? Maybe late this week before y'all take off for the basketball tournament?"

"Let me give you a call, Truman," Austin said. "I need to see some people first."

"I got you. Say, you have one of my cards, don't you? Let me get you another one."

Blatchford reached into another drawer on his desk, and Austin rose from his chair as the grandfather clock in the office began to chime the hour.

"Here you go," Blatchford said. "Ain't that thing loud? But I got to where I don't even hear it. Listen, I know you're high from the win last night, but you got to do it again in the tournament, right? No time to let down, is it?"

"It seems like it never is. One thing after another."

"Come on," Blatchford said, "you wouldn't have it any other way, and you know that's the truth, Austin. 'Fess up now, Big 'Un. Get mad at the next one before it gets here."

17

The witch lay, face to the sky, in the thicket at the western limit of the graveyard of the Alabama-Coushatta Nation and looked through an opening in the sycamore leaves and pine needles at the half-moon in its steady slide toward the earth. A bird waked by something in the night croaked above and then with a rustle of wings settled back into its roost to wait for the light of morning.

The witch shifted from one shoulder to the other against the damp ground, still cold in late March, and looked at the glowing hands and numbers on the watch. Just before the hands touched four and twelve the moon would vanish into the mouth of the earth, and full darkness would come, lasting until the time the sun began to push itself up into the sky far enough to send first light to all that slept below. When that darkness came between the earth's eating of the moon and the first waking of the sun, the witch would be able to move and no human eyes could see anything being done in the world.

The witch did not mind the cold. It was good to feel the heat of the body being drawn into the earth and the blood slowing in the veins and the light dying in the eyes as the dark time approached. The breath slowing and the sound of the heart becoming each moment more faint, the fingers curving into the palms of the hands and the smell of the body blending into the odor of dirt and stone in the nostrils made a sweetness come in the mouth, a taste of berries shrivelled by winter and of meat long dead in summer heat.

A soft groan rose from the witch's throat, the sound a dog makes as it scratches a sore so raw the pain is sweet, and the witch knew it to be a good thing. The witch let the groan come again and shivered to watch the sound float up toward the opening into the sky between the sycamore leaves. The groan stopped at the level of the treetops for two slow beats of the witch's heart and then flew toward the dying half-moon with the speed of a dart from a cane blowgun, its poison a thin whistle in the night.

The last light of the moon vanished, and the true darkness came, and the witch rose from the earth-bed in the thicket as though pushed up by a force from the ground itself. The sleeping bird in the tree above rustled once and was silent again. Arms outstretched, the witch moved to the edge of the cover of trees and brush, paused at the opening into the clearing of the burying ground, and spoke the first word of the chant of the berdache.

"Chikmaa, People of the Nation. The Dark Thing is here still. Chikmaa."

Having warned of the approach as Abba Mikko had required from the foundations of time, the witch crossed the open space slowly, the bag for death-earth slung on a thong from the shoulder.

The grave of Chief Emory Sees the Water was nearer than that of the child, and the witch headed to it first, stepping forcefully onto the swept and sprinkled space which surrounded the raw mound. In the morning light those who had watched to guard against the visit would see that they had failed, and they would despair again at the evidence of their weakness, the footprint of the witch.

The witch began at the head of the grave of the dead chief, going by feel in the darkness, tossing aside that which had served the old man in life, the coffee cup and razor, the comb and bowl for food, the unworn dress shoes, the unfastened belt and the wooden-handled fork and knife.

Moving quickly now, the witch swung the leather bag from shoulder to ground and began scooping handfuls of loose earth from the head of the grave into its open mouth, hissing once as a razor blade set as a trap between two small stones sliced the flesh of a palm. Blood would be left now unless all of the earth which had caught it was put into the bag, and the witch scooped more from the grave earth than was first intended.

The grave of the dead child was smaller, had fewer items arranged upon it, a rubber ball, a few cards slick-faced to the touch, a pair of rubber-soled shoes, and the witch finished quickly, knocking these things aside, crumpling the cards into wads of cardboard, and scooping handfuls of dirt into the leather bag, heavy now with the old chief's death-earth.

Done with it, the witch moved three times around the small grave, face toward it and then four times reversed, so that the last thing the spirit of the dead boy would see was the berdache who had killed him refusing to honor him in his leaving from this world.

Well before the sun pushed the first beams of the new day into the land of the Alabamas and Coushattas, the witch was deep in Lost Man Marsh on a grassy hummock surrounded by water. In the night that remained the witch sang the song of the berdache full of death, shuffled in the dance to no drum, no flute, no rhythm, and ate the earth from the graves of the killed ones, smearing the red dirt on the hands, the cheeks, the lips, the teeth, apart from all men and unseen in the darkness.

18

The door to Richard Peter Prongle's office was several feet beyond the counter where those having business with the principal of Annette High School had to stand as they waited for recognition by one of the women in the outer room. Neither of them ever looked up when some visitor approached the counter, Austin knew, so he stood waiting for a full minute before he cleared his throat and made a scratching noise on the top of the barrier with the stack of papers he was carrying. Two students already lined up cut their eyes at Austin for this expression of impatience.

"Be with you in a minute," the woman at the desk nearest the counter said, her gaze firmly locked on the set of attendance forms in front of her. "Hold your horses."

"I'm trying to, Peggy," Austin said, "but they're about to pull the reins out of my hands."

One of the students began to snigger and cut off the sound abruptly as though a hand had suddenly grasped her by the throat.

"Oh, Mr. Bullock," the woman said, looking up from her forms. "I thought you were one of the kids."

"Students," corrected the older woman at the far desk, nearer the pebbled glass door to the principal's office in the power location and thus allowed to speak in single words rather than sentences. She wore a black pants suit and a small man's tie which matched the bluish tint of her hair.

"Students," the younger woman amended.

"That's me, in a manner of speaking," Austin said. "I'd like to see Mr. Prongle for a few minutes."

"Quiet time," the woman in the pants suit said.

"What's that?" Austin said. "Quiet time?"

"Mrs. Givens means he's having his quiet time." Peggy said, putting the communication in sentence form. "Every morning he takes an hour to think by himself."

"I see. Rather than do it with somebody else. Well, could you ask him if I may intrude briefly?"

Givens shot the left sleeve of her suit coat, looked carefully at the watch displayed by the movement, and nodded at the other woman who immediately punched a button on her telephone which buzzed faintly in the closed office behind the frosted glass door.

"Mr. Bullock would like to see you," she said softly into the receiver, and everyone on both sides of the counter waited for the principal's response. In a minute the glass door swung open and Dick Peter Prick, as Coach Mellard called the principal behind his back, stuck his head out.

He had his coat off, but his white shirt shone like a snowbank in the sun, and he aimed a broad smile at all who might see it. "Austin, on your off-period, I see. Please come in and set a spell."

The principal waved a hand toward the waiting students on the far side of the counter, gave each of the secretaries an approving look, and ushered Austin through the door and to a chair in his office. Like a Hapsburg prince, Austin thought, receiving the morning visitors from a regional capital. I know he's going to ask what he can do for me.

"Hey, guy," Prongle said, "congratulations to the coaching staff again and particularly for your contribution. Crucial, really crucial. I don't have to tell you what this does for school morale."

"Thanks, but the kids did it. We just handed them towels and water during the timeouts."

"Hey, listen, if you expect me to buy that, Austin," Prongle said with a rich laugh, "think again, fellow."

"Well, like they say, it was a team effort."

"It always is, isn't it, Austin," he said as his voice dropped an octave into the sincere range, "any signal advances always are. Tom Peters has made a study of accomplishment, group and so-called individual, and that's precisely what he's discovered. His new book's a great read. I recommend it without qualification."

"Yeah. I've heard a lot about him, off and on, over the years."

"Can't go wrong with Peters. Good stuff. Solid." The principal paused and looked toward a small table which held a coffee pot and three mugs. "Coffee while we talk? And what can I do you for?"

Bingo, Austin thought and spoke aloud. "No, thanks. The reason I'm here is to ask permission to miss one, maybe one and a half days next week. I'll get my classes covered, of course."

"Oh, what's up? Doctor's appointment? Illness in the family?"

"Nothing like that. No, it has to do with Alabama-Coushatta business. Something they want me to do."

"Can't wait until the weekend?"

"No, has to be during business hours. It involves a trip to Washington, and that means I'd have to be there all day Monday, maybe a little more."

"The grapevine has it, Austin," the principal said, propping himself back in his chair and fixing Austin with a look he might give a sophomore caught cheating on a chemistry exam, "that you're the new chief now that the old one's died." He moved forward in his chair with a sudden lurch as though to spook the sophomore into spontaneous confusion. "What's that going to involve?"

"That's only technically true, Dick. It's customary because of family connection that I'd be next in line to be stated chief of the Nation, but I don't want the job."

"You see my concern. It's a question of duelling responsibilities, given your appointment at Annette High. All teachers, as you'll remember, sign a conflict of interest declaration along with the annual contract. Right?"

"Sure. I do that every year."

"Guards against double-dipping," Prongle went on. "Keeps the focus on what's primary. The education of our students, first and foremost. I take that seriously."

"I couldn't agree more," Austin said to a spot on Prongle's forehead. "That's why I'm here to talk to you."

"Tell you what, Austin," the principal said, placing both hands before him on the desk with a little slapping sound. "You make it one day, not a day and a half, be sure your classes are covered and that you're back in time to take home room duty early Tuesday morning, and I'll approve. How's that, my friend?"

"Just what I expected, Dick. I knew you'd see your way clear for most of it."

135

"Great, then, Coach." The principal rose and stuck out his hand. "I'm looking forward to the state tournament. And Austin, in your dealings with the bureacracy on the reservation, I do recommend Peters. I'd lend you my copy of Thriving on Chaos, but I've not quite finished it. Go to the library. They'll have several."

"I'll get one to read on the plane," Austin said. "Thanks for the tip."

Two new students were standing at the counter when Austin came through the door of Prongle's office, one he didn't know and the other Juanita Two Tongues, the granddaughter of a Coushatta member of the Nation's council.

"Abba Bullock," the young woman said as he walked past, nodding her head until her dangling earrings jangled.

"Only in a manner of speaking, Juanita," he said. "Just barely."

"You see how the berdache came," Albert Had Two Mothers said to Austin, pointing toward the grave of Chief Emory. "He wasn't wearing no shoes."

"Who put up the string around the grave?"

"Cooper Leaping Deer had the idea. It was a good one. You can see how everybody's stomped around right up to the edge. Hadn't been for that string, you wouldn't be able to see where the witch had walked by now."

It was late in the day, and a mist of rain had begun. Already drops of moisture were hanging on the twine strung in a square around the grave site, and by the time the all-night downpour to come was finished, the only marks remaining on the sandy soil of the Alabama-Coushatta graveyard would be the depressions and small gullies left by water running on bare ground.

"He has big feet," Austin said, looking at the marks leading up to, around and away from the grave. "Whoever he is."

"That's what he wanted to leave. He can make his feet any size he wants, the berdache can. He don't have to even walk unless he wants to. He can fly up to the thing he wants to get and float in the air like a humming bird. We told you that."

136

"Yes, you did. McKinley Big Eye used to give us kids all the details."

"This witch might be a woman, too. He just showed big feet to let us know how he had got to the grave and fooled us. He's just laughing at us. The berdache always wants the People to know when he gets ahead of us."

"I don't doubt this happened. I can look at Chief Emory's grave and see that. But a man did it, my elder. And a man, maybe the one who left these footprints, maybe somebody else, is who killed Chief Emory and that little boy."

Albert Had Two Mothers had painted a broad stripe across his forehead when he first heard of the witch's visit to the recent graves, and now he gently picked at he dried paint with a forefinger as he stared at Austin. The white stripe would provide protection against the charm of the witch and serve at the same time as an announcement of his defiance, but Albert's skin was that of an old man and it itched. He wouldn't remove it, though, Austin knew, until the identity of the berdache was established and the witch was destroyed.

"You don't need to tell me it's a man, Austin Bullock," Albert said. "That's the form he'll have taken when we catch him. But inside that man will be the witch."

"All right, my elder. I can buy that. But right now we've got to tell the sheriff about this." Austin pointed toward the grave and then in the direction of the spot where Charlie Sun-Singer was buried. "Maybe this will help persuade him to see the truth about what's happened."

"You ever see opossum when he's run into a nest where hornets live, Austin?"

"No, my elder," Austin said and waited for the instruction he knew was coming.

"Opossum does what has always served him well when he was in trouble before. Maybe when a rattlesnake got too close, or when he saw a hunter coming his way when he was on the ground and too far from a tree to run away and climb it. Opossum falls down and closes his eyes and lets his mouth hang open, and he holds his breath and stays real still. You know why?"

"Yes, so the snake or the hunter will think he's dead and not do anything to him."

"I'm glad you remembered. And that works for opossum most of the time, his little trick. But when he tries that with the hornets, they

137

don't care if he's already dead or not. They sting him with the little poisoned darts in their tails while he lays there making like he's dead. And by the time opossum comes to know he's got to move or die, it's too late. That poison from the darts gets in his meat and his bones and his head, and then opossum really is dead, and he ain't fooling nobody no more. You know what the worst thing is, when that happens to opossum when his trick don't work?"

"No, what's worse than being dead, my elder?"

"The hornets don't even eat him," Albert Had Two Mothers said. "They just fly back off to their nest where they live, and they don't use dead opossum at all. He just rots. He don't feed nothing. Not even the buzzards will eat him, see, because of all that poison the hornets put in him."

"Thank you for the story, Albert," Austin said. "I'll keep it in my mind."

"I hope you will," the old man said, his voice returning again to normal level after it had chanted in the old way the account of opossum and the hornets' nest. "It's a lesson in it, and it's a good thing for a man to remember when he gets to trusting things too much. When he gets to believing that stuff is going to happen like it ought to, instead of just happening the way it does. You know what I'm talking about."

Austin didn't say anything else about the topic except to nod twice as Albert looked sharply at him. After a few more minutes of conversation about the arrogant ways of the berdache, he headed for the headquarters building of the Alabama-Coushatta Nation with the old man to join the other members of the council, Truman Blatchford, and the two men from Houston interested in mineral rights in the swamp land of the reservation.

He would save for later the story to tell to the old man of the time when black bear fell so in love with the sweet taste of honey he followed the bees too deep into the marsh and couldn't find his way out and home again. Black bear couldn't keep up with the bees, he didn't find honey in the swamp, and he starved to death far from his true home. Austin hoped he wouldn't have the opportunity to give his elder a lesson in what the legends of the people still have to say, but it was tempting to have his turn.

138

Except for Bronson Sings War, the other men of the council were waiting in the room with the plywood-topped table and the collection of metal auditorium chairs furnished by the government when the building had been constructed in the thirties. The room itself had been intended by the architect from the Bureau of Indian Affairs as a place for the members of the tribal government to meet on a regular basis to conduct business and listen to advice from federal spokesmen.

It hadn't worked out that way over the last fifty years or so, however, since the council preferred to construct sweat houses when they felt the need for communication and enlightenment, so the special little room stayed empty except for the occasions it was necessary to meet with visiting blank eyes. Then one of the council members entrusted with keys to the building room would unlock it, chase out any wasps or house martins that had moved in since the last time the door was opened, and the council members, dressed in their best outfits, would receive guests of the Nation within.

They were there when Albert Had Two Mothers and Austin Bullock entered, ranked along the two sides of the table and unspeaking in the presence of the three white men as they stared across the plywood surface in front of them.

Truman Blatchford sat between the two strangers, and he popped up from his metal chair as though a jolt of electricity had just hit him when Austin and Had Two Mothers came through the door.

"We just got here," he said. "We haven't waited long. Just got a chance to introduce these gentlemen to the council right before y'all came in."

Truman looked toward the man to his right and kept talking. "This here is Mr. Martin Utz, and the other gentleman is his colleague, Mr. Clarence Denver. Just like the city, just like it sounds. They are with a subsidiary of an international concern called, I believe, Netcon. Idn't that right?" The man to his right, the one with the eyes hooded like a Cherokee's, nodded in agreement.

Albert Had Two Mothers, on his best behavior, stuck out his hand like a white man, and Austin fell into line behind him.

139

"These gentlemen are the second chief of the Alabama-Coushatta Nation and the new stated chief," Blatchford said, finishing up his introductions, "Mr. Albert Had Two Mothers and Mr. Austin Bullock."

"You're the new head man, right?" Martin Utz said to Austin. "Just took office?"

"Technically, just technically."

"What they want to talk about is a little project that may make you folks some money, Austin," Blatchford said, "like I told you the other day in my office."

Blatchford paused and then added, "Did I mention that Austin here went to Rice University on a basketball scholarship? He's the man that took Annette to the state championship back when God was a little boy, and he's fixing to do it again, too. Right, Austin?"

Austin shrugged and sat down on one of the metal chairs. "Truman tells me you're interested in mineral rights, Mr. Utz." One of the old men of the council said something in the language of the Nation to the man sitting beside him who blinked and said nothing in return.

"Two Tongues only just said it's hot in here," Albert Had Two Mothers told the white men. "It wasn't no secret he was saying."

"Maybe we're interested in poking around some," Martin Utz responded to Austin. "Bring in a small crew for two or three days or a week and see if it's worth spending any more time here than that."

"Arco has contracted with the Nation for the oil rights for the next fifty years," Austin said, "for what that's worth."

"Which is nothing," Utz said. "I know that. Netcon is not into fossil fuels, Chief. We're looking for deposits of real low level industrial grade bauxite and beryllium with an eye to lowering production costs in one of our industries on down the road. Clarence can tell you more about that than I can. All I know is it's probably not worth spending any real money on. Am I saying it right, Clarence?"

"You are," the other man said. "The whole process is about to be superceded in the next couple of years any way, and I don't know why management is still looking for this kind of thing. They should listen to the engineers and save us all a headache."

"I see," Austin said. "You realize the Department of Interior has to approve of any business ventures involving use of reservation lands, don't you?"

"I so informed them," Truman piped up quickly.

"We already knew it," Utz said. "But the feds don't get involved until a proposal project is far enough along to specify formally. You people can look at what you've got as much as you want to before you have to call them in."

"That's right," Talmadge Blue Hand said. "We learned that in the oil deal."

"What we want is permission for a four or five man crew to spend a week over there somewhere in the woods," Utz said, "and find out if we need to talk any more. Us in this room."

"Say you found what you're looking for," Albert Had Two Mothers said, "How much money are we talking about?"

"Total?" Clarence Denver said. "Or your part? Depends on lots of factors."

"Both," two of the old men said in one breath.

"Total, less than a million dollars, if we find something. Your share, thirty percent. But like I said before, it won't last two years if we find you're sitting on all the stuff in North America."

"We better do it fast, then," Talmadge Blue Hand said, "before it all spoils in the ground."

"It's your call," Martin Utz said. "We'll let you talk about it by yourselves, of course, but we've got to get back to Houston tomorrow. We got other places to visit."

"Y'all know where I'm located," Truman Blatchford said. "You folks know me. I talk to everybody, and I shoot straight."

"No doubt," Clarence said.

The meeting broke up in a few minutes, and Austin walked outside with Albert Had Two Mothers to watch the white men pull away in their rented Lincoln toward the highway to Annette.

"No reason to say no," Albert said, "that I can see."

"Is there any reason to say yes, my elder?"

"What's four blank eyes with little shovels and a computer going to do bad to Lost Man Marsh?" the old man replied. "Thirty

141

percent is three hundred thousand dollars, and I think he means every year they out in that swamp digging."

"Thirty percent of nothing is nothing."

"You learn that in school, huh? There at the Rice University? You got to take chances now and then, Austin. Just like Dirty Boy did when he took that ride on the back of the horned snake."

"Didn't it eat him before he got to the shore of the other world?"

"Yeah, but he had forgot his magic chunk stones," old man said. "Remember? That's what did him in. He didn't have to mess up if he had kept his wits about him."

"That's what I'm talking about."

"Well, all I know is you got to ask these people in Washington the right questions, Abba Bullock. And then help the Nation get some of that Yankee money."

"Tell me the whole story of Dirty Boy again before I take off for that country inside the beltway, my elder. Help me see what I'm getting into."

"I'll give you the long version, but first you got to tell me something. What is this beltway you just mentioned? I hear about it all the time on the television."

"It's like the loop in Houston. It's just the word they use for the highway that goes all the way around the city."

"I knew it wasn't a real belt," Had Two Mothers said, "but why don't they just call it the loop? Why a belt?"

"Maybe it sounds more important. Like calling a company Netcon. I don't know."

"No, that's a good name, Netcon. I like the way it sounds. Arco, that's good, too. But beltway for loop, that's pushing it."

"I guess you're right, my elder," Austin said. "Now when they first saw Dirty Boy he was living in the woods by himself. Isn't that how it starts?"

"He was an orphan," the old man said, his voice beginning to lift into a chant. "One day he come up to the edge of the village. Not here. Back before the Nation came to Texas."

19

Austin called Laura's dormitory room from a telephone near the American Airlines counter in the Houston Intercontinental Airport. It was a little before 8:00 p.m. on Friday, so he was surprised when she answered on the second ring.

"Why aren't you out drinking beer or listening to some pedant talk about pottery markings?" he said. "Aren't you getting all the good out of your educational opportunity?"

"I was taking a nap so I could go out later. I pulled an all-nighter for a poly-sci paper and needed some downtime."

"How white of you. Listen, I'm going to be in Washington, D.C. until Tuesday. So if you need to get in touch I'll be at the Hotel Washington on 15th and Pennsylvania."

"Wow, is that near the White House? Why are you going to be there? Is it about the poor little boy and Chief Emory?"

"I don't know to the first question. And, no, it's not about Chief Emory and Charlie Sun-Singer. That's local. I'm talking to a man in the Department of Interior about a project the council is all hot about. They figure all of us Alabamas and Coushattas are going to get rich."

"Are we?"

"Not a chance. One other thing." Austin paused and shifted around to turn his back to a man at the next telephone speaking in what Austin guessed to be Arabic. "Your mother called this week, and she says she's coming for a visit in the next few days."

"To see me?"

"Probably, I guess. She's into something called Life Consequences, and she wants to discover where she went wrong in her choices. She says she's working on some kind of connecting graph and needs to plot the decision points. Or something."

"It's not inner child stuff now?"

"She didn't mention inner child, no. But maybe she'll show up at Rice looking for you, and I wanted to let you know, just in case."

"I do want to talk to her eventually about things, but I don't know if this is the time. I mean really, pop psychology. It's sad."

"Well, that's for you to work out," Austin said, watching the Arabic speaker hang up the phone next to his and immediately begin to punch numbers into it again. "You and your mother. Not me."

"I know. Have a good time in Washington. Say hello to the president for me," Laura said. "Abba Bullock."

"If I see the Great White Father, I will for sure."

Austin hung up the telephone and walked toward the concourse, joining a line of people waiting at the metal detector for a tall man in a Stetson to remove his belt, his silver tipped boots, and an assortment of neck chains before technology would declare him safe for boarding. The more he shed, the angrier he looked, Austin noted, like a rattlesnake in the spring molting season, unused to its tender new skin and undecided whether to rattle or strike first.

Better not do it, Friend Rattler, Austin thought, stepping around the clot of people at the metal detector, they'll pull your fangs and put you in the Hermann Zoo to let folks admire your pretty colors. Just take it all off, smile, and step aboard.

Austin had always liked flying, ever since the first experience he had of it his senior year in high school when he had taken his first trip out of Texas, that time as a member of the High School All-South Basketball Team bound for Memphis to play the All-North bunch. That had been a night flight out of Houston, too, and the sensation of leaving the earth into a sky sucked free of light had been deeply satisfying to him, although his seatmate, a hulking blonde kid from Leggett, Texas, had refused to look out the window the whole way, insisting that if he continued to stare straight ahead the experience would be just like a bus trip.

The blonde center hadn't been able to fool himself, though, and had had a miserable time in Memphis before, during, and after the All-Star game in the Mid-South Colliseum. "I just keep feeling my stomach floating," he had confided to Austin during a time-out in the second half of the game against the All-Star team from the North. "I can't think of nothing else."

"Maybe that's why you can't stop that center from Indiana," Austin had told him. "Try thinking about winning."

144

"All I can think about is falling out of the sky and dying," the boy from Leggett had said in 1966, his eyes popped so wide they looked like oversized blue marbles. "You think they maybe'll let me ride the bus home?"

The change to Eastern time made it almost midnight when the flight arrived at Dulles, and Austin decided to take a taxi to the hotel rather than try to figure out the bus schedule at such a late hour. The driver, whose skin was close to the shade of Austin's own, looked sharply at him and said something in a language unknown.

"Try English," Austin said. "That's what I always end up doing."

The taxi driver gunned his engine and didn't say another word all the way in from Dulles to the northeast corner of Pennsylvania and 15th, two blocks from the White House.

Austin got up early enough the next morning to have a full breakfast in the dining room of the Hotel Washington before the time for his appointment with an official at the Department of the Interior. He looked around him at the other diners to see if he could recognize anybody he might have seen before on a political talk show on television. Only one person was a possibility, a man in a dark suit, but he was middle-aged, balding, and gray-faced, and could have been a body-double for any school administrator Austin had ever seen.

The man made a big production of ordering grits with his eggs, explaining to his companion that the Hotel Washington's dining room was the only place you could get them within walking distance of the Executive Office Building. A professional Southerner, Austin thought. Nobody ever said a word about corn in any of its forms when eating back home, but give a certain kind of blank eyes a chance to blow the bugle, and you'd think he was raised right in the middle of a great big patch of it. Austin lowered his head and ate.

The man Austin had talked to on the phone, a Mr. Fondren in Interior, was in his office even though it was only a few minutes after nine o'clock on a Saturday. There was no receptionist behind the desk in the outer office, and Fondren had the door to his room open to watch for visitors. He was through it before Austin let the door to the corridor close behind him. Hand extended, he came forward at a half-trot, already talking. He had a full head of prematurely gray hair and looked to Austin to be about sixteen years old.

"Austin Bullock," he said, "Chief of the Alabama-Cherokee in Texas. Am I right? Please come in and sit down."

"Mostly," Austin said. "The title's largely ceremonial, and the Alabamas and Coushattas are related to the old Cherokee Confederation, but we're a tribe in our own right."

"Of course, Chief Bullock. I knew that. Please excuse my misstatement. I've just this instant located the file on your people, and I confess I've not put the beady eye on it yet. No help in the office this morning, I'm afraid."

"I want to thank you for meeting me on Saturday like this. I realize it's an imposition and off-schedule."

"Not at all. Not at all," Fondren said, waving a hand. "We all stay so busy there are never any weekends for us in Interior. I wouldn't have it any other way, though, I assure you. I thrive on the pace, so long as I can get an hour every day for some racquetball. Do you play?"

"No, I've never tried that sport."

"You should. I recommend it. It's a real toner, I've discovered. I began it way back at Amherst and kept going right through Harvard Law and all my time in Interior. A real lifesaver."

"I can see that," Austin said in his most up and positive tone. "Thanks for the testimonial. I'll give it a try the first chance I get."

"Do," Fondren said. "Do." He bounced a pencil on his desk, gave Austin a huge grin, and leaned forward in his chair. "You're here in a pre-proposal mode, I take it. A possible use of ceded land in Texas."

"Well, maybe even a pre-pre-proposal mode at this point. I don't know. What I'd like to discuss is an approach the Nation has had from a corporation named Netcon. It concerns some proposed surveying of a swamp area on the reservation. They're interested in mineral rights, they say."

"I'm sorry, Chief Bullock, but I don't want to hear about that right now. Interior isn't interested until the RFP stage."

"Well, what can you tell me about Netcon?"

"Nothing, I'm afraid, and I won't try. Interior has learned over the years that it's work-heavy and paper-intensive to enter any discussion, slash, consideration about possible land use, revariance, or cost-analysis before the RFP stage. We have to husband our human resources and not be drawn into what-if questions until the document has hit the desk."

"On behalf of the tribal council, I just want to learn what I can from you about Netcon before we go any further. You know, any prior dealings they've had with lands administered by your department, anything you can tell me about the organization."

"Nothing," Fondred said in a regretful tone. "Even if I knew, I'm not at liberty at this point, pre-proposal, to make an assessment of any entity or private player. You understand the policy implications, I hope."

"I think I'm beginning to. Can you give any advice at all to me to take back to the council?"

"Essentially no, except the best wishes of Interior and our encouragement to the people you so ably represent." Fondren put his pencil down in precise parallel to the edge of his desk and directed a smile Austin's way.

"Well, I guess it's RFP time down home. And then you can talk to us about Netcon."

"You bet," Fondren said. "You bet, Chief Bullock."

Austin got up from his chair and began to move toward the door, and Fondren briskly came around his desk to follow, his hand out for a farewell shake.

"Your first time in DC?" he said "If so, you may want to check out the Smithsonian before you leave town. They've got a world-class display of Native-American artifacts up and running just now."

"That sounds interesting. I may just do that. Is that close to the Vietnam Memorial?"

"Not cheek by jowl, but you can see one from the other."

"I bet," Austin said. "I would have guessed."

As he left the building and headed back toward the hotel in a light drizzle, Austin realized he probably should have mentioned the deaths of Chief Emory and Charlie Sun-Singer to the Interior man. No, he told himself, waiting at an intersection for a walk/don't walk light, that would probably fall into the jurisdiction of Justice, and Interior would for damn sure have nothing to do with that.

20

Crippled Sparrow had known witches before. In fact, one of the old women who had raised him in Oklahoma after his mother had been killed by a drunk white man in Yellville had been reported to be a witch by his classmates in the reservation school. He had watched her closely, hoping to catch her strangling a cat or eating rat poison or mixing magic powder, but Roy, as he was known then, had detected no sign of the witch in the old woman.

He had finally asked her once if she was a witch, assuring her that if she was, he considered that to be a good thing and nothing she should continue to conceal from him. He would like to join her in her hidden life, contributing what he could to advancing her work against people on the reservation and pledging himself to learn all she might be willing to teach him. Maybe she would tell him a magic way to make his dwarfed legs longer, he remembered saying to the old woman, in exchange for his doing whatever she wanted. Stealing a baby from its mother's house, setting fire to the car of somebody the old woman despised, throwing dead animals into people's wells: these were a few things that came immediately to Roy Blending's mind as possibilities. He had barely finished listing them before the old woman had hit him on the right side of his head, backhanded, with a pinewood knot she had been about to put into the fire.

When Roy came to, he found himself tied with rawhide strips to a mesquite stump behind the house where he lived with the old woman and her sister, and it wasn't until the next morning that he was released, covered with dew and insect bites, both his arms numb from the shoulders down. It took until sundown for the feeling to return to them, and it was then that he became convinced that the old woman really was a witch, though one who wanted no help from him in her activities.

He had deep respect for her for what she had done to him, and he never lost it, even though he was able to get her power contained by telling the white social worker who saw him once or twice a year that the old woman and her sister made him do things to them that he didn't understand. That story got him moved to another household and the two old Cherokee women put in the Knox County jail for six months, a result that satisfied Roy Blending on all counts. But the old woman was the first witch he had known, and she had taught him something. He felt the debt.

So years later when Roy, now Crippled Sparrow and educated in Native American myth, legend, and the moral terrain of the dominant white culture, began some dealings with the Hopi and Navajo in the Southwest, he was prepared to negotiate with all manner of witches from a position of authority.

He had met them, known them, and turned the ways of witches to his advantage for years: Bad Thing in the Santa Clara Pueblo, Tin Mouth of the Taos, Look for Him from the Colorado, and several others less powerful and famous. He came to own them all, at least for long enough to get what he wanted at the time.

But it wasn't until he had come to the tiny Nation of the Alabamas and Coushattas, a people in Texas so detached from the roots of their origins they had to hire a consultant to show them how to build their past into a tourist trade, that Crippled Sparrow had found the opportunity to create his own witch from the ground up.

His venture into the East Texas backwoods of the Alabama-Coushatta reservation began as a straight business deal. The president of the Coushatta County Chamber of Commerce was visiting South Florida with his wife and childred and had caught one of the festival shows Crippled Sparrow had produced and directed for an off-shoot branch of Seminoles near Kissimmee. Recognizing a good thing when he saw it, Don Kepple offered the sawed-off little Indian running things a flat fee and expenses to come to the reservation in

Coushatta County and investigate development possibilities there for an outdoor pageant.

"These old boys haven't done a thing with themselves," he told Crippled Sparrow, "and they're just sitting on a ton of local color possibility. I just want you to come take a look-see. They are just not pro-active on their own."

Between gigs, Crippled Sparrow expressed reluctance and the need for money up-front, but in his mind he was already seeing the Airstream heading north. He could use the same dramatic structure he had sold to the Seminoles, changing the names of deities and tribal heroes and inventing the ones he needed to fill in any gaps, and be out of East Texas before the first of the winter rains started.

Once in Coushatta County, he realized larger opportunities and broadened his scope, particularly after he was approached by the man in Houston, Martin Utz, about a brand-new wrinkle which promised to make the pageant creation business look like small potatoes. Sammy LeBlanc had put Utz on to him, and Crippled Sparrow had not been surprised to discover that the old connection still had life in it. Make new friends, but keep the old. What he had done for Sammy in getting that ex-wife in New Orleans off his back was still paying dividends. There's no man more grateful than one whose ex has had her mouth stopped for good.

"What we want you to do," the man had explained to Crippled Sparrow in the suite in the Galleria Hotel in Houston, "is find a way to throw a scare into the people there on the reservation. One that'll last for a little while, long enough for us to do what we need to. We want these people to feel like staying close to home for while. We want them inside the house. We've lost something out there and need to find it. Bad."

"In keeping," Mr. Bloodworth, one of the two other men in the sitting room of the suite, said, "with the traditions of the tribe. It has to look like it belongs with their history and mindset."

"You're talking mythic consequence," Crippled Sparrow had said, sipping at the Campari and soda in the Waterford crystal glass, "you mean the logic of the legendary."

"I like your vocabulary," Mr. Bloodworth said.

"I believe you've done post-secondary work," said the third man, the one called Clarence. Everybody had taken another drink.

Crippled Sparrow had identified the one he wanted his second day in the Nation of the Alabama-Coushatta, the member of the people he thought of to himself as his witch-in-waiting. The encounter came when along with two old men of the council and the Chamber of Commerce man, Kepple, Crippled Sparrow had driven in a Chevrolet van up and down every navigable road and pig trail on the reservation, getting to know the territory.

The vehicle had just forded a creek, narrowly avoiding sliding into a hole too deep to climb out of in two-wheeled drive, when one of the council members pointed ahead to the right and said something to the other old man sitting beside him.

"Who's that?" Kepple asked. "Is that Tucker Pop-Eye? What's he got in his hand?"

"I expect it's a rock," one of the old men said. "That's generally what he's carrying around with him."

"He's fixing to throw it at us," Kepple said, flinching away from the window of the van and sliding down into his seat as the man at the side of the road came around in a left-handed pitching motion.

Everyone in the van watched a star-shaped crack appear in the windshield and immediately vanish in a burst of red the shape of a flower blossom.

"It was a turtle," Albert Had Two Mothers, one of the tribal council, said. "Not no rock."

"Yeah," the other old man said, "a rock would have come on through that glass."

"What's wrong with him?" Crippled Sparrow said, looking back through the rear window of the van at the huge man who had moved to stand now in the shallows of the creek. "Is he drunk or crazy?"

"It's hard to tell," Albert Had Two Mothers answered. "Tucker Pop-Eye is drunk now and then, but he's crazy all the time."

"Why is he just standing there with his arms folded?" Mr. Kepple said, easing up from where he had slid down in his seat. "Like he ain't done nothing?"

"He's waiting," Had Two Mothers had said. "He's waiting for what he just hit with that turtle to blow up."

"Blow up?"

"Yeah. Tucker Pop-Eye thinks he's back in Vietnam a good bit of the time. He's looking to see if this shipment he just throwed the grenade at is going to blow up or get through."

"A shipment of what?" Crippled Sparrow said.

"Whatever them Viet Cong are bringing down the Ho Chi Minh Trail today," Albert Had Two Mothers said. "That's what Tucker done told me several times this road here is we're riding on."

"I'd like to meet him," Crippled Sparrow said. "See if I could give that veteran some help."

"He don't want no help," the other council member said. "He done told them social workers and them government nurses and doctors that a long time ago."

"They ain't come back, neither," Had Two Mothers said. "Not after the way Tucker he told them."

"No," the other old man said. "You right about that."

"I wouldn't want to change his thinking," Crippled Sparrow said. "See, I wanted to serve my nation in the Vietnam conflict, but I couldn't pass the requirements."

"Too short," Albert Had Two Mothers said, looking toward the other two men in the van for confirmation. His fellow council member nodded, but Mr. Kepple pretended not to hear.

"What's he got inside his head?" Crippled Sparrow said. "What darkness, what flashes of light? What visions?"

"I expect it ain't nothing but a couple of burned-out light bulbs, poor fellow," Mr. Kepple had said and pointed ahead to the left of the road. "Look there at that stand of dogwood, Mr. Sparrow. Idn't that as pretty a picture as you'd ever want to see?"

"Yes," Crippled Sparrow had said, fixing in his mind the image of Tucker Pop-Eye reared back to throw the turtle in his hand. "I can see great banks of flowering trees as background to a scene in the pageant. We'll use that for sure."

"In the old time the people didn't like Rabbit," Crippled Sparrow said to the big man sitting on the ground in the clearing deep in Lost Man Marsh. It was cold, for as late in March as it was, and the bole of the fallen oak on which he sat was sucking all the heat out of his body. Tucker Pop-Eye didn't seem to be feeling it, although he was seated flat on the mud, at least two hours after midnight. Crippled Sparrow shuddered and went on.

"They wanted to get rid of Rabbit, wanted to shut him up. They didn't care how much he had already done for them, scaring off the Choctaws with the gourd rattles and the broken arrow points that time. The people weren't grateful. They were selfish." Crippled Sparrow paused and looked carefully at the dark bulk of the huge man sitting before him. He couldn't make out his eyes in the shadows. "Like the two Viet Cong that had found the secret medals in the hole in the swamp. The two you had to get the medals back from, the big one and the little one. Remember?"

"Some people made fun of the uniform," Tucker Pop-Eye said in a rumbling voice, "when I got off the plane in L.A. Little girls in them flower dresses hollered at me."

"You remember what the council tried to do to Rabbit, the first thing, my brother?"

"The rattlesnake," Tucker Pop-Eye said in that voice that sounded full of rock chips and broken cane shafts. "The snake always comes first."

"Yes," Crippled Sparrow answered, beginning to rock back and forth on the log as he spoke. "The council told him to get a rattlesnake, show us what a good hunter he is, and maybe the snake will bite Rabbit when he tries to pick it up. Rabbit found the rattlesnake, and he fooled him. He asked to measure him, and when the snake said all right, Rabbit laid a stick down beside him over and over until he got to the head like he was counting the times he laid it down. Then he stuck the sharp end of the stick through the snake's head and killed him and brought him back to the village. Then who was the fool, my brother?"

"Them protesters," Tucker Pop-Eye said. "Them hippies."

"Yes, my brother. And the council of the People thought to get Rabbit stung to death by wasps and they sent him out to bring back a

153

sackful of the stinging things. And Rabbit took the sack from the old men and he found the wasp nest and he told those poison things, he said, I dare you to fill the sack up and they did, because a wasp won't take a dare. And not a one of them stung Rabbit, and he took the whole hive back to the village and let them loose in the old men's faces."

"Them wasps did some stinging then," Tucker Pop-Eye said. "He hollered when I slapped him across the face and mashed his nose back into his head. That cadre leader."

"The council wasn't through with Rabbit yet. Somebody thought to use alligator. I believe it was Chief Emory Sees the Water. He said Rabbit should go kill an alligator and bring it back to the village and they'd cook it for a big feast and make Rabbit feel at home again. So Rabbit went and he looked," Crippled Sparrow said, shivering in the night air. "Rabbit found that alligator not far from where we're sitting right now, my brother, over in Long King Creek, and it was a big one with just its eyes sticking up out of the water."

"You couldn't see them hardly ever," Tucker Pop-Eye said. "They was little men and women, and they laid down in the dirt and dug holes and tunnels everywhere. The whole ground sounded like a drum. I could jump up and down and hear it booming off in the woods a half a klick from where I was standing."

The big man rose from the center of the clearing in Lost Man Marsh and jumped twice, the soles of his feet hitting the muddy ground with a slapping sound. "Listen," he said, stopping abruptly and crouching forward with a hand to his ear. "Hold your breath. Yonder, way off, hear it? That booming noise?"

"Yes, my brother," Crippled Sparrow said. "I hear it under where we are, under where we're living."

"It's tunnels everywhere," Tucker Pop-Eye said, sitting back down. "You know how to look for them."

"Rabbit knew how to listen," Crippled Sparrow answered. "He wasn't the fool they thought he was. He wasn't the dummy they wanted him to be. He called that alligator up out of the water. He said he wanted him to help Rabbit move a log to the village, and the alligator said he would because he liked to show off how strong he was, how there wasn't anybody his match."

"All them big shots wanted more stuff to put on their clothes," Tucker Pop-Eye said. "Stripes, some of them wanted. Bars on their shoulders. Stars. Leaves. We was supposed to get them for the officers.

We had to fool them alligators and them wasps. Snakes, little bitty ones you couldn't see."

"Rabbit had to handle that last test," Crippled Sparrow said. "That big one, the alligator. You know what his name is, don't you?"

"The last one I got to fool and bring back?"

"The big alligator, the one they figure will pull you under the water until you drown. Drag you off to a hole to get ripe, so he can come back and eat you when you're all soft and rotted. That one."

"I'll know him when I see him, I reckon."

"He calls himself a name. The council wants to put all manner of decoration on his clothes. Stripes, beads, feathers," Crippled Sparrow said. "Medals."

"What's the alligator call himself? You can't tell which is which. They all look the same. That's why the only thing to do was to kill all of them. The big and the little. The old ones and the young."

"Yes, like you did with the old one by the water and the little one in the marsh. When you got the medals back they had taken from the place in the ground." Crippled Sparrow paused and looked up into the shadowed face of the man across from him as though he were a cat which had heard a rustle in a small crevice in a wall.

"Abba, the council wants to call him," Crippled Sparrow said to Tucker Pop-Eye. "Abba Bullock. That school-teaching coach, Austin Bullock. That's the name he goes by. But his real name is Alligator."

"It was real dark at night there all the time," the big man at the center of the clearing said. "Everywhere you looked, you couldn't see no moon. You couldn't ever see a star in the sky."

21

After walking around the mall for two or three hours and looking at the capitol building and the Washington Monument from the steps of the Lincoln Memorial, Austin had decided to get his ticket changed and return to Texas a full two days early. Fondren had been no help and Austin knew he wasn't likely to find anybody else in D.C. who would commit an act of opinion in the next couple of days, either.

The fact that the government man wouldn't say yes or no to Austin's request made it easier, anyway. When he got back to the reservation he could tell the council he had done all that was possible, and the next step was up to them. Maybe that would take him out of the equation and give him some space to tend to his job uninterrupted for a week or two. Let the old men decide whether or not to allow the people from Netcon to poke around the swamp in search of God knows what.

Maybe if he was lucky, by the time the state tournament rolled around to take him out of town for three days, Sheriff Lewis would have found who committed the one murder he recognized to have been done, and Austin would be able to return to the life he lived between his house on Peachtree Street and the Annette High School building on Penry. Then if he were really lucky beyond all measure, Albert Had Two Mothers would realize how unsuited Austin was for the job of stated chief of the Alabama-Coushatta Nation and take it on himself or farm it out to somebody who at least lived on the reservation.

Hold those thoughts, Austin Bullock told himself on the way back to the Dulles airport, make them come true. Let my medicine be strong, Old Ones in the sky and earth. I'll even sing my manhood song for that and speak aloud with the spirits of Fire and Water.

"Did you say something?" the taxi driver asked, staring through the rearview mirror into the backseat. "You did say Dulles, right?"

"Oh, yes. I was just talking to myself."

"That's the only one that'll listen to me, too," the driver said and pushed the car at a little faster rate toward the country outside the beltway.

By the time Austin had driven the fifty miles from the Houston Intercontinental Airport to Annette it was well after dark. When he made the turn onto his street he could see that the lights were on in his house and a Chevrolet Cavalier was parked in the driveway. His stomach took an instant plummet when he saw the car was a rental and realized that probably it had brought his ex-wife to town.

She was sitting on the sofa beside Laura, looking at a stack of papers and photo albums on the coffee table before them. They had been drinking Diet Cokes and eating a pizza, the remains of which lay in a torn box on the floor by the table.

"Daddy," Laura said. "I thought you weren't coming back until Monday night."

"I wasn't, but I got through early. So here I am. Hello, Ellen."

"I don't usually eat this kind of junk," Austin's ex-wife said. "But you can't find anything else in Annette. Certainly nothing macrobiotic."

"You're right about that. A barbecue sandwich, maybe, when the Pig Stand's open, maybe some catfish."

"Spare me," Ellen said. "I didn't intend to intrude, but Laura convinced me it would be all right to search through these albums for match points, with you out of town."

"Without a doubt. Go right ahead. My schedule changed all of a sudden." Austin looked down at the album opened to a double page of photos of Laura as a child and Ellen as a younger woman in a series of various poses and dress. "What do you mean match points? You aren't talking about tennis, surely?"

"Lines of convergence," Ellen said, "where two or more decision vectors touch or cross."

"Oh," Austin said and looked at Laura who refused to meet his gaze. "I see, I guess. Maybe."

"How was Washington?" Laura said. "Did you see the prez out for a jog?"

"No, not this time. Maybe on my next visit. How's school?"

"It's part of the calculations," Ellen said, "you have to do with key dates and consequential actions, slash, results. What the graph tells you can be confirmed by photographic evidence. If any exists, I mean. Look, I'll show you one to let you see how it operates."

She gestured for Austin to walk around the table to get a better look and then she turned the album toward him. He took a step and looked down at the photo Ellen was tapping with her index finger. "This one," she said. The back of her neck looked more vulnerable than ever.

The picture showed the three of them before a cage in a zoo, Laura as a two-year-old standing in front of her parents, Ellen to the right of Austin, him thirty pounds lighter, grinning into the lens almost twenty years ago. Over his shoulder behind wire mesh at the top of a cement wall stood a polar bear, reared up to see over the people between it and the camera.

"Hermann Park," Austin said. "A long time ago. Laura can barely reach my knee."

"I can't believe I was ever so small," Laura said. "Look how I've got my hands up to my eyes."

"You used to do that whenever you saw anyone aim a camera," Austin said. "Trying to copy the person holding the magic machine."

"Four beings," Ellen said and wrote the number on a sheet of the stack of papers on the table. "Fourth month of the year. I've already checked the date of the picture. April, 1974. Look closely now." She bent further over the table and tapped the point of a pen on the photo.

"See my right hand? How the fingers are showing?"

"Yeah," Austin said. "You're holding a brochure or something. A piece of paper, maybe."

"Can you see my thumb? Is it visible?"

"No, I guess not."

"All right, then. Four fingers on the dominant hand. Four, four, four, four. Four fours."

"You can see all five fingers on my hands, though, both of them. Laura's, too. I can't see the bear's."

"That doesn't make any difference, Austin," Ellen said, her voice rising a notch. "It's not your Life Consequence we're analyzing here. It's mine. And there are four fours showing, and one of the fours is behind literal bars, one is behind the bars of complacency, one behind the bars of innocence, and the other one, me, is behind the bars of psychic dependence and ignorance."

"You see all that in the picture?" Austin said, straightening up and looking at the top of Ellen's head bent over the table. The part in her hair looked as though it had been drawn by a draftsman with a T square.

"That, and a lot more. Notice where your eyes and Laura's are directed. Straight into the camera. Now look at mine and that poor bear's behind you. Mine are several degrees off to my right, and so are the bear's. What were we searching for in the distance, that captured animal and I? Did we know where we were trying to focus in that fourth month of the fourth year of the decade in the fourth year of my marriage to you?"

"Oh, mother," Laura said, getting up from the sofa and walking into the kitchen. She turned on the faucet and let the water run hard into the sink.

"That's just the photographic record," Ellen said. "It only confirms what the numerical vectors of consequence prove. Do you see that, Austin? Can you admit that much at long last?"

"Ellen," Austin said, moving toward the door, "I admit all kinds of things. Truly, I do. But I don't want to go into a long confession of my shortcomings just now."

Laura was still standing at the sink, but she had turned the faucet off and was looking over her shoulder into the living room. Austin avoided her eyes.

"Why don't you stay here tonight with Laura?" Austin said to his ex-wife. "I've got to go out to the reservation, and I plan to stay with somebody out there."

"No, thank you," Ellen said. "I've already checked into the Quality Inn on the new highway. I keep my own location."

159

"Quality Inn, huh?" Austin said, pursing his lips and looking toward the ceiling as though trying to figure something out. "I believe I know it. Isn't that the fourth one after the first stoplight? Or maybe it's the first one after the fourth stoplight. Either way, it's a hell of a deal numberwise."

There were no lights at the cattleguard entrance to the reservation, and no lights on the highway in either direction for miles, so the occasional illuminations in the small houses scattered along the way stood out in the darkness Austin Bullock traveled. Now and then as he slowly passed the dwelling places of the Alabama-Coushatta people, he could see figures moving in the lighted windows, shadowed and outlined in the night, and he wondered what was on their minds. Television shows out of the Houston stations, a car that wouldn't start or run right, the next day's work if there was any, how to get a drink in a dry county, the thing the husband or wife hadn't done, a child not back home yet, the death of Charlie Sun-Singer deep in Lost Man Marsh, some easy money from the blank eyes if they weren't lying again this time.

He turned off the highway south on the dirt road that would lead him past Bobby Crow Fly's place, thinking that if Bobby was home and sober he would ask him for a bed for the night. Bobby was Austin's age, and the children were all married and living in their own government-subsidized dwellings, and Bobby's wife kept a neat house. Austin knew he should feel guilty about choosing a place for the night on that basis, given his own housekeeping habits, but somewhere along the way, maybe in his time at college, he had begun to notice other people's dirt and clutter, and he didn't want to lie down in it. He knew he wouldn't sleep well out of his own house anyway, and the thought of feeling someone else's sheets and pillows under and around him in a strange bed made him feel a queasy surge in his belly.

"I'm a picky bastard," he said aloud as he neared the clearing in the pine thicket where Bobby Crow Fly's house sat, "but I know what will and what won't let me get some sleep."

A little later, recognizing the stand of huge sycamores at the bend in the road just before Crow Fly's house, Austin spoke out loud again. "And give me dreams," he said. "And give me dreams."

The only light in the house was a dim glow from one of the rooms in the back, and after slowing the car to look, Austin decided not to turn into the yard. In bed already, he thought, Bobby and his old lady, and the last thing they need to see now is that schoolteaching Coushatta who moved to town and is back for a one-night free room and breakfast. Why won't he just lie down in the bed he made for himself where the blank eyes live?

I'll take one more shot at a free stay in a clean place, he thought, Lawanda and Tommy Bear Killer's new little house on the road past old Tom Sylestine's. They're too young to be in bed yet, at least for the night, and if the visiting shaman parked in front of their house hasn't sucked all their electricity out to keep his trailer cool and his little hog content, Tommy and Lawanda will still have their lights on and will invite their old teacher in.

It was a full two miles from Bobby Crow Fly's place to the turn-off to the even fainter dirt road that ran by the Bear Killer's new little house. Austin drove it at a little over fifteen miles per hour, cutting his headlights so that only the amber glow of the parking bulbs lit his way. He rolled the window down to listen for night birds hunting on the chance he might be able to hear over the quiet hum of the Japanese engine. Maybe he'd be able to listen to an owl strike a rabbit or a nesting bird. Maybe a bobcat would be on the hunt for what it could turn up in the darkness, and he'd hear the single cry as the prey made its last sound in this world.

The night air was cool, and Austin shivered as it touched his face and chest, but he didn't roll the window back up. He rode that way, his mouth opened slightly as he listened closely for things in the dark, but he didn't hear a sound but his own all the way to within a hundred yards or so of the clearing in the thicket where the new little government house sat.

He saw the glow of lights well before he reached the area where the trees began to thin and the underbrush was pushed back from the one-lane road, and he slowed the car to a crawl when he saw the silvery reflections off the rear and right side of the Airstream trailer up ahead. After nosing the Honda off the road and behind a clump of yaupon bushes, he killed the engine and stepped out of the car, easing the door shut.

As he walked to the edge of the house clearing, Austin could see that the trailer was dark and all the light was coming from the house, and it was just as he stepped out of the cover of the ring of loblolly pines that the cry began to crawl into the night air. It began in a low guttural range, but Austin could tell it came from the throat of a woman even before it reached a level of shrillness that could not have come from a man. It broke off, began again even lower at the beginning this time, and persisted longer than the first time he had heard it.

Austin moved toward the window on the right side of the house, the one lit most brightly, stumbling once over something in his way, something metal and unmoving when his left foot encountered it, and reached the corner of the house at the same time the sound began to crawl out of the woman's throat again. He could feel its vibration in his hand on the windowsill as he leaned to look into the yellow light of the room.

It was a message of pain, and it came from the wife of Tommy Bear Killer, but from what Austin could judge its source was something she had wanted. He started to back away, ashamed for his intrusion and embarrassed at his stupidity, when he saw the table. On it lay a length of rubber tubing, a lit candle and spoon and plastic envelope and hypodermic needle, and the table obscured most of the scene before him, but he could see Tommy Bear Killer's face as he knelt behind the woman lying on her back with head toward him.

Bear Killer's eyes stared flatly ahead, the pupils widened as though to let all the light in the world directly into his brain, and he pulled back steadily on the woman's knees, holding her legs up and apart to allow the man between them space for what he was doing.

The man who called himself Crippled Sparrow held his mouth in the shape of an O, opening and closing it like a child blowing spit bubbles or a balloon fish feeding on small prey in clear tropical waters. His eyes were closed, and the lashes lay on his cheeks like those in a cosmetics advertisement, long and straight and black.

As the muscles of his bare shoulders filled and flexed, the low cry began to crawl again from the woman on the floor, and Austin

162

stepped carefully back from the house and the window, turning away from the light and toward the cool air of the night where surely some owl, floating on soundless feathers, would have found prey by now, or a fox, lying quiet in a thicket, would have outwaited a small animal too impatient to hide.

All the way to the car he held his breath to listen.

Near midnight, Austin ended up in the southeast portion of the reservation where the road ran out at the edge of Lost Man Marsh. He stopped the car at the end of the last hard piece of ground, just before the water began to creep so deeply into the earth that no step could be considered certain and no member of the Nation would trust fully what the appearance of things promised.

He killed the engine, stepped out of the car, and looked at the constellations in the night sky, automatically beginning to search for the arrangement of stars that, according to the stories old McKinley Big Eye used to tell, outlined the figures of Hunter and Pigeon Hawk. Had Charlie Sun-Singer looked for them, too, as he waited not over a mile away for the man who would kill him in Lost Man Marsh?

Did the stars in the sky, the holes poked at the world's beginning in the black blanket by Abba Mikko to let people know there was still light behind the darkness, yet speak to the Alabamas and Coushattas?

According to his cousin, Thomas Fox Has Him, Charlie had been a boy who still looked for the signs the old men of the Nation had declared existed in the world for reading by those willing to search for them. Maybe the boy had seen some pattern in the lights of the sky that night he had died, had thought even as his life was being torn from him that Abba Mikko presided over it all with a plan. A way to explain how the water became part of the earth, the darkness shaded into light, the pain of death dissolved into sleep, and the dreams and stories of the Old Ones proved the truth of living in a body made of bone, flesh, and blood.

"I hope you felt Abba Mikko touch you, Sun-Singer," Austin Bullock said aloud in the language of the Nation and stepped from the last piece of solid ground into the mingled water and earth of Lost Man Marsh.

Moving forward into the muck of the swamp, listening to the mixed sound the water and mud made together as he stepped, he

163

continued until he reached a hummock of vegetation and earth rising a few inches above the surface. He sat down upon it, fixed his gaze upon the figures of Hunter and Pigeon Hawk in the pattern the points of light made above him, and began to recite their story aloud in a strong voice so that Charlie Sun-Singer might hear if he were listening.

"Hunter had looked all day and found no deer. His luck was not good, and the magic sabia bead in his pouch and the red paint he had put on his cheeks were not working. His charms didn't help.

"He built a fire and threw tobacco on it to keep away the bad spirit, and he thought he would fix the holes in his moccasins while he waited for things to get better.

"Pigeon Hawk flew down and sat on the same side of the fire with Hunter to keep him company. Owl flew down from the very top of a dead pine and landed on the other side of the fire Hunter had built.

"'Throw Pigeon Hawk to me,' Owl said. 'I want to kill him. If you help me do it, I will show you how to see at night.'

"'Do not do it,' Pigeon Hawk said, 'and in the morning I will give you good hunting and your medicine will work again.'

"So Hunter kept Pigeon Hawk safe all night by never going to sleep. And in the morning Owl was blinded by the sunlight and flew up into a hole in a tree to escape it in darkness.

"Pigeon Hawk could see in the light, and he flew up to the hole in the tree and killed Owl.

"Because Hunter had saved him during the night when Owl had his power, Pigeon Hawk flew down to the ground and gave Hunter a feather from his right wing tip.

"'Keep this in your headband, and your hunting will always be good.'"

Austin Bullock stopped speaking to Charlie Sun-Singer, the dead boy in the marsh, and then he pointed at the heaven above and said one more thing. "Look at the stars," he said. "See Hunter's headband, see the wing feather of Pigeon Hawk near the back of it. See that, and your medicine will always be good, little warrior of the Nation."

In a little while, Austin left the hummock and turned back for the hard ground at the edge of the swamp. He would sleep in the car and leave the windows open so he could smell all night the way earth and water mixed together in Lost Man Marsh.

Wood smoke was already pouring from the kitchen flue of Albert Had Two Mothers' house, early as it was on Sunday morning, when Austin pulled his car up. That was not surprising, though, since Austin had never visited the old man at any hour day or night and found him asleep or showing signs of having recently being in that state.

By the time he had opened the door and stepped out of the car, the screen to the house was already pushed back and Albert Had Two Mothers was peering out at him.

"Why are you here, Abba Bullock? I thought you was in Washington talking to the head blank eye."

"I have been, my elder," Austin said and followed the old man into the front room of the house. "I'm back already."

"Did it go that bad? Did the negotiations fall through? Did you catch him lying to you?"

Albert gestured to his wife who had stuck her head in from the kitchen, lifting his hand to his mouth and making a drinking motion.

"I wouldn't say he lied. The Interior man wouldn't say yes and he wouldn't say no. Not until we get together a formal proposal for anything we want to do with those people from Houston. I couldn't pin him down."

"That's good, then. They can get their crew in there in the marsh, and we can get that little lawyer lady to working on the papers."

"I guess so," Austin said, taking the cup of coffee the old woman offered him and remembering to nod his head twice in thanks as she retreated to the kitchen. "I just wish we knew what they're after."

"Some kind of mess. It don't make no difference. There's nothing in that water and mud we're using. If they dug up the whole thing and carried it off, we wouldn't miss it for as long as it takes a mouse to run across the floor. You know that, Austin."

"Yes, you're probably right. But that marsh has been the way it is for as long as the Nation has been here. And before. That's bound to

165

change if they get their trucks and backhoes and bulldozers to work in there."

"We got to be modern, young man. We got something to sell that the blank eyes want, then we got to be up to date."

The old man paused to sip his coffee and look closely at Austin as he sat in a cane-bottomed chair across from him. "I tell you what's bothering you," he said, his milky eyes fixed on Austin.

Austin took some coffee and waited to hear.

"You think about old times too much. You read all them history books and make them kids in the high school pay attention to them, and it's give you a funny way to look at things."

"I'm not the one that puts store in things such as stated chiefships," Austin said, keeping his voice in the mild range. "Or wants to go into a sweathouse to hold business meetings."

"That's different. You got to use the structures you already got. I'm not talking about government. I'm talking about money."

"I know you are, Albert. I just don't want to see things change in the Nation when they don't have to. You never get back what you had once it's gone."

"I don't want to keep this old leaking roof," Albert Had Two Mothers said and pointed above his head. "Neither that old Ford pickup that won't start unless it's a real hot day. You ask anybody in the Nation. They'll tell you the same thing."

"Most of them would," Austin agreed. "Most of them would, all right. But that doesn't mean we have to hurry up to give these Netcon people everything they ask for without thinking about it first."

"You got to grab the catfish before he backs into his hole. He don't show you his nose but once."

"One other thing that's on my mind, my elder, and yours, too, I expect, is the dead boy and Chief Emory. Both of them were killed down in that same part of Lost Man Marsh. I keep wondering about the connection between what happened to them and what these Houston people are so interested in."

"Now here's the way I see it," Albert Had Two Mothers said, leaning forward in his cane-bottomed chair. "I have put my mind on this and tried to dream about it, but nothing ain't come to me when

I'm sleeping yet. But here's something I know. When a blank eye gets into the middle of some of our business, not everything is connected anymore. Don't say nothing yet to me, Abba Bullock, until I show you what I mean."

"I wasn't going to."

"Well, good. Now, see if it's just us, just the people we're talking about, then everything is all hooked up, just like you always been told in the stories. If a bird flies up from a tree limb somewhere in the woods, its wings make the air move and that'll carry to the ear of a Coushatta or Alabama four or five miles off and make him think about the way he's living his life or maybe he'll get sad or happy. You understand that, don't you?"

"That's what the old stories say," Austin answered. "McKinley Big Eye let us all know that."

"I still go along with that. No matter if I drive in a car or watch the TV set or eat at a hamburger store in town. It don't matter. That stuff don't touch the middle of the circle. But, see, Austin, when the blank eyes get into the figuring, them strings that hold everything together for the Nation, they get all stretched out and twisted and you can't tell what one thing causes another thing to happen. You following me now?"

"I can tell you've been thinking about it, my elder."

"Good. Then you know what I'm talking about. What this all means is that we got to give these blank eyes the benefit of the doubt. Don't go blaming them for what happened to our two people that's been killed just because everything's happening at the same time. Wait up little bit before you start up seeing this and that being part of the one thing."

"At least until the money's passed from one hand to the other."

"Something like that," Albert Had Two Mothers said. "Now, you want some more coffee before you leave and go talk to that little lawyer lady yonder in Annette?"

"I'm going to let you and the council do that. I've got a lot of work to do this week before I go to Austin for the state tournament. Besides, I just heard a crow fly up somewhere in the swamp. His feathers are making my ears ring and telling me things."

167

"Sometimes it's just a bird changing tree limbs, Abba Bullock, that's all."

"I guess sometimes it is," Austin said. "One thing else I wanted to ask you about before I leave, though."

"What's that?" the old man said, standing up from his chair to let Austin know it was time to go.

"It's this consultant the Nation's hired, the one that calls himself Crippled Sparrow. How much longer is he going to be around?"

"They got what the little man calls the dress rehearsal to do next week. Then he says he's got to go help them Indians in North Carolina or somewhere. He's going to come back for when they open up the pageant for the blank eye tourists, though. First of May, it's going to be."

"It'll be good when he's gone," Austin said, "from what I can tell."

"They tell me he knows this here show business. He's got these kids learning all kinds of dances and ways to do. All this stuff the tourists want to see. New kinds of stuff."

"I have no doubt about that," Austin said and left the house of Albert Had Two Mothers. He hoped when he got back to Annette he'd find his own place empty of Ellen and charts and graphs and old pictures and calculations about lines of convergence.

22

"I figure two more days," Martin Utz said, looking out the window of the Quality Inn at the parking lot of the Walmart next door. People were unloading from cars and pickups and heading for the door of the huge flat building even though it was well before the noon opening time on Sunday. "Three, tops."

"Until what?" Clarence was sitting in a chair beside a round table with a plastic top, pointing a remote toward the television and flashing back and forth between a soccer game and a documentary on the Discovery Channel about DNA.

"Until I can get in that Lincoln, drive back to Houston and fly the fuck out of this goddamn state for good. That's what."

"You aren't enjoying learning about new minority groups, broadening your experience and all like that?"

"Three days," Martin repeated. "Tops."

"It'll take longer than that," Clarence said, clicking the remote steadily, "before we can leave. Mr. Bloodworth will want it where he can see it before he turns us loose."

"They've located it already. They told us right where to dig. Soon as the head redman gives us the word to bring in the crew, we'll get it out that night, no problem."

"I still don't know why we had to deal with those people in the first place," Clarence said. "It won't take over a few hours for the whole operation. Just go in and do it."

"Bloodworth's careful, that's why. People come to him because he's careful. He won't take chances. Everything's always clean when he finishes a job. It's a turnkey deal. And nobody's jabbering about what they seen going on because he's fixed it so they believe what he wants them to. Besides, you're talking about some big equipment. Way we got it fixed now, when we vacate, these fuckers will thank us for the hole we leave, rather than asking questions and getting in the way. They'll think we're coming back with a shitload of cash to put on their Indian asses."

"It's nice to be appreciated," Clarence said. "We're operating like it's intact, of course."

"What's to hurt? It'll all be there. Just scoop it up once we get down in there wherever it got to. So it's busted up a little. You can't hurt it."

"Right," Clarence said. "I understand that. But it did hit hard. Kicked up that other treasure trove on the way in. Opened it right up to public view."

"Yeah. I still don't believe that. What something like that says to me is there's a plan, right? Operating all the time. Making stuff happen all connected up like. It's weird."

169

"I hate to undermine your faith in order and regularity, Marty," Clarence said, still watching the DNA documentary, "but there's not one thing that has to do with another thing in this world, except what comes already hardwired together."

"You telling me this whole business, the shit coming loose and falling on a goddamned Indian reservation and Bloodworth happening to know this little magic runt redman who just by chance is running his own game out there at the same time and them coins or whatever being in the spot in that mud and water where it hit, you're telling me it was all an accident? There ain't nothing making it happen like that?"

"That's what I'm telling you, exactly. That pretty well sums it up."

"I feel sorry for you, then," Martin Utz said. "I don't know what I'd do if I didn't know there's something somewhere watching out for me and making things go right. Me, I'm special."

"I just grit my teeth and hang on. Depend on myself the best way I can."

"Looking at this thing, you can tell me there's no overall plan working? Bullshit. But it finally ain't no big deal, right? I mean where it landed finally. We got them back, didn't we? Every last one of them coins they took out. Nothing lost, nothing to worry about now."

"Tell that to this Indian schoolteacher."

"He knows what's good for him, he'll stick close to his blackboard," Martin said, moving toward the window overseeing the parking lot. "And stop poking around and asking fucking questions. Hey, come look at this one, Clarence. I swear to God when she got out of the car I felt this window shake."

"Not just now," said Clarence, clicking the remote. "I'm about to get this guy to kick a soccer ball up the DNA spiral. Create a whole new species, maybe."

"You're missing a real specimen. I shit you not. She has literally got a plate on her car says TON 306. I guess you'd call that an accident, how her license plate is saying all the time what she is. Me, it's part of that big plan I was telling you about."

"Coincidence, sheer coincidence. Like everything else. It doesn't mean a thing."

Laura's note was bright and chipper. "Calm down, old fellow" was the subtext beneath the information that she was taking her mother to observe one of the rehearsal sessions being conducted by the little drug-shooting shaman-for-hire. "Mom's really interested in what I told her about Crippled Sparrow," it read, "and we're going to watch him work with the performers on the water dance segment of the pageant. That's the one scheduled for today. Back in time for supper."

Austin wadded up the piece of paper and wondered how in hell he was going to be able to forbid Laura from ever speaking to Roy Blending/Crippled Sparrow again without achieving exactly the opposite effect. What she said in the note about Ellen's sudden concern with activities on the reservation was hard for him to believe. The last time he had taken her out there was years back, when Laura was no more than a toddler, for his mother's funeral. By that point in their marriage, Ellen had become so put-off by what she called the "whole redman thing" that she had stayed in the car during the entire time in the Nation, through both ceremonies of burial. When he had returned to her in the car, Austin had found her almost comatose from the August heat and Laura playing outside in the dirt with a pile of pine cones and acorns she had gathered.

"She won't stay in the car," Ellen had said, "no matter how I beg her to. Look at her. She's reverted to looking just like the rest of them. She's just covered with dirt, and her hair is as straight as string hanging in her face. Look at her eyes. There's no pupil."

A long time past, he thought, just before the Hunter's Moon almost twenty years ago, and now mother and daughter visit the Nation to watch a four-foot high consultant get the Alabamas and Coushattas organized. Laura was easy enough to understand. For her, the Nation was good material for developing mythic views and cultural connections. For her mother, maybe a line or two would cross somewhere in the woods and swamps of the reservation, and she'd find herself another life consequence or a decision point or whatever the hell she called the current system she was trying to live by.

Austin headed for his bedroom to change clothes and leave for work. Maybe he could find some sense in leading tenth graders through the Great Depression and the New Deal, or better yet, see

171

some purpose in showing five high school basketball players how to bring in the ball against a full-court press being put on by a team averaging a half-foot taller per man.

Thomas Fox Has Him would, for the last two weeks, come closest to remembering it when he was sitting in the biology lab in Annette High School. It was in that place, twice a week in the hour after lunch when his class met there, that he thought most about his cousin, Charlie Sun-Singer. That was true, he realized, because it was there he could look through the microscope and see the tiny creatures swimming before the lens and realize things so small could exist and not be seen in this world by the ordinary eyes of a human being. But they were there, seen or not.

Charlie Sun-Singer, so young when he died, had always believed in things that could not be seen or heard or touched, and he had thought that way since the time he was old enough to speak. The first time Thomas Fox Has Him really noticed him, this small son of his mother's brother, six or seven years younger than he, was on a day when Thomas had gone into the swamp to search for ginseng plants to sell to the blank eye who ran the store at the edge of the reservation.

Charlie was alone, sitting on the bank of Long King Creek and staring so intently into the moving water that he had not been aware of Thomas coming up behind him until the elder boy touched him with the toe of his shoe.

"If you're watching for perch," Thomas had said, "you're not going to see them in water that shallow, little boy. They stay in pools."

"It is not fish I see, my cousin," Charlie Sun-Singer said. "I listen to the little man inside that rock." He pointed toward a gray stone streaked with reddish lines, rising up in the middle of the creek, the main stream breaking around it. "There, where the red bars hold him."

"That's just a rock."

"Yes. He is inside it, though."

"What do you think he says, this little man?" Fox Has Him said, staring at the side of his cousin's face. "Tell me his words."

"He waits. He has waited. He will wait."

"For what?"

"For when the red bars are washed away by Long King Creek and he is able to live again with his people."

Thomas had squatted for a time beside the small boy, his breath held to listen for some sound the water made to fool Charlie into thinking he heard a voice, but nothing came to him but the splash and play of the creek, and he left soon to look for the ginseng root, aware that the boy had not realized when he was gone.

Now in the laboratory in the high school building, the silver and black microscope before him, Thomas Fox Has Him peered deeply into the lens to search for some form in the specimen in view which would let him hear again the words Charlie Sun-Singer had said to him a little over two months before. It had been late in the afternoon, the sun already sunk behind the tree line, the light fading so quickly that Thomas was afraid it would become dark before he had finished putting the hundredth shot from the free-throw line through the outdoor basket which stood in the yard near his house.

He did that every day, and he had done it since he had begun playing basketball six years ago on the junior high team in Annette. He did not consider himself a believer in charms or sabia beads or blue jay feathers kept in medicine bags, but he could see no reason to break the pattern he established, particularly in his senior year when it looked like Annette had a chance at going all the way to the state championship in Austin in March. Free throws were given for the taking, and a man was a fool not to get them all.

He was at seventy-six and was retrieving the ball to step back to the line when he saw, at the corner of the half-court he had marked out with white stones many years ago, the figure of a child kneeling just outside the boundary. Thomas was not surprised to find someone watching him at his daily ritual. Ever since he had first begun playing on the junior high team, people of the Nation, young and old, would gather at times to see him put the ball through the circle, but this was the first occasion on which Charlie Sun-Singer had done so.

Maybe his young cousin was beginning to show an interest shared by other boys of his age. A good thing, Thomas remembered thinking as he picked up the basketball and bounced it on the hardpacked earth of the half-court, maybe my strange little kinsman is starting to grow up and will spend some time with others for a change, instead of wandering all day alone in the woods and marshes.

"Seventy-six," Thomas Fox Has Him said in a kind voice to the boy just beyond the boundary line, "twenty-four more to make, my cousin." He had already walked back to the free-throw position and was seeing the ball in his mind intersect the circle of the basket when Charlie Sun-Singer spoke.

"The sky vomited this morning," he said, "just before the sun touched the middle one of the three cypress trees in Lost Man Marsh."

The dip of the knees, the automatic movement of all the muscles of the body, the front edge of the rim bathed in a light which made it stand out from all things around it, the release into the perfect curve of movement which the ball must travel...

The metal of the basket made a flat clanging sound, and the ball came directly back to Thomas on the fly. Still seventy-six, and it had felt right, and the dying sun continued its downward journey beyond the tree-line.

He put the ball up quickly again, and this time the net snapped as it should. Thomas walked toward the goal to retrieve the ball for the next shot.

"When the sky spit it out, the thing fell down into the marsh," Charlie Sun-Singer said then as he watched his cousin go back to the line. "It splashed in the water and mud, and pieces of the marsh flew up into the air and got on all the leaves and limbs of the trees. When I went to look, I could see the hole it made."

Number seventy-eight came immediately, and Thomas Fox Has Him felt the true movement stirring within his flesh and bone. "What was it?" he asked. "Did the top of a dead cypress break loose and fall?"

Then the little boy, his strange cousin who chose to wander alone in the parts of the Nation where no one lived in a house or planted a garden, said no it was not a dead tree top, it was something else from the sky, it was a... And his word came when number eighty of that day's hundred free throws did not go through the net for Thomas Fox Has Him and his ear heard what was said by the boy, but his mind stopped listening and bound itself around a rubber ball and a circle of steel with string hanging from it. It had taken until full dark to get the hundredth.

Thomas Fox Has Him leaned forward in the school laboratory over the microscope, fitting his eye more closely to the flexible piece of rubber and adjusting the focus of the lens by a delicate sliver of movement. Before him in the gray soup of the specimen of water he had brought from Lost Man Marsh, a shape detached itself from the mass around it and swam in his view defined as a thing apart from all else. Thomas could feel the word which Charlie Sun-Singer had said to him before he rose from the edge of the outdoor court to walk away into the coming darkness of the twilight of that day over two months ago. It stirred.

Like the swimming shape in the lens, which now resolved itself into the form of an egg rounder at one end than the other, the word pushed at the edge of the mass in the mind of Thomas Fox Has Him, hesitated a beat longer, and then moved before the eye of his memory, coming fully into view as itself and nothing else.

"Pod," Thomas said aloud. "He said it was a pod, a wing pod."

He looked one last time at the shape beneath the focused lens of the microscope, elongating slowly as it drifted toward another form near it, and then Thomas sat back and reached for a pencil. He would write it down now, what his dead cousin had told him had been vomited by the sky into Lost Man Marsh, and he would show this written word and tell Charlie Sun-Singer's story to his coach, his teacher, to Abba Bullock of the Alabama-Coushatta Nation, and he would do it today before he touched another basketball again.

23

It was not supposed to be this far, the village, the collection of hooches these people lived in. It had a name, the lieutenant had told him what it was called, something that sounded like smacking your lips together and saying bang in the middle of the smacking somewhere. The sound it made when the lieutenant said it was like a man eating a sweet, a pudding with raisins in it good enough to groan over, but in the middle of it, one of the raisins was a pebble and you had to spit it out or break a tooth trying to chew it.

Don't go by names, he told himself, as he eased forward another step in the sucking mud and weeds. Never look for a thing by what it's called. They can change that. One man will say it one way, another mouth will not make the same sound. They had accents, too, all these people, so you couldn't listen to one say a name and hear the same sound come from a different voice heard through a wall made of bamboo and grass and dirt and know both of them were talking about the same thing.

It didn't seem like it ought to be that way in this place of rice paddies and lizards and stinging ants where these people lived, but it was that way back in the Nation. A Coushatta would use the same word for a thing as an Alabama, but you could tell by the way his mouth handled it which people he belonged to, where his mother gave him birth, on which side of the sleeping room his father lay when he dreamed.

Go by what your eyes tell you, look at the compass they taught you to use in the Special Forces school, listen to the way the birds fly up when they hear something coming. These things will not lie to you. In the same way the grunting of hogs or the lowing of cattle or the crying of a baby mean each time one thing and not another. If a thing cannot talk, it will not lie.

So the hooches should be here, within one klick of where he now sank to his knees to lie flat in the earth mixed with water. He opened his mouth and let his tongue taste the elements of the place where he lay, and that told him he was not mistaken about where he was, the thing he had come to, and he knew that again the words they had told him were wrong.

It was always hard not to listen when the officer spoke directly into his face, holding his eyes steady while assigning the mission and describing the location where he must proceed, the next set of hooches, mostly situated by water, sometimes at the edge of a great stand of underbrush and trees, always to be approached in the dead of night after the moon, if there was one, had dropped.

Again he had let himself be directed too much by the words spoken to him. He had let them get inside his head in the part which he always wanted to keep in darkness. He had not trusted to the sounds that things make when they fly up afraid, to the way water, earth, stone, and vegetation tasted in his mouth and told him the true path to take, the glow of light that played always about the edges of the target he sought when he at last found it, the light that was in the darkness that only he could see.

He would wait, sinking deeper into the mud and water giving beneath him as he lay. When the moon dropped below the tree line, he would move according to the way the compass pointed and the taste of earth told him, and he would come upon the hooches, this village with the name like smacking something sweet with a thorn hidden in the middle of it. He closed his eyes to wait to see.

"I saw him again today," Menard Stands Steady said to his mother. She was at the kitchen stove, turning pieces of meat over in an iron skillet. It was pork, fatty, and it made a popping sound each time a new side met the hot metal. Menard flinched when a drop of grease from the pan touched his cheek.

"Move back," his mother said, "and you won't get burned. Where is your brother?"

"He's on the porch," Menard said, rubbing the spot on his face where the hot grease had hit, "cleaning the mud off his shoes. Ow."

"Did you clean yours?"

"I didn't step in the marsh. I walked on the dry spots and looked where I was going."

"Who did you see?" his mother asked and reached for a pot on the back of the stove.

"Tucker Pop Eye," Menard Stands Steady said. "He was lying down in the swamp again."

"Maybe he fell. Tripped on something or slipped down."

"No, he did it on a purpose. Me and Brazos watched him do it. He was careful when he was laying down there in the mud and water. He took his hands and put some mud all over the back of his head."

"You didn't say anything to him, did you?" Menard's mother turned away from the frying meat and looked hard at him. "Did he know you were watching him?"

"Nuh uh. Me and Brazos was hiding down behind a log, like they do when the cops are fixing to do a bust on TV. Tucker Pop Eye didn't see us watching him."

"I'll bust you," she said. "You boys leave that man alone. Don't go around trying to look at him. You hear me now."

"We don't. He just showed up where we was at. He looked just like a big old alligator laying down in that mudhole. Dirty and wet all over."

"Don't go back there again. Go get your brother. It's time to eat."

"He sounded like one, too, old Tucker Pop Eye. He grunted like a hog." Menard Stands Steady went to the front door of his house, calling his brother Brazos by coughing as deep in his throat as he could, but it still wasn't close to the sound Tucker Pop Eye had made as he lay at full length in the mud and water of Lost Man Marsh, smearing dirt all over the back of his head and neck and squeezing his eyes shut tight.

24

He had most of them going now, at least the ones who had spent time learning the three lines on the handout he had given them two days ago. All of them were arranged in a circle, facing inward, and were moving three steps to the right, pause for two beats, then two more, pause for two beats, then one step back to the left.

The young ones had it down, the dance part at least, and were getting into it. Of course, none of that bunch had learned the chant, because that involved reading something, and the ones who had done that part of the assignment were the older women who couldn't tell their right foot from their left. They stumbled and moved the wrong direction and bumped into the person on the left and then overcompensated and lurched toward the right into the one on that side.

The worst thing about teaching, always: having to depend on somebody else to put into the world what existed pure and precise in his own head, a chain of movement and sound clicking together like a string of beads run through the fingers one by one by one, when it was right.

At least the old man pounding on the drum head was good. Lucky for me, Crippled Sparrow told himself, I've got one this time who won't be distracted by movement. From now on, I'm going to insist on a blind man to set the beat. Look at him leaning over that skin, working that boom boom boom. He's got to lose the sunglasses, though, before the dress rehearsal. Can't have an anachronism gumming up the works.

"People," Crippled Sparrow called out, "listen to the beat. Feel that drum pulse. Let the rhythm tell you where to go. Don't think about what you're doing. You belong to the dance, it doesn't belong to you."

Hopping down from the top row of the outdoor bleachers, he rushed down the center aisle toward the dance ground in what looked like a controlled fall. He centered himself behind one of the women who had been having the most trouble in maintaining time with the others and grasped her with both hands just above the hipbones. She shied away, but Crippled Sparrow dug in with all ten fingers and began to count rhythm in a strong bark.

"One and two and three," he said, hopping in perfect synch with the low booms coming from the blind man's drum. "Let your belly do the thinking, let your belly do the thinking."

Satisfied with the rhythm he'd established in the set of buttocks before him, he stepped back and looked sharply about him from side to side at the circle of weaving Alabamas and Coushattas. "Coming along," he said, "coming along."

It was then he saw two new ones in the small crowd of onlookers which usually showed up each time he worked his actors, or, as he liked to call them publicly, the tribe's representatives of its mythic past. Two women standing at the fringe of gawkers, one the daughter of that hang-around-the-fort schoolteacher, and the other an older white woman, wearing a calf-length dress much too purple and busy with design to do anything for her but to point up the defects in her appearance.

He waved and started toward them, studying the white woman as he proceeded in their direction. Reddish hair, a good dye job, green eyes that had probably once been fine before the light went out in them, not much of a bustline but good body carriage, fingers a mite short for her build, and an overall effect just a little this side of stable. My kind of girl, he thought, or at least close enough for East Texas.

"Colita, it's so good to see you again. You've brought a friend with you. Welcome to my little workshop on the dance. Don't we look awful?"

"Not at all," the girl said, turning toward the white woman. "Crippled Sparrow, this is my mother, Ellen Felder."

"I could be polite and say I don't believe it, but she could be no one else but your mother. I can tell now where you get your soul."

He extended his right hand toward the white woman, palm up as though he were offering her something small he had been holding in a clenched fist, and when she touched her hand to his, Crippled

Sparrow moved back a sudden half-step and jerked his head up and widened his eyes.

"Your aura," he said, "is very powerful, like an ember. You've learned to focus your energy, haven't you?"

"I hope I have," the woman said in a small voice. "I've been working on my lines of convergence, the intersections."

"Ah," Crippled Sparrow said, fixing his gaze on the pale green eyes before him and staring as though he saw a thing hidden deep within. "Yes, yes, of course. You must come with Colita to the dress rehearsal and lend us what you have."

He waved his hand in a circle which he meant to include the ring of dancers shuffling behind them to the beat of the drum, the dance ground itself, and the sky above them all.

"We need a spirit. We ache for it."

"All my direction is inward," the white woman said. "The energies are from within or they're nothing. The first step in Life Consequences is to give up on anything that suggests an external explanation for your own individual situation. You got yourself to where you are. And it's your task to find out how." Ellen Felder fixed Crippled Sparrow with a pleading look. leaning forward as she spoke. "Am I explaining it clearly? I haven't had much experience yet in talking about Life Consequences to people who aren't already familiar with it."

"Perfectly," the little man said in a mellow tone, thinking to himself that she was worlds edgier than he first thought. She'd be a real hoot to be around. "The only thing different between what you're saying and what I know to be true is in the language. The externals. And as you say, what matters is the essence within, not the trappings of words."

"Right," the woman said, smiling beside her daughter who had begun to get a look of intense suffering on her face. "You understand it immediately."

"What's to understand? I eat food, it becomes my nourishment without need of a single thought. The body is the consequence. The consequence is the body."

181

Crippled Sparrow smiled at the women and turned his back to watch the circle of mythic representatives wheel about the muddy dance ground, their rhythm a ragged counterpoint to the blind man's drum. A mother-daughter combo? he asked himself. Too much to dream, but what a line of consequence it would be.

"You don't mean there was a plane crash, do you?" Austin Bullock was saying to Thomas Fox Has Him. "People would have heard about something like that if it happened. There'd have been flight plans filed and radio contact, probably, and I don't know what all else."

They were in the locker room at the end of practice, everyone else gone but Coach Mellard back in his office waiting to see Austin just two days before the Annette basketball team was scheduled to leave for the big fieldhouse on the University of Texas campus where the state tournament was to be held. About every two minutes, the door to Mellard's office would open and the coach would stick his head out to see if his point guard and his assistant coach were still talking. They had been at it for twenty minutes, and he needed to talk to Austin Bullock, but he was afraid to interrupt.

Who knew what kind of tribal thing the assistant coach and the young player were going through? Maybe Austin was using some kind of Indian folklore or something to motivate the kid who had to be right for three days in a row in a strange fieldhouse in front of a bunch of people he'd never seen any of before. Better not break in on this thing, no matter how much he needed to hear Austin tell him things were going to be all right. Stay out of the kitchen while the cook's at work. Let the big dog feed, and all that stuff. Wait until it boils before you lift the lid.

"Be with you in a minute, Coach," Austin called the fourth or fifth time Mellard opened the door to the locker room. "We won't be much longer." Mellard closed the door and forced himself to pick up a ten-pound hand weight from his desk and begin to do right arm curls.

"So it couldn't have been that," Austin said to Thomas Fox Has Him. "A plane crash, could it?"

"No, my elder. Charlie Sun-Singer said a pod. It came from a plane, but not the plane itself. The plane had two engines, he said."

"What does that mean, Tom, a pod? He didn't mean an engine housing, did he?"

"No, I thought so, too, at first, when I remembered what my cousin had told me, but it is not that. I know now."

"How do you know? Did you go find it in the marsh?"

"No, Abba Bullock. I did what you would do," Thomas said. "I went to the library and looked in books and magazines. I had to go to the library in town, too, before I found it. I got the information off the Internet. I hunted for pictures of planes with two engines and something that looked like a pod."

"I'm proud of you, Tom. Just like a research paper you would do in history class. What'd you find out?"

Fox Has Him reached into a gym bag on the floor by the bench where he was sitting and pulled out a sheaf of papers and began leafing through them. "The search engine was good. I found news stories and articles about what I wanted, and I wrote down what it said in an aviation magazine about the 2190 series of the two-engine plane with the name I can't pronounce. It's Japanese. And then I made a hard copy of a picture I found of it. See, you can look at it."

"Tell me what you wrote down," Austin said, taking the copy Thomas offered him.

"It says for three model years they attached a metal carrier beneath the fuselage because there wasn't enough room provided for transporting baggage and stuff. They changed it pretty soon because three different times they know of the baggage pod had worked loose in flight and had almost come off when the plane landed."

"This thing here?" Austin said, pointing to a tear-shaped bump on the underside of the aircraft pictured on the photocopied paper. "It looks big. Over ten feet, maybe."

"I think so. It's got to be that. I figure somebody was flying that model, and the pod worked loose over the Nation and fell down into Lost Man Marsh. That's what Charlie saw make the big splash and the hole in the mud and water. He saw the plane."

"Huh. Could be, I guess. But you don't know whether or not Charlie got a look at where it landed. Actually saw this thing he called a pod?"

"I was shooting free-throws when he told me," Thomas Fox Has Him said in a low tone. "I didn't listen well, and I wouldn't let him keep talking. I wanted to get the last shot in before it got too dark to see. And now..." He stopped talking and began fanning the edges of the sheaf of papers back and forth in his hand, making a rustling sound in the silence of the locker room.

"And what?'

"And now I keep seeing that last shot go through the net over and over, and I know it never counted for nothing and never will."

"Don't think that, Thomas Fox Has Him," Austin said. "You've done good work here. Work that will help your cousin more than anything anyone else could have done. I am very proud of the way you have behaved. You are like Lodge Boy in the old story on the day he saved his village from the Choctaw when nobody would help."

"Y'all about finished out there?" Coach Mellard called from the door to his office. "Is it gonna be much longer?"

"No," Austin answered. "Tom and I are through here. We see where we've got to go now, and all we have to do is make ready for it."

"Is that the one with the wolf head stuck up on a pole?" Thomas Fox Has Him said to Austin. "Is Dirty Boy in it, too?"

Austin told him that it was, that was the right story, and as they left the locker room, he began from the first and recounted the tale in words as close as he could remember to the ones McKinley Big Eye had used for him almost forty years before.

25

The first time Cake Golson saw a squeeze coming had been a half-mile or so back, just after the shoulder on each side of the narrow road had started turning to mush. So he had to keep the trailer rig in the middle of the roadbed, no cheating to one side or the other, and the give was going to have to come from the two trees, one on each side of the way he was taking. One of them was little enough, though, to let him ease the side of the rig right into it, ripping it loose from its roots with the bumper on the roadbed side like a dentist pulling a bad tooth.

That one was easy. The two up ahead were different. Both were hardwoods, oak probably, and they looked to be eight or nine feet around, maybe more, jammed up close enough to the roadbed to make it tight for even a pickup to squeeze through. No way this rig was going to push one of them fuckers over, no matter how much you gunned it. Cake eased off on the gas pedal and put the transmission in neutral.

"Can't make it," he said to the man sitting in the passenger seat beside him, the squint-eyed guy Mr. Bloodworth had told him to meet at the motel in Annette. "Looky yonder."

"What? You mean the trees? Get up a little speed and bust on through. No problem."

"Not no, but unh uh. They too stout and my rig's too wide. I try that, and we'd be stuck here for good. I flat guarantee you that."

"Leave the road, then, and drive around them," the man said. "You can run over those bushes and weeds and shit off to the side there."

"Look at that ground," Cake said, staring mournfully from one side of the roadbed to the other. "That's pure-dee mud and water. Ain't no bottom to it. We'd be up to the door handles in two minutes, the load this rig's carrying."

"What the fuck, then? I'm supposed to sit here, pulling on my dick?"

"Cut one or both of them trees down, only way to let us through here. Probably just one'd do it. I can put my wheels up on the stump if it's cut low enough. Go right on through."

"You got a cutter, then? What do you call it? An axe?"

"Not hardly," Cake said. "Wouldn't no axe do her. Take a power saw to get them things down. Big'un, too."

"Don't tell me. Let me guess. There's not a power saw within fifty miles of here, right?" The man leaned forward in his seat, twisted around to look directly into Cake's eyes, the expression on his face a happy one as far as Cake could tell. He grinned back, then realized that the narrow-eyed man was not really smiling but setting his teeth like a man about to bite into something he didn't really want to eat, but had to.

"Yessir, we got one in the bed of the pickup Dwayne's driving yonder behind us. It's a Poulan, too, and big enough to take down anything in these woods."

"I can't believe it," Martin Utz said. "You're not trying to tell me somebody thought ahead around here, are you? Because if you're claiming that, I know you're lying."

"I ain't claiming nothing, no sir, and I ain't lying, neither. Dwayne just never takes nothing out of the bed of that pickup, and I know that Poulan chainsaw is in there from a pulpwood job he did back in the fall."

"That's more like it, then," Martin said. "You're coming clean with me now, and I do appreciate the straight talk. Let's get that fucking saw started up."

"Yessir. I'll step back there and talk to Dwayne." Cake moved to open the truck door and then paused to look at the man dressed in new and unwrinkled clothes. "But ain't these trees technically on government land?"

"The government's not here," Martin said, looking around him in an exaggerated way at the undergrowth and swamp surrounding the rig, "as far as I can see." He leaned forward and turned the knob on the glove compartment in front of him and watched papers, maps, screwdrivers and fuses tumble out onto the floor. "Do you see any government agents hiding here in your treasure chest, partner?

186

Because if you do, I'd really be grateful if you'd point them out to me. I mean me being new around here and all."

"No sir," Cake said and stared down at the mess the man had just made on the floorboard. "I reckon not. But's there an old Indian man up yonder leaning up against that red oak on the right side of the roadbed. Maybe he'll want to say something against us cranking up that Poulan."

"Where?" Martin said, cracking the door open on his side. "Oh, yeah. Suppose he's carrying a bow and arrow? I'm just scared to look."

Fucking shithead, Cake Golson thought as he killed the engine and stepped outside the truck onto the roadbed, careful to keep from getting his boots into the ooze just a foot away, I'd like to come up beside your head with a goddamn monkey wrench. See how you'd talk with your fucking jaw broke.

"Go tell that other one to get the saw ready," the man said without looking back at Cake. "I'll go talk to the Last of the Mohicans up here and get him straightened out."

The Indian leaning against the red oak was an old one, dressed in bib overalls and wearing a dirty gray felt hat too big for his head. Cake could see that it had two feathers in the band, one a long black one, probably from a crow or a buzzard and the other shorter one was blue touched with white at the edges and top. Probably from a blue jay, Cake figured, and then he turned to walk back to the pickup to tell Dwayne about the Poulan chainsaw.

As he walked past the trailer, Cake checked the chains holding down the backhoe and saw that they were all in place and tight against the load riding the chest-high bed. One thing this morning was going right, then, he told himself and then spoke to Dwayne. The man sitting beside him—tall, thin. with a fringe of blonde hair ringing his bald head—was staring straight ahead at Cake so hard that he looked behind him to see if somebody was following. Nobody. He cleared his throat and said Dwayne's name again.

"Boss man up there wants us to get that chainsaw back yonder cranked up."

"Why?" Dwayne said. "Is it something he wants cut?"

"No," the tall man sitting beside Dwayne said, the one the other one had called Clarence, "he just wants to listen to the music it makes."

"Who? Cake?" Dwayne said.

"Martin. The man you're working for."

"Uh huh," Dwayne said. "I get you."

After they had pulled the Poulan from beneath a tarp in the bed of the pickup and Dwayne had checked the level of gasoline in the tank, the three men walked past the truck rig and stopped just short of the oak tree where Martin and the Indian were standing. Neither man was saying anything. Martin was looking at the trunk of the tree, and the old man with the hat decorated with feathers was staring into the woods on the other side of the dirt road as though he saw something happening in the vines and underbrush of the swampy thicket.

"Chief Crazy Horse here says these two trees have got names," Martin said to the three men in front of him. He was looking at Clarence. "Just like they was human."

"That's nothing strange," Clarence said. "My mother had a name, and she wasn't human."

The Indian man touched his right hand to the brim of his hat and nodded at the three men with the chainsaw. "Howdy," he said. "My name is not Crazy Horse. He got that wrong." He nodded toward Martin. "I done already met y'all before. Remember? It's Albert Had Two Mothers."

"You say you have two mothers?" Clarence said. "Twice unlucky, two times cursed."

"I only had one," the old Indian said. "It's a clan name. It goes back to the old ones. In the time before Texas."

"Sounds like Eden," Clarence said. "But I'm glad you got that straightened out for us. I'd still bet you're unlucky, though."

"Nobody'll take that bet," Martin said. "Nobody with any sense."

"That oak there," Albert Had Two Mothers said, pointing across the narrow road with his left hand, "is Thunder Man. This one here," he jerked his right thumb over his shoulder toward the tree behind him, "is Stone Woman."

"I believe I was married to that bitch at one time," Martin Utz said. "Tell these lumber cutters how the trees got their names, like you told me. Go ahead. Clarence, I want you to pay attention."

"Dirty Boy was an orphan," the old man began, his voice picking up a rise and fall quality as he spoke. "He didn't have no father, nor no mother. He hunted by himself and lived by himself. One day he come upon the den where a Big Man-Eater lived, and he wasn't home. So Dirty Boy he picked him out a pretty stone, a red one, that had thunder in it, from a bunch of other rocks the Big Man-Eater had lying in a pile there in his den. And he come out of the den onto a trail and began to walk on it, and the Big Man-Eater saw him."

"He was stealing this rock, huh?" Dwayne said.

"You hush," Clarence said. "Let the narrator work."

"The Big Man-Eater he knowed Dirty Boy had his red stone because he could hear the thunder in it. He started after him, and he was fast, so Dirty Boy was going as hard as he could down that trail. He figured he would be caught soon, but he wasn't going to quit without giving the Big Man-Eater a run.

"About then Dirty Boy heard the thunder in the stone start up in that leather bag he had throwed it in. It was crashing around and making sounds, and directly Dirty Boy could understand what it was saying. That red stone didn't want to be kept in that den no more, it didn't want to belong to the Big Man-Eater who wouldn't let it outside to be in the air and light.

"That stone it told Dirty Boy to call Thunder Man and Stone Woman. It said to holler out loud, and them red oak trees would help him. Dirty Boy commenced to hollering, and them trees standing yonder they heard him. Back then they was far apart, one way down there in Lost Man Marsh and the other one, it was Stone Woman I believe, it was up on that ridge yonder where you can see that stand of long-leaf pines now."

The old man turned and pointed back behind the truck-rig toward a hill rising beyond a bend in the narrow road, and everyone except Martin looked in the direction he indicated.

"See yonder?" Albert Had Two Mothers said. "Just the tops of them two trees?"

"Yeah," Dwayne said. "I see some long-leafs poking up."

"Stone Woman and Thunder Man heard Dirty Boy calling, and they could hear the thunder in that red stone, too, and them trees pulled up their roots where they were standing. They walked toward each other and when they got to the right spot they put them roots down, and there you see them standing here where we are this minute."

"Dirty Boy got to the spot right after Thunder Man and Stone Woman was in the new place and he ran right between them, on up the trail where this road is now, carrying that red stone with thunder just booming inside of it."

"How did that do him any good?" Cake Golson asked. "Couldn't that thing still catch him?"

"No," the old Indian said, shaking his head so hard the feathers rustled in his hat band, "the Big Man-Eater couldn't fit between them trees, but he didn't know it. See, Thunder Man and Stone Woman had stopped with just enough room between them so he couldn't get through. When he tried to run between them, and he was going as fast as he could, why he just knocked his brains out on Stone Woman and tore off his right arm on Thunder Man. See way up yonder on Stone Woman where that scar is now? It used to be head high to Big Man-Eater before the tree growed all that ways since that story time. That scar there is where his head hit and knocked his brains loose. They scattered all out through here, and won't no bushes or weeds grow here more than knee-high now. And that swamp water…" The old man leaned forward slowly and went into a knee bend. "See how it's kindly a red color? Been that way since the day the Big Man-Eater's brains got scattered all out through here."

Straightening up, the old man looked from face to face of the hearers of his tale, a half-smile on his face, and stopped speaking as though to wait for any questions that needed to be cleared up. Nobody said anything for a while until finally Martin turned toward Clarence.

"That's why they got names, see, these two trees by the road. You get that?"

"I do get it," Clarence said. "Man interpreting the phenomena of nature. I love a legend, not to mention a myth."

"You reckon that red rock was worth anything?" Dwayne said. "Maybe it was a ruby or something."

"The natural curiosity of the human animal," Martin remarked. "Say, chief, do you suppose you could go with Clarence off there into the woods and look for that arm that monster lost?"

"There ain't nothing left of his arm out there," Albert Had Two Mothers said. "That's all just swamp and sawvines if you step off this road."

"I don't know about that," Martin Utz said. "Maybe it's turned into a rock formation or something. Petrified wood, say. Could be a remnant left. You two go see."

"Reckon it might've?" Dwayne said.

"Let's go, Dad," Clarence said, taking the left sleeve of the old man's shirt in his hand and giving it a tug, "It's time to test the theory."

Albert Had Two Mothers stepped off the hard road into the mud of the swamp and let the blonde man lead him away from the others, picking his way gingerly and looking down as best he could to find the harder spots to walk on. He hated to see his shoes get that wet, though, knowing that the leather would dry as hard as iron later and rub sore spots on his feet. Maybe they won't make me go too far, he thought, watching the man called Clarence step aside to let him move into the lead. That's good, letting me get in front. I can pick where to go.

He was lifting his eyes to look for when they would get to the first hummock where he could tell the man it was time to go back when Albert Had Two Mothers heard the saw crank. A big sound, like a steel mouth to eat something, and when he began to turn to see what the men on the road were doing, a big white light came on inside his head like the sun and he heard a great crashing, the noise a Big Man-Eater might make plunging through a stand of saplings after something he wanted to catch.

Albert Had Two Mothers tried to think how to make his mouth name words, but there wasn't time before the Big Man-Eater broke the last sapling and the sun dropped off the edge of the earth and everything was darkness and all the sounds stopped like a birdsong cut off before it could finish.

191

Back on the road, Martin Utz stood with his fingers in his ears against the scream of the unmuffled Poulan chainsaw and watched Clarence pick his way up from the swamp, hopping from what he took to be one hard spot to another, guessing wrong about two-thirds of the time. The mudline reached well up the thigh of his right leg and almost to the knee on his left.

"I have ruined everything I'm wearing," he said to Martin as he stepped up on the roadbed. "This stuff will never come out."

"Why didn't you just lie down in it and roll around some?" Martin said. "Get an even coat of that shit all over. Make you look balanced."

"Stuff stinks, too," Clarence said, sniffing at his fingers. "Smells funky."

"Well?"

"Well, what?"

"Will that crazy old Indian be up here in a few minutes hugging that tree so we won't cut it?"

"Not unless he has gills, he won't."

"Face down, is he?"

"Old people will wander off and then faint and fall into mud puddles. It's in the papers all the time."

"I don't read the human interest sections," Martin said. "I'll take your word for it."

"Timberrr," Clarence said.

26

He could see a squad of NVA regulars from where he perched in the tree where the forest began at the edge of the clearing. The one he had chosen was a little exposed, but the way three branches grew from the trunk about twenty feet up made up for the fact it stood apart from the others. The branches started almost at the same point and made a pocket shaped like a large cup which allowed him to rest his back against one limb and still see around the trunk to the road. He had been able to tie all of his gear to the other branches, and he didn't even need to use a hand to hold on while he reconned the section of the Ho Chi Minh Trail before him.

The squad of NVA had been in two armored vehicles loaded with munitions probably, on the way south, but now they were stopped to inspect some obstacle in their way. Maybe it was a crater from one of the B52 strikes. Or one of the squad suspected mines ahead, he couldn't tell from this distance. Had my scope I could see everything, he thought, but that was gone and had been for a long time, he couldn't remember how. Had he traded it? Was it lost somewhere when the moon was down one night during a long range patrol? It didn't matter. Anything he really needed to see he could get close enough to. Some things you know you'll always have, some things you rely on, and they are a comfort.

Two of the squad left the trail and started coming toward him, moving slowly, stepping carefully in the rice paddy, one behind the other so he could put his feet where the first one had walked. They think it's mined, he thought, and they won't look up above ground level no matter how far this way they come. Even if one of them did, he can't see me the way I'm fixed up here. They could come right up to this tree and look up the bole, and all they'd see would be vegetation. Nothing shiny, no metal, no marks on the trunk where I climbed it. Nobody can tell where a lurp has been. I learned that better than any of them in training. I knew it before I got here. I was that way back in the World.

He looked away from the two walking through the paddy toward the trail to see what the rest of the squad was doing. One of them had gone back to the second vehicle, an enlisted man probably, and was lifting something to his shoulder, looked to be a handheld anti-tank weapon from this distance, short-barreled, shiny parts along the top edge, sighting devices, maybe. What would they want with that, he asked himself, and then he looked back at the two men picking their way through what they thought was a minefield.

The one behind was lifting his hand with something in it, and as the lurp focused on that, the man brought it forward against the head of the one in front. He slumped straight down, like a building collapsing when the bottom floor is dynamited and all the ones above begin to settle, and he stopped on his knees balanced straight up in the mud and water of the rice paddy. A flash of sunlight bounced off something hanging around his neck, and as the man behind him brought the thing in his hand hard against the head of the man in front again, the recon lurp in the tree realized what the shiny thing bouncing against the man's chest was.

Dog tags. U.S. Army issue, taped together so they won't jingle. He's a grunt, one of ours.

The NVA squatted to look at what he'd done to the man in front, slipping to one side a little in the paddy and putting out his hand to catch himself. He said something out loud at that point and shook his hand in the air and then wiped it on his pants, standing up to turn back toward the trail, not looking again at the grunt he'd just clubbed. He walked back the way he had come, stepping carefully in the same places as before, the way you were supposed to in a minefield.

The lurp in the tree felt for his Kay Bar knife, but told himself no, the squad on the trail was too close and one of them was watching the NVA come back toward them. Not enough time to get there, do it and return to concealment without stirring up everything. The mission, that was the important thing, and he couldn't compromise it by allowing himself pay-back for the grunt lying on his face in the rice paddy. It would be sweet, though, to feel the surprise in the NVA as he hooked his fingers in the facial mask and pulled his chin back to hold him while he slipped the Kay Bar between the ribs to reach the heart from behind.

One thing he would do, he told himself as he slid down the bole of the tree on the side away from the squad on the trail, was see about the grunt, get his tags before one of them did and take the ID back for the desk soldiers to deal with.

He reached the ground and lowered himself into the mud and water of the rice paddy and was almost to the place where the grunt was lying on his face by the time the NVA stepped up on the road by the armored vehicles. They'll be jabbering at each other and messing with that piece of ordnance, and they won't see me even in the broad daylight if I keep low enough, he told himself. I'm glad the sun is shining at my back and it's hours until the dark comes. It makes it better to do it this way right under their noses when they ought to see me.

He felt the white buzz beginning in his ears, and the taste of metal started up in his mouth, and he sucked at his teeth to get a little spit going before it all dried up like it always did when the good thing began and he could see everything, all the bits and pieces, lying out there before him waiting to be picked up.

The grunt was lying with his arms flung out to the side like a man who had been trying to keep his balance when he felt his feet begin to go out from under him, and his head was turned a little to the right, resting partway on a clump of vegetation. His headgear had been knocked off when the NVA had hit him the second time, and it was lying a little in front of him, so when the lurp raised up from the mud he could see the leaf insignia and the blue and black markings on the patch. An officer from a division he didn't know, and the major was blowing bubbles from his mouth into the muddy water of the rice paddy.

The lurp reached out a hand and turned the man's head a little more to the side, feeling the slick blood on his fingers as he did. The officer groaned and coughed, and water came out of his mouth.

While that squad is up there on the trail, laughing about wasting this major, I'm going to pull him out of here up into the trees, the lurp said to the white buzz in his head, and I'll do it in the middle of the day when they can see me if they'd look, but they won't. Because I'm better, he told the buzz. Because I'm better, and nobody does my job like I can do it. And when I take on a mission, it gets fucking done, I don't care if it is a pissant officer I'm hauling out of here, while the NVA slopes up yonder point their anti-tank weapon at a goddamn tree.

The white buzz was louder now, and his mouth was full of the taste of pennies, and he savored that while he dragged the major through the marsh toward the dark cover of the trees.

195

27

"Mother," the younger woman was saying, "I don't want to talk about it any more. You do what you want to. You always have before. So why should it be any different now?"

"I wish you'd let me drive, Laura," the mother said. "Every twist and turn of your emotional state is being revealed in the way your body is reacting to the physical world surrounding it. The motions of your feet on the pedals, the turns of the steering wheel, the toss of your hair as you fight through this thing—it's all a manifestation. It's a consequence."

"No shit," Laura said, easing up on the accelerator of the rental car. "Where you'd get that huge psychological insight? Out of one of your books? Or on a tape you ordered off the Home Shopping Network? Did it come to you in a dream?"

"You're angry. I sense it."

"And I was trying so hard to disguise my true feelings. How did you ever guess?"

"I've developed my emotional antenna over the years. At one point I didn't understand anything. A long, long time of seeking has led me to this open space. There's a road behind me, and it's long and twisted and full of false starts and dead ends, but it ends up here in this car and at this time of Life Consequence, and I thank myself for it. No one else deserves any credit."

"Jesus Christ," Laura said and sped up again.

"You say that name, yes, and he was a prophet hooked on circularity, but the true guide is within, and it comes from understanding convergence."

"One more time. Jesus Christ."

"What upsets you, I know, and you aren't ready to accept the truth yet, but it's this. When Honey-Suckle spoke to me, and I understood and answered her and acknowledged the truth she offered, it was then you reached your limit of belief. That was the kicker for you, deny it or not."

"Mother, you and a pot-bellied pig were grunting back and forth at each other on the floor of that RV for fully five minutes. And then when you began crying and leaned down and hugged it, good God!"

"If you'd understood what she had just told me, how she had answered my question, you'd have done the same thing. She changed my life, to put it simply. You don't know enough to judge. And, my poor little girl, do you know what else?"

"I'm sure I don't. I don't know anything about anything, obviously."

"Precisely," Ellen said, looking ahead of the car at the lines on the highway rushing toward her, "you know too little, and here's the important thing. You know too much."

Neither woman spoke again until the city limits sign of Annette, Texas, appeared on the side of the road, and Laura slowed the car to the posted limit.

"So you're still determined to just go out there and move into that trailer with him?"

"I don't ask you to understand what you can't yet. Just take me to the motel for my things, and I'll drop you off wherever you want. The lines of consequence are converging now, and I have no choice in the matter. I never did and never will, and I embrace what's there for me. Consonance is all."

"How do you know you're doing the right thing, Mother?" Laura said as she pulled to a stop at a light and turned to look at the woman beside her. "And don't just tell me what you said before."

"I've got to, darling. It's the truth, and it's come to me at long last after all the circles and the arcs and the cycles and the retrogressions in my progress. Honey-Suckle has told me where the convergence of the lines will be and when, and Crippled Sparrow agrees with her completely. It's the final true crossing."

"I'm going to find Daddy," Laura said, turning the car left on 59 toward the Quality Inn. "That's what I'm going to do."

"You can't. Austin is lost to the world, and he's lost to himself. He'll wander forever alone in a circular motion. He'll end up where he began, as he always has."

"Move that fucking truck," Laura said, leaning on the horn of the rental car, "move it, goddamn you."

197

Thomas Fox Has Him hadn't spoken since he had gotten into Austin's car in the Annette High School parking lot, and it wasn't until they had crossed the cattle guard marking the boundary of the reservation that he finally said something.

"The road which comes closest is the one that starts by Long King Creek," he said.

"The little one," Austin said. "Not the one by the owl tree."

He nodded, and Austin slowed the Honda to look for the turn-off. It was easy to find. Whatever had recently gone before had swung wide to make the turn, running over three or four pine saplings on one side of the opening and leaving the tracks of double wheels in the loam where they grew. The saplings and sawvines were beginning to lift from where they had been crushed into the roadbed, and Austin steered the car around them as he followed the track the truckrig had taken.

"It's dry here," he said. "The road is."

"Lots of water later. The closer you get to Lost Man. It's always wet out in there."

"It's because the man who is lost is crying," Austin said. "He never stops, the old story says, the way McKinley Big Eye used to tell it."

"Charlie Sun-Singer liked that one. He would dig down where the ground looked dry on top and show me the water coming up." Thomas Fox Has Him paused and looked through the windshield at the narrow road curving ahead, its ruts cut with the wide tire marks of the truckrig. "When I would let him."

Austin picked his way ahead, conscious of the narrow wheelbase of the Japanese car, trying to straddle the rut the truck had left in the roadbed, keeping his attention on the edge where the thicket lining the way sent runners of vegetation out and over: yaupon, palmetto, sawvine, wild flowers. The trace was narrow, and he drove slowly for almost three miles.

Fox Has Him saw it first and spoke its name in the language of the Nation. "Tali Itto," he said. "Stone Woman."

The sawdust from the chainsaw was heaped thickest on the right side of the roadbed, but it covered most of a three-foot wide

198

swath of the way, reddish yellow as it lay in its drift like strange snow, except for the place where the tire tracks compressed it into their own symmetrical shape.

The stump of the red oak was low, probably less than six inches, and its area was at least five feet across, Austin judged as he brought the car to a stop. The sawyer had thrown the tree at an angle almost perpendicular to the roadbed, and it had jumped the stump as it had fallen, leaving a four foot section of bark and wood still attached on the far side. The trunk had kicked up as it had toppled, because of the large mass of the branches at its top, and it had skewed to the side, lashing the loblolly pine standing next to the oak with enough force to uproot it on the near side. The pine now leaned at about a thirty degree angle, the sawvines on its trunk torn loose from the earth, their exposed roots white in the sun.

Thomas Fox Has Him left the car and walked to the fallen tree, placing his hand on the end of the reddish bole where the saw had made a flat surface, roughened now and exposed to the air and light of the empty space where it had stood. He brought his hand to his face and turned toward Austin.

"It does smell good," he said, "the inside of this oak tree where it's been cut. If I keep my hand to my face, I smell only the heart of Stone Woman and not the gasoline from the saw."

"Let me smell," Austin said, moving toward the bole of the tree. "I would like that, too. And when it is all finished, this thing that is happening, we will make sure, you and I, Thomas, that no one splits up this red oak tree for firewood or that it just lies here and rots."

"Yes," Fox Has Him said, scooping up a handful of the sawdust and offering it to Austin, "someone will build something from her, a house maybe, or shingles for a roof. Abba Bullock, smell how sweet the heart of Stone Woman was, like a flower."

They could hear the sound of a heavy duty engine revving well before the car reached an opening in the thicket which would let them see what was happening up ahead in Lost Man Marsh. Austin pulled the car as far to the right of the road as he could and still avoid sinking a wheel into the soft margin of mud and water. It was going to be a long ride in reverse when he had to leave, he thought, getting out of the car and motioning to Thomas Fox Has Him to make no sound. The engine of the unseen machine revved again, this time to a new high, and he heard someone yell something he couldn't understand. A shout in a different voice came as he and Fox Has Him began to walk toward the source of the activity, staying close to the left side of the roadbed, Austin in front.

Something splashed off to the side in the marsh, but when he looked, all he could see were bubbles rising to the surface of the dark water. A muskrat, probably, or a beaver, the water too shallow at this point for an alligator of any size to be able to hide. Hachonchoba, Old Monster Lizard, Austin said to himself, stay deep for now, we have no quarrel with you.

He pointed ahead toward a stand of high palmetto bushes and looked over his shoulder at Fox Has Him who lifted his hand in response. Crouching, they slowed their pace and stepped off the roadbed, moving in an arc through the marsh toward the palmettos, reaching them and squatting to look through the sharp-pointed fronds.

The truck and heavy trailer were parked in the road ahead of a blue pickup, and off-loading ramps extended to the ground where the tracks of the backhoe began. They led in a long curve to where the machine with its huge tires now sat about sixty yards into the swamp, its shovel digging into the earth and water with every roar of its engine. A waist-high mound of mud and vegetation marked the right limit of the hole the machine was gouging as the operator leaned forward to peer over his controls.

He yelled something at the man standing to the left of the backhoe and in front, and the man turned to answer, his mouth moving soundlessly, and Austin strained to get a better look at his face. No one he knew. Nor was the operator as far as he could tell at this distance, but there was no doubt about the identity of the third man, the one on the far side of the excavation, leaning forward to peer into the hole after each shovelful was removed by the backhoe.

Martin Utz, the Netcon man at the council meeting, the one with the flat eyes and the nose like a Cherokee's. He was wearing a white baseball cap and a khaki safari jacket well covered with gobs of mud from the hole in Lost Man Marsh, and he was giving the backhoe operator hand directions without pause as he leaned to look over the edge.

Where was the other one, the tall one with the fringe of blonde hair, Austin asked himself, turning his head to look at Thomas Fox Has Him. Wasn't it likely he'd be here ?

Fox Has Him was staring at something above Austin's head, not toward where the machine was working, and his mouth was open as though he were about to speak. A voice came from a little behind Austin and to his left, from beyond the last one of the stand of palmettos and near the base of a longleaf pine.

"What've we got here? A field trip with the teacher?"

The other man from the tribal council meeting was leaning against the trunk of the nearest pine, looking down at Austin and Thomas Fox Has Him with a smile on the bottom part of his face. From the nose up his expression was as blank as the surface of a cattle pond. He was holding a handgun, like those Austin had seen before only in photographs: square, stubby, and made of something that looked more like plastic than metal.

"I think it's nice," the blonde man said, gesturing with the firearm for Austin and Thomas to stand, "your taking education out of the classroom and into the workaday world where all of our young people are going to have to live their lives. I say yes to close teacher-student involvement. Don't you, Mr. Educator?"

Austin stood up, sensing Thomas stepping closer to him and feeling a little dizzy as though he had just waked from a deep sleep and raised up too quickly in bed. He could see himself moving in slow motion. His mouth felt too dry to speak.

"What's the gun for? You don't need to be waving that around."

"I beg to differ, learned sir. I believe I must be prepared for any predator that might show up out here in the wilderness like this." He waved the gun in a small circle that included the stand of palmettos, the marsh around them, every place he had ever found himself. "Who knows? We might come across hostile Indians out here in the woods."

"Abba Bullock," Fox Has Him said.

"See," the blonde man said, taking a step back. "There's one just jumped up right beside you. Think I ought to turn him into a good Indian?"

"No," Austin said, lifting his hands to shoulder level, "we'll do what you want. Don't be stupid."

"The eternal cry of the school teacher, eh? All right, I'll go along just this once. But you better give me an A in conduct, or I'll act up in class."

He waved the gun again, this time toward the sound of the backhoe at work, and moved away from the pine. "Let's go over there and show Mr. Utz what I found, Chief. You and Little Beaver walk in front. We'll take a look up close and personal at the hole you're just dying to see."

The three men on and around the backhoe didn't see them approach until the blonde man with the squared-off gun called out to the one in the muddy safari jacket. He looked away from the hole in Lost Man Marsh reluctantly at the sound of his name, and at the sight of Austin and Thomas Fox Has Him he placed both hands on his hips and glared as though he were an executive who had just been shown a budget deficit by his chief accountant.

"What the fuck? What's this?"

"Look who I just found cutting class. The teacher and one of his star pupils."

"What're you talking about, Clarence? What're they doing here?"

"Like I told you, Martin, I found them over there hiding in the bushes trying to spy on our experiments here in the mudhole."

"I knew this fucker was trouble as quick as I looked at him," Martin said, jerking his head at Austin, "back there in that dump when we talked to those old boys that looked like a bunch of homeless Mexicans."

"He's not homeless, though," Clarence said. "Remember? He's got his own nice little place there in town. Not too neat sometimes, though, the way he keeps it. He's going to be their new chief. He's an intellectual, too. I bet he owns a book. Or did once, before he traded it for firewater."

"Yeah?" Martin said and then spoke to Austin. "The fuck you doing here?"

"I live here. What are you digging for? And don't tell me it's bauxite."

"I believe he saw me do the old man," Clarence said. "Out there in the mud and water. And I don't know what this kid's here for, but it's for a reason."

"Shit," Martin said. "They just keep popping up, these fucking Indians, don't they?"

"You want me to keep on digging?" the man operating the backhoe asked. "Or what?"

"Fuck yes. What do you think you came from Houston for? Fire it up."

"When do you want me to do it?" Clarence said. "Just say the word."

"Does everybody have to ask me everything at the same time all at once?" Martin said. "Can't it be one thing at a time for a change?"

"That's why they call you the boss," Clarence said. "The burdens of office and all that stuff. Strategic planning and so forth and so on."

"No," Martin said. "Not now. Wait'll we get it out of this goddamn mud, and then we'll take care of these next two in line. Maybe they'll be the last ones we got to deal with. I hope to fuck they are."

"All right," Clarence said. "I prefer to eat one dish at a time, anyway. Lend me Dwight for a couple of minutes."

"Dwayne," the man who had not yet spoken said. "Lots of folks get that name wrong. Mostly, though, they say Wayne, not Dwight."

"Understandable," Clarence said and gestured toward the bed of the pickup. "Get some of those plastic ties out of the duffel bag there, Wayne, and bring them over here to me and our visitors."

"Dwayne," the man said, moving in the direction of the pickup.

"Dwight," Clarence said.

"When you get through with that," Martin said, yelling to be heard over the roar of the backhoe, "call that runt Indian on the radio. Get his ass over here."

"Why? We know where he is. And I do believe he's busy about now."

"Why is because I want to get every damn thing taken care of today, and I don't give a shit if the little fucker's busy. He ain't going to be busy long."

"Ten-four," Clarence said. "Whatever and whenever."

Martin moved back to his spot on edge of the growing hole in Lost Man Marsh, leaning over as far as he could without slipping down inside with the shovel arm itself. Up on the seat of the backhoe, Cake Golson wished the foreign-looking little bastard would back off and give him some room, but he told himself to just keep thinking about getting back to Houston before dark. Keep focused, eyes straight ahead, don't see nothing but the hoe doing its job, one bite at a time.

"You and your little friend pick out a small tree apiece," Clarence said to Austin and Thomas Fox Has Him, nodding to his left toward some pine saplings at a distance growing out of a hummock halfway between the location of the hole and the roadbed, "and sit down with your backs to it. Dwight, you put a plasti-cuff on each of them once they've made their selection and've put their arms behind their backs."

"These them?" Dwayne said, lifting what he had in his hand for inspection. "These here plastic things look kind of like a big old twist-tie?"

"The very ones, and you found them all by yourself. I bet you didn't even finish high school, did you, Dwight?"

"It's Dwayne. No sir. I went to the eighth grade."

"Hardly even shows. You should be proud of yourself."

Austin looked at Thomas Fox Has Him's eyes as they began to walk through the mud and water toward the hummock, Clarence several yards behind with the gun pointed loosely ahead. The boy looked to be going into shock, the pupils of his eyes large and unfocused despite the brightness of midday. He stepped into a hole beneath the surface of the marsh, stumbled and almost fell. Austin grabbed him by the elbow and Thomas leaned against him, breathing as though he had just run up and down a basketball court three times without stopping.

"Hold on, Fox Has Him," Austin said in the language of the Nation. "Something will happen. Remember when Abba Mikko helped the six brothers."

"That's not real, my elder," the boy said. "That blank eye's gun is real now. That's the only thing. Everything else is a dream."

"No, everything is real, not just the gun. What used to be and what is. It's all here now. All at the same time."

"Hey," the man behind them said, "I'm enjoying the linguistic treat. Keep talking that stuff. It's like being in German class. I wish I had a tape recorder."

28

"The cannibal was hiding in the river, remember?" Austin was saying to Thomas Fox Has Him. The pine sapling was large enough that Austin had to lean forward as he sat with his back against it, his arms around the trunk behind him and his hands fastened so that the tops of them faced each other. The right one was going numb, and he flexed his fingers to see if he could feel them. Some, a little. He shifted his weight and felt relief in that hand and new pressure in the other.

"The brothers had found the strange canoe by their house. It had markings on it they couldn't read. The canoe was red, and the markings were yellow. I forget which brother found it that morning."

"The youngest one," Thomas said. "Wasn't it?"

The tree to which Dwayne had fastened Thomas was much smaller than Austin's, so the boy could sit up straighter, but he was slumping down anyway.

"Lift your head, Fox Has Him," Austin said. "Yes, it was the youngest one, come to think of it. He was getting water for the cooking."

Dwayne and Clarence had gone back to the hole to stand with Martin Utz, watching the shovelfuls of earth and water pile up as the backhoe worked. By twisting his head and looking down and back, Austin could see past the tree to where they were all standing. Utz was talking continuously to the others, not looking at them, but at the hole before him, leaning further over at each load the hoe lifted from the marsh.

"One of them pushed the canoe away from the shore into the river, and it started moving against the current like somebody was paddling it. It got a ways upstream and stopped and stayed at one place. It just sat there, and the water couldn't move it."

The shovel of the backhoe hit something solid in the hole and made a clunking sound, like a bucket on a rope hitting a stone in the bottom of a well, and Martin Utz yelled at the man at the controls who immediately cut the engine back.

"Get down here and jump in that hole," Austin could hear Utz yelling. "See if that's it."

"They found the pod," Thomas Fox Has Him said to Austin. "They'll get it out now."

"Maybe," Austin said. "Maybe not."

"They're going to shoot us, Abba Bullock, after they get it out."

"We don't know that," Austin said, looking down and back at what he could see of the men clustering around the hole in the marsh. "Not yet."

"It's full of water," Cake Golson was saying as he gingerly sat down on the edge of the hole to begin his slide to the bottom. "I can't see nothing."

"Feel for it, numbnuts," Martin Utz said. "You can tell by the shape if that's it."

"The brothers went one by one to see why the canoe was stuck in that one spot in the river, not moving with the current," Austin said, turning his head to look at Thomas Fox Has Him. "Until all of them but one had gone and not come back." The boy was looking straight ahead and squinting as though he were trying to make out letters on a sign too far away to read. As Austin watched, Thomas leaned forward slowly, pulling steadily at the bond fastening his arms behind his back around the tree. Nothing moved.

"The last brother decided to go look for the five who had not come back, Tom," Austin said. "But unlike them, he carried some fruit to eat on the journey to keep his strength up. I believe it was peaches."

"Persimmons," Thomas Fox Has Him said. "That's what I always heard it was." He slumped back against the pine tree to which he was bound.

206

The man at the bottom of the hole full of water said something to the others which Austin couldn't hear, and Martin Utz let out the shrill cry a man might make when seeing his lotto numbers match the ones in the newspaper, and Austin thought he felt something touch his hand, the right one which was almost numb. He moved his fingers, once, twice, and the touch came again, and suddenly his hands moved apart, the connection of the plastic cuffs binding them gone.

He brought his arms forward and had begun to twist to look behind him when a large hand completely covered with the brown mud of Lost Man Marsh appeared beside his head, its index finger pointing ahead and to the right. He saw Thomas Fox Has Him lurch forward away from the sapling behind him, and Austin began to crawl in the direction the finger had indicated, toward a hummock of earth and brush poking up twenty or so yards away, the sound of Fox Has Him's ragged breathing following close behind him.

Lowering his face into the surface of the marsh, he pushed as quickly as he could with his legs, his arms, his numb hands toward the screen of thicket ahead. It was persimmons, he told himself, Thomas was right, not peaches at all, which the sixth brother took on his journey to bring the others back.

It was a new piece of equipment the NVA squad was bringing down the trail, the lurp realized as he watched them work with the small tank they had unloaded from the trailer behind the first armored vehicle. We don't have anything like that, he told himself as he lay buried in the mud of the rice paddy, only his head from his nose up above the surface of the water, a piece of ordnance that digs itself in with an attachment to its own cannon. It's got to be Soviet, and they're warehousing them in China, maybe Laos. How many? How does it work? What size is the crew? How self-contained is it?

The officers would ask those questions and more when he showed up back at the base from his long range patrol, he knew, and he lowered himself further into the earth and water thinking about it, knowing how excited they would be and how much they would want to grill him over and over, hoping he would remember another detail each time they made him retell it. Too much to remember, to have to talk about over and over to every new man they would bring in to question him, with their tape recorders and notebooks and their blank eyes.

The part of the mission I don't like, the lurp told himself, the shit part that comes at the end, like being in school having to talk to people about stuff that was already over with, fucked, blown-up, and dead.

The squad leader was giving directions to a man sitting up on top of the small tank, operating the controls which moved the attachment on the cannon. As the man on the ground moved around the hole where the tank was digging in, light flashed off the dark glasses he was wearing, and the lurp thought about putting a round right between the lenses and watching the officer slump into the mud of the rice paddy and the other two in sight scramble to get into the vehicle where they could clank the hatch shut.

Too close and there was too much light, and the other man in the squad had moved back down the trail toward the north where another detail was likely to be right behind. Maybe I can slip around to him before the next ones show up, the lurp thought, and leave a message, a little wake-up for the new slopes coming down the trail.

He had begun to back up slowly in the mud and water, careful to make no sound, feeling the slightest suggestion of the taste of metal beginning to form in his mouth, when he saw the three men come out of the cover on the trail to his right. The one behind the first two was the other member of the squad, the one he had seen leave the ones at the tank, and he was carrying an automatic weapon at ready.

No insignia on the first two that he could see at this range, but he could tell by the way they were walking they were Americans, obvious even with the shoulder slump a captured man always shows, the way he drops his head and looks at the ground just in front of him, flopping his hands like he's forgotten what they're used for.

Too far to see their eyes, but the lurp knew what you'd find in them, the way the thousand-yard stare opened them up deep enough you could see all the way through to a man's skull if you looked long and hard enough.

Flyers, for sure. Maybe a chopper pilot and a gunner knocked down by small arms fire. Came too close to where the grunts lived, in among the vines and snakes and stinging ants and Charlie, and now had to pay the price. See how the other half lives all the time, every fucking day.

The one in front, the big one, kept looking at the other American, the lurp could see, as they moved closer to where the rest of the NVA squad was working around the tank. He's the pilot, the other one a kid scared shitless, maybe wounded when the chopper came down, and he knows he's a fucking dead man. If the pilot keeps thinking about him, worrying about how the kid's taking it, he can keep his own shit together a little longer, maybe right up to the time they put him on his knees in the rice paddy and open up his brain pan with a round or two.

The lurp leaned forward and made his face touch the surface of the paddy, letting the water wet his lips, and when he looked back up, the squad leader was giving orders about the American prisoners, pointing this way and that, making the rest of them scramble to do what he was saying. They weren't going to kill them right off, then. Maybe wait until later when the tank was dug in and they could spend their time and enjoy it.

One of the squad got something from the smaller of the two armored vehicles, and the tank went back to work, while the slope with the automatic weapon took the Americans away from the rest of them to where some small trees stuck up out of the paddy. The direction was toward where the lurp lay buried in the mud and water, but the slopes were too interested in backing the captured pilot and gunner up to a couple of the trees and lashing their arms behind them to look anywhere else.

The way the Americans were tied placed the sides of their faces at a ninety degree angle to the lurp's position, and he could see the older one begin talking to the kid when the two slopes rejoined the rest of the NVA squad. Trying to talk him down, probably, telling him about some shit back in the World, the way the streets looked in some little town in Ohio or Michigan or one of those places, Christmas time, drinking beer at a ballgame, a good meal cooked by a woman, something.

The NVA squad up by the tank began jabbering, and one of the enlisted men, the one on top of the tank, jumped off and ran around to the front of the vehicle where the mud was all piled up beside the place they were digging in.

Something clicked in the lurp's head, right behind the middle of his brow and deep enough inside that he felt it at a point at the center of where the white buzz always started, and he jerked his chin up twice sharply, like a man trying to cure a crick in his neck. It didn't help. The sound had begun, and he tasted the coppery bitterness well up under his tongue.

Fuck it, he thought, knowing the burden was shifting again onto him, the mission rising up from the horizon before him like the red ball of the sun at dawn after all the clouds in the sky had already turned from darkness to color, the shades of yellow and gold and pink pushing away at the blackness which let a man close his eyes and sleep.

When he looked down, his hands were already moving and he could feel the muscles of his thighs beginning to flex. Am I going to proceed, he asked his body, am I going to crawl to within seventy-five yards of that NVA squad by that tank and cut those Americans loose? Am I going to lead them back to the ridge cover with the major? Am I going to have to do it all by myself here in the middle of the day?

His body did not answer. It never did. But it took him along.

29

After they had reached the hummock by two angled crawls, one to put them even with the mound of earth and trees and the other to put it behind them, screening a possible view from the men around the excavation, Austin raised his head from the surface of the marsh to look back and verify what he already knew.

Thomas Fox Has Him was close behind, his eyes squeezed to slits against the muck through which he crawled, giving his face a look of intense devotion to his task. Six feet behind him came a figure of mud, of water, of reeds and swamp grass, of Lost Man Marsh itself. In his teeth he held the cut plastic bindings which had held Austin and Thomas to the pine saplings, and in his right hand flashed the blade of the large chef's knife he had used to do the job.

He saw Austin's eyes on him and gestured forward once with the hand holding the knife, and Austin turned his face back to the surface of the marsh before him and the line of trees marking the ridge rising from the water two-hundred yards ahead. He crawled, Tom and the man of marsh and mud behind him, and he heard the engine of the backhoe rev just before he reached the solid ground of the pine island.

Several yards deep into the thicket of the ridge, he stopped and turned toward Thomas Fox Has Him. Despite the long crawl, the boy's breathing had calmed, and he looked no more winded than if he had just finished playing an eight-minute scrimmage in practice.

"You're right, Tom," Austin said. "It was persimmons, ripe ones, the sixth brother carried when he went after the others."

"I thought so, Abba Bullock. I thought I remembered what it was."

"What did they hit you with?" the man with the chef's knife said, holding the plastic ties out toward Austin. "A handheld rocket or small arms fire?" He spoke in English.

"I don't know," Austin said. "I couldn't tell what was happening. It was too fast."

"I got another one up in here." The man gestured ahead into the thicket. "He's a major. I can't tell what outfit, though, and he don't know. He's talking out of his head."

"Is he bad hurt?" Austin said, looking sharply at Thomas Fox Has Him who seemed to be wanting to say something.

"Hit in the head a couple of times. He doesn't know who he is right now. Where's your dog tags?" He pointed toward Austin's chest and turned to look toward Fox Has Him. "You had them on back on the trail when that slope brought you in. Did they take them off?"

"I guess so," Thomas Fox Has Him said and touched his throat. "They're gone."

"They want to ID you," the mud-covered man said. "NVA always take the dog tags. Generally, the Cong won't." He paused and slipped the chef's knife into a scabbard on the belt around his waist. The scabbard was homemade, and the black leather belt was something a man would wear with a dress suit. "Let's go further on up in there where the major's lying down. Maybe you can get him to talk some sense."

He looked at Austin as Thomas turned toward the heart of the yaupon and sawvine thicket. "You the officer, ain't you?"

"Yeah, I am."

"I want that tank," the man said. "I don't care what your rank is back at your base. I'm going after it, and I'm bringing it back. You ain't telling me no."

As Crippled Sparrow steered the Honda dirt bike around a rut in the roadbed, he could see a man he didn't know rigging a cable from the backhoe over the top of a pile of dirt. The man was having trouble balancing on the edge of the hole on the other side of the dirtpile, and Martin Utz was chewing his ass for being slow.

"I believe they've found it," Crippled Sparrow said to the rider behind him on the bike. "I've noticed that the closer my business associate comes to getting something he wants, the meaner and more unhappy he gets. It's a cultural thing."

He cut the engine, and he and the woman dismounted. "Let's go see," he said. "It might be payday."

Crippled Sparrow hopped off the road into the marsh with no hesitation, splashing through the mud and water in his knee-high boots toward the backhoe in a gait as close as he could get to a trot. The woman stopped at the edge of the roadbed, looking down at the watery surface with reluctance. "Come on," he called back at her. "Don't be afraid to get your feet wet."

"Is it snaky?" she said, stepping off and sinking to midcalf immediately.

"You're not afraid of snakes," the little man said. "Even right up close. I know that for a fact."

Clarence turned away from the lip of the hole and watched Crippled Sparrow and the woman approach. "Look who's showed up," he said to Martin Utz. "The pig lover."

"You called him, didn't you?" Martin said, not looking away from Dwayne in the bottom of the hole, fumbling with the end of the cable running from the winch on the backhoe. "You knew he'd come running."

"But not with a gash."

"What? What you mean?'

"Trim, snatch, cunt. Whatever you want to call it. One of them's on the way out here."

At that, Martin swivelled his head around toward the roadbed without moving his body, as though after checking all alternatives, he had selected the perfect position for watching events in the hole and was not about to chance losing his fix on it. When he saw the woman coming toward them through the marsh, he moved his lips like a man about to spit out something stuck to his tongue.

"Ptuh," he said. "Who the fuck is that?"

"Ellen," Crippled Sparrow said, edging around Clarence to see into the hole. "She believes in the lines of convergence or consequence or conveyance. Something like that."

"Watch where you're stepping," Martin said. "She's about to run into a convergence she ain't going to want to believe. I'll tell you that."

"Why'd you bring her out here?" Clarence said. "You just want to make more work for us, is that it?"

"Well, she's with me now for a while, but she doesn't even realize there's a world outside of her," Crippled Sparrow said. "She won't know a thing that's going on, I guarantee you."

"Not for long she won't," Martin said.

"You found it?" Crippled Sparrow said, pushing close enough to the crumbling edge of the hole to make his foot slip. "It's down there, huh?"

"Don't be so eager," Clarence said. "You're going to get a chance to see everything right up close now in a little while. So stop and smell the diesel fumes."

The woman came nearer, almost up to the side of the backhoe now, the line of mud on her pants just to the top of her knees, and Dwayne in the bottom of the hole gave the cable a final jerk and looked up toward Martin Utz. "I believe I got it fastened tight enough around it now, this here cable. Tell Cake he can start winching her."

"Just wait down there a minute," Utz said. "We've come this far we can slow down for a little while."

"I hope I'm not in the way," the woman said to Clarence, the only man looking at her as she put one hand on a tire of the backhoe and leaned to the side to lift one foot for inspection. She began to pick at the dark mud clogging the tread of her shoe.

213

"Oh my no," Clarence said, running the words together. "We're honored by your presence."

"Who are you?" Martin Utz said. "Just for the record."

"Ellen."

"You got a last name?"

"I've had several. Now I've decided not to use one any more. I want to simplify my life."

"I'm all for that," Clarence said. "Break things down to their elements, I say. There's a time for this and a time for that. A time for digging holes and a time for putting dirt back into holes. Isn't that the way it goes?"

"What?" Martin said. "How what goes?"

"You know, that book in the Bible. A time for this and a time for that and a time for the other thing. On and on, a great long list of it."

"Talk some sense, Clarence," Martin said and then, leaning to look down into the hole at Dwayne, "O.K. Come up out of there. We got some more for you to do up here on top."

"What about the cable?" Dwayne said, tugging again at his handiwork and looking with satisfaction at where it was attached. He patted it twice.

"Leave it like it is," Martin told him.

"You know where you found them before," Clarence said to Dwayne as he hunched himself up and over the edge of the excavation, scrambling out to stand and face the others. "There in the duffel bag. I hope we don't run out. I didn't bring enough for more than a football team or so more to show up out here."

"Put them there with the other two," Martin Utz said, "if there's trees enough left over for it."

"What?" Crippled Sparrow said, stepping back and looking up into Utz's face, the expression on his own that of a child just informed the promised trip to the video game parlor had been called off. "Do you have a problem with her being here? If you do, hey, no sweat. We're out of here, my friend. Pronto. Chop chop."

"I love it when they talk that talk," Clarence remarked. "That Native-American lingo."

"I'm about through talking to anyfuckingbody else this trip," Martin said. "Get him out of my face, Clarence."

The blonde man reached behind his back under his loose shirt and brought the dull-black Mac 10 around in front of him, holding it flat in both hands as though presenting an item of interest for examination. Everyone except Martin and Cake Golson up at the controls of the backhoe turned to look toward it, forming what looked like a circle of children on a playground clustering to see a Gameboy or a condom someone had brought to school from the drawer by mommy and daddy's bed.

"Look what I found," Clarence said. "I call him Simon, and Simon says the runt and the cunt come go with me."

"Oh, no," the woman said, lifting a swatch of hair that had fallen across her face back away from her eyes. "A firearm."

"Bingo," Clarence said, and the circle broke up as Dwayne started for the duffel bag in the bed of the pickup parked on the road.

"Not me," Crippled Sparrow said, peering intently at what Clarence now waved in a tight little circle. "I'm in this thing with you people. I'm here, goddamn it. Please. I did every thing you asked me to. Now, didn't I? You ask yourself if I did or not."

"You're in it, all right," Martin Utz said. "But not with us. Not no more. Everything's moving too fucking slow. Come on, Clarence. Stop playing."

The blonde man pointed in the direction of the hummock with its clump of pine saplings with his left hand and placed the muzzle of the weapon up against Crippled Sparrow's forehead just below where the part began in his hairdo. The little man shook his head until his braids swung, describing little circles over his shoulders with the weight of the beads worked into their ends. "I'm not leaving this hole," he said. "No way I'm going to."

"You shall return to it," Clarence said. "In a while, don't worry. Ellen, you take him by the hand and go get your feet all muddy again."

"Yes sir," she said, taking Crippled Sparrow's left hand in her right and tugging. He resisted at first, pulling back as though he were a child being led by his mother into the dentist's office, and then, slumping, gave in, letting Ellen pull him with her toward the pine saplings rising from the hummock.

"You can't see them from here," Clarence was saying as he followed behind the man and woman holding hands before him, "but not far up there are a couple of guys I think you'll find fascinating. They're very ethnic."

Crippled Sparrow seemed to be having trouble walking in a straight line, and as he wavered from one side to the other, he was kicking up much more mud and water than Ellen, who looked to be using all her concentration to move precisely ahead. Clarence dropped back a step and moved to the side to avoid Crippled Sparrow's splashing and as he did so he could see clearly over the little man's head the two saplings where Dwayne had fastened the schoolteacher and the boy. They must be slumped down, all worn out by their day, he told himself, as he stretched to see their shapes on the other side of the thin tree trunks. It wasn't until the two people ahead of him had gotten within fifty feet of the mound of earth and vegetation that he let himself admit what he couldn't see.

"Oh shit, oh dear," Clarence said aloud, "they're gone," moving now to swing around the man and woman blocking his way, slipping as he tried to run in the muck of the swamp and falling forward to his knees but reflexively keeping the automatic weapon up at eye level out of the water. Getting a purchase on something solid with his right foot, he came up, wet from his chest down, and lurched forward around Crippled Sparrow, jostling him hard enough with his hip as he went by that the little man fell forward face down in the marsh, pulling the woman to her knees beside him.

Clarence was by both of them, within a few feet of the clump of trees on the hummock, bumping the automatic against his chest to knock off the water that had splashed up on it when he fell, and he was feeling the ground beneath his feet grow more solid as he neared the mound when something to his left moved beneath the surface of the water.

As he turned to see, beginning to bring his left hand around to steady the gun, the marsh not three feet away roiled, heaved and parted, and a mass of brown mud, creepers and grass rose up head high and surged over him, solid, slick and grasping as it rolled him tumbling back and to the right.

He could see the black shape of the automatic weapon rise up from his hand as he went down, outlined and revolving slowly against the bright background of sky, and he watched that as long as he could until the brown shape came between him and the light. Somebody was

216

screaming in a high voice, the runt probably, and then that cry cut off like someone had hit a switch, and the sound then was a low roaring with bubbles somewhere in it, and the only colors were dark greens and marsh-brown and black.

30

At first, back near the trail, again buried at full length in the rice paddy, the lurp thought the woman riding behind the man on the motorcycle was VC herself, a hell-bitch, worse even in her own way than one of the men. The kind who left an armed grenade in one of the baskets they carried their babies in, so if you went into a hooch and leaned over to see if the kid was lying inside asleep or maybe dead and touched it the whole thing went up and took your head off.

He had never seen that, but it happened. One like that would pass up burying her own dead baby to do that. Or say "no VC, no VC" when grunts came into the village and then go ahead and let one of them fuck her and act like she liked it just to get the chance to shove a spike into the back of his head when he closed his eyes to come.

But as soon as the little VC in the white boots stopped the motorcycle and the woman got off to follow him to where the NVA squad was gathered around the tank, he knew she was American. A nurse, probably, judging from the fatigues she was wearing, or maybe a reporter or correspondent dumb enough to let herself be captured. They'll turn her out, the lurp told himself, seeing that her hair was wrong, too, for VC, too light and curly. She ought to have killed herself well before now, but a civilian will never do that. They're too close to the World not to hope for something to save them. They always believe somebody will turn up to get their asses out of the shit they stepped in. They pray, they beg, they say please.

The tank looked to be about dug in, judging from the height of the pile of mud and vegetation in the rice paddy on the far side of the road, and the lurp could see the squad leader gesturing to the others as the VC from the motorcycle approached, followed by the American woman. It would be a hard thing to get the armored vehicle out of the nest it had been digging for itself once it moved into position, working by himself, he knew, and he closed his eyes for a few seconds to try to get it started in his head, the picture that would rise up and show him what he had to do to serve the mission.

Nothing came fixed in place yet. Not blank, but a series of random shots, like photographs in no order, just one after the other being flipped over in somebody's hand as he watched them turn before him. A man in a dark uniform seen from behind, running as he fell. A kid three or four years old looking up with big eyes, a rice bowl in his hands. A naked woman up on a table, dancing from side to side, her feet not moving as her small breasts jerked up and down out of time with the music playing behind her. An officer looking over his head as he gave orders in a voice that sounded like it was coming from the soundtrack of a movie. A Kay-Bar knife being sharpened on a whetstone, its edge a silver thread of light.

Shaking his head twice from side to side, the lurp opened his eyes to look back at the people around the tank and saw that three of them were crossing the road, stepping up and out of the paddy on the far side, moving in a direction that would take them straight to him if they maintained it and kept coming. Two were in front, the short VC from the motorcycle, walking beside the American woman, pulling at her hand to keep her moving. A few steps behind was one of the NVA regulars armed with a handgun the lurp couldn't identify at this range.

He let the lids of his eyes come together again, holding back the desire of his body to take a deep breath, and he saw what he was waiting for, the picture which told him what he needed to know and how to handle it. It rose up strong and bright, the edges of each thing in it outlined by a hard rim of light that vibrated with a buzzing he could hear so clearly it made the roof of his mouth itch.

The first scene of the movie had the NVA regular at the center of the focus, and he was already moving to the side, off-balance, his feet sliding away from under him, and his weapon was hanging free in the air, turning slowly above the earth as it hung suspended in the upper right quadrant of the picture.

The projector made a clicking sound in the lurp's head, and the VC in the white boots filled the screen, his mouth open to scream, that sound not there yet, as he turned away from the taller American woman, losing his grip on her arm as he tried to scramble backwards in the sucking hold of the rice paddy.

Opening his eyes, the lurp allowed himself a breath, then another deeper one, as he waited for the feature to begin, knowing already from the preview he had been granted what part he would soon begin to play in the film. What would be the next scene, he wondered, listening to the moan begin to start deep in his throat and chest, would it be taking the woman back to the cover of the ridge with the pilot and the gunner and the wounded major? Or would the director jump ahead in time to the scene with the rest of the NVA squad and the special tank?

Don't hurry it, he told himself, it's always better to wait and see what comes next, that makes it more of a surprise. Don't let yourself know what you know before you need to know it. That way it goes too fast. He listened to the sucking sound of the feet of the people coming toward him through the rice paddy. Each one of them had a necessary part to play in the story of the mission. Nobody could be left out. Nobody would be. Nobody.

Dwayne was stepping off the roadbed into the marsh, trying to put his feet in the same places where Clarence had been, thinking water moccasins were likely to have moved away from where people had already walked, when the high scream came from up ahead where the three of them were in front of him. He flinched so hard when the sound cut the air that he dropped two of the plasti-cuffs into the mud and water, clutching the other ones to his chest in reflex as he looked ahead to see if he could tell what that crazy fucker with the funny pistol was doing to the woman who had just hollered.

She was the only one he could see standing. The little sawed-off Indian with the long braids of hair looked shorter than ever, with only the part of his body from the chest up visible to Dwayne. He was turned toward the roadbed, his mouth open so wide Dwayne could see inside it at this range, and the sound of screaming came from it again, this time cut off abruptly as the torso of the little man jerked backward and down as though something big had seized him by the legs underwater from behind and was taking him beneath the surface of the swamp.

"Alligator," Dwayne said out loud in an ordinary tone of voice, his legs feeling heavy and weak, and then again louder, "Alligator," and then a third time finally in full volume, "Gator, gator."

The woman standing beside the spot where the Indian midget had vanished had not moved, staring down beside her at the marsh as though she had noticed a flower growing in the mud and was trying to remember the right name for it. The other one, Clarence, the one who called him Dwight and Wayne wrongly on purpose, was nowhere.

Flicking the handful of plastic-cuffs he had saved from falling in front of him like a man shaking water off his hands, Dwayne began to turn back toward the roadbed behind him, feeling life and strength return to his legs as he moved. The plastic-cuffs came down like white dogwood petals and floated on the surface of the water.

"Gator," Dwayne repeated in a cracked voice, slipping and churning as he climbed back toward the road rising before him and seeming to move away as he flailed for it. "Oh, a goddamn big one, goddamn big one, shit."

"What you saying?" Martin Utz yelled from the hole on the other side of the road. "Where's Clarence?"

"It's done got two of them," Dwayne said, clambering across the ruts of the road and coming to a sudden stop before he reached the marsh on the other side. Teetering on the edge, he looked down at the water, up at Cake Golson on the backhoe and back down at the water again as though it might have moved during the time his eyes had left it to find Cake.

"Jesus Christ, Cake," he said in a high whine, "I didn't know they was any in here big like that."

"A what?" Utz said. "A what got them?"

"Not that woman," Dwayne said. "She's still standing there last time I looked. Them other two fellows. That's the ones got eat."

By that time Martin had reached the roadbed and was staring in the direction of the hummock and its stand of saplings where Clarence had been taking Crippled Sparrow and the woman. He could see her, but nobody else, as he swept his gaze back and forth across the marshland before him. Her back was turned to the road, and she was moving steadily toward the place where the first two, the Indian schoolteacher and the boy, were tied to the little trees sticking up out of the mound of earth.

"She's walking off," Dwayne said. "It ain't got her yet. See yonder."

"I can see that, dumbass," Martin said and gestured ahead into the swamp with one hand as though pointing out a site for possible land development. "Go after her and see where Clarence and that runt went."

"You got a gun?" Dwayne said. "To make me?"

"No, I never carry."

"Fuck you, then."

Cake Golson climbed down off the backhoe, leaving the engine running and tension set in the cable stretching from the winch into the hole in the marsh, reaching the roadbed in a series of great splashing jumps.

"You see the gator, Dwayne?" he said, standing squarely in the middle of the road and looking over his shoulder from where he had come and then toward the back of the woman almost to the hummock by now. "Did you eyeball it?"

"Nuh uh. I seen what he did, though, to that little runt Indian. I don't want no part of the son of a bitch."

"That's awful shallow water for a big one."

"Tell that to them two that got pulled under. Sure as hell deep enough for them fuckers. You don't see them no more, do you?"

"Will it let them go?" Martin said. "As soon as it stops being mad?"

"Oh, yeah," Dwayne said and laughed with the sound of a man clearing his throat. "When it gets them into its den and turns them loose to ripen up, it will."

"Ripen up?"

"You see," Cake began to explain to Martin Utz, "a bull gator like that one appears to be can't chew nothing with the kind of teeth it's got. Meat's got to loosen up a good bit before it can worry it on down."

"Don't tell me nothing else about it. I believe I got it the first time through."

Utz looked out over the stretch of water and marsh grass between him and the mound of earth which the woman had almost reached by now, forging ahead steadily and rising up higher with each step as her footing became more solid near the trees. "Clarence," he called and began to beat the flats of his hands against the sides of his legs. "Yo, Clarence."

It didn't seem possible, he told himself, after all that stone-crazy fucker had gone through that it would end up like this, him being eaten up in a swamp by a big wet lizard and not even getting off a round. You would think that what finally got Clarence Denver would be somebody with a sawed-off shotgun or taking himself too heavy of a speed ball pop or something else that made sense, not a reptile that would drag him off under water to keep him in a hole until he got dead enough to eat.

No time to get all soft about it, he told himself, but he knew he'd miss Clarence. All you ever had to do with Clarence Denver was to get him pointed on the course you wanted and he'd get there straight as a laser beam, the pupils of his psycho eyes no bigger than a pencil point. He did what and who he was told, and Jesus Christ could he make a computer hum like a son of a bitch.

Martin called the name one more time, watching the woman reach the mound of earth and walk steadily across it to the marsh on the other side without even looking at the trees where the two local Indians were tied. She's not thinking about anything but herself and getting her ass out of here, he thought, shaking his head at the selfishness of the bitch. I hope it gets her, too.

"All right," he said and turned back toward the two men standing in the middle of the roadbed, "let's get that sucker out of the hole. What's your name, Cake, climb back up on that machine and start cranking."

The man he had addressed looked at the other one and spoke. "You still got that rifle in the truck, right?"

"Well, yeah," Dwayne said, his gaze fastened on the spot where he had seen the little Indian disappear beneath the lid of scum on Lost Man Marsh. "But it still ain't got no shells in it."

"Naturally," Cake said. "I don't know why I even asked you."

"Them damn boys of mine shot them all up at a bunch of starlings in the yard. How's I to know we might want to use it?"

"You ain't carrying?" Cake said to Martin. "Nothing at all?"

"I already told him I wasn't. I don't do gun stuff. That was always Clarence." Martin turned back toward the water and called his partner's name one last time, prolonging the sound until all his breath was gone. "Clarence," he called until he startled a nesting marsh hen enough to cause it to fly up with a cackle.

"Well," Cake said. "I don't know about getting back in that water again."

"You want your money, don't you?"

"Sure. But I want to be able to spend it, too."

"That crocodile is busy putting Clarence and the runt in his pantry. He won't be around to bother us while we get the stuff out. Get on out there on the backhoe. Go on now, do it."

"It's a gator, not no crocodile," Dwayne said. "See, their jaws work different. One goes up, one goes down. I don't remember which is which."

"Dwayne," Cake said, looking deeply into the water of the marsh toward the east as though he might be able to see beneath it if he stared hard enough. "Watch all up and down this here road. You see anything fixing to cross it you holler at me, you hear?"

"Right, sure," Dwayne said, standing on tiptoe and beginning to swivel his head back and forth. "You go on ahead. I sure hope it ain't more than one of them fuckers, though. I mean on this side here, too."

"We'll do it fast," Martin Utz said. "We'll be out of here in thirty minutes. We got to be. It'll work out. It's supposed to. It's part of the plan."

Cake plunged back into Lost Man Marsh and made for the backhoe in a churning run, gobs of mud from the bottom kicking to the surface at every step.

"Can an alligator walk on hard ground?" Martin asked Dwayne, "or do they have to stay in all this water and swamp shit?

223

31

The VC kept wanting to float. The NVA with the sidearm had gone down like a rock and stayed in the mud of the rice paddy below the surface as though the body had been fastened to the bottom with wires. But the little one kept bobbing, and each time the lurp released his hold the body began to move slowly upwards in the water like a half-filled balloon.

It wasn't until he thought to wedge the head and shoulders of the VC under the legs of the NVA regular that things began to hold together and stay where they were put. For some reason, the VC had long hair which he had twisted into braids, and that was a puzzle, a thing the lurp had never seen before on one of them. Maybe he was a special of some kind, the braids a sign of rank the lurp hadn't run across yet. He'd watch for the next one.

The braids did come in handy, though. After he had tied them together around the leg of the NVA regular, everything seemed solid, even when he tugged twice, hard, and the lurp felt able then to slide away and leave them where they lay. By the time they did come up to the surface of the rice paddy, tied together and puffed up with gas, he'd be long gone.

The lurp moved slowly away to the east, his face toward the roadbed again, making no more noise in the waters of the rice paddy than a snake swimming, pleased to see almost no wake behind him as he angled away from where he had taken down the two slopes with the American woman. He still didn't know what she was, nurse or correspondent, but she had listened to what he had told her, showing no surprise that he was there in the paddy. In shock, probably, but she had the sense to get rid of any insignia she might have been wearing when she was captured. Not a sign of patch, stripe or tag on her that he could see.

She had taken off for the cover of the ridge without saying a word or even looking at him after that one time, marching in a straight line and not looking back, on her way to where the rest of them were hidden in the brush and trees. The ranking officer, the first one he had rescued, was probably still talking out of his head and no help to anybody, but the pilot would know what to tell her, know how to handle an American woman who had just missed buying the whole thing, guts, feathers, and all.

The lurp raised his head far enough to see the rest of the squad up on the trail and allowed himself a glimpse at the way they were moving around in jerky starts one direction and the other, looking back and forth from the spot where the one had seen the VC go down to the tank across the barrier of the road, its engine still running while they tried to figure out what to do now.

He didn't have a whole hell of a lot of time, he knew, to get the rest of it done and the tank run off into cover somewhere before another contingent came down the Ho Chi Minh Trail. They traveled in small groups, like a series of blood clots breaking loose bit by bit as they moved through an artery, and he knew he could take advantage of that as he had done before. But it was getting on toward dark, he told himself, turning his head to one side to look at the shadow of the blades of marsh grass, and business always picked up once the sun went down. Then the blood clots came in a steady stream, building and growing and surging until somebody had a heart attack.

Up on the road, one of the NVA regulars left the other two and moved toward the tank, making enough noise splashing through the rice paddy for the lurp to hear it clearly where he continued to slide eastward in the mud and water on his side of the road. The taller of the remaining two was stretched out as high as he could get, scanning back and forth across the spot where the VC had made his last noise, his shape outlined perfectly against the sky as he surveilled the rice paddy.

It would be nothing, less than the snap of a match stick, to take him out with one round with the sniper's rifle, the lurp told himself, but for some reason he didn't have the weapon with him anymore. He wondered where it had gone, that and the .45 automatic he had always carried, not regulation and too heavy for most people's taste, but he had always taken comfort from the lump it made against his right leg, like something that had grown there, like a big tumor. Not a grenade left, either, not even a piece of wire for close work.

He tried to think about where everything had gotten to, all his gear, slowing his sidling progress for a moment, but nothing came into his head where the white buzzing was except the Kay Bar knife he still had fastened to his belt. He couldn't remember the enemy having taken his weapons from him, not even that time in the big house on the old French landowner's plantation, and he wouldn't have just forgotten his tools, left them somewhere and walked off. He was trained not to do that. How would you forget your hands some place? How could you misplace your eyes?

Make do, he told himself, sliding steadily in the mud and water of the paddy. Invent what you don't have. Get the job done. Carry out the mission.

Behind him the engine of the backhoe was roaring and the cable was making a singing noise in the winch, but Martin Utz was having a hard time getting his attention drawn up to a tight focus. Dwayne was skittering back and forth on the road, craning his neck to be sure he saw the alligator or crocodile or whatever the fuck it was that had bitten the life out of Clarence Denver and the runt Indian with the pigtails in his hair, should it decide to crawl across the road and sample the buffet on this side of the table. How fast would it move, Martin wondered. Lizards were quick as hell, he could remember from his youth, closing his eyes and seeing himself as a child watching one flicker up the wall near the pad where he lay on the dry dirt floor in San Diego.

Alligators are just big lizards, right? And if that was true, all it would take to miss seeing the one which had got Clarence scamper across the road was to blink. Fuck all this water on the ground, and fuck all this wet. The goddamn thing could be right behind him ready to bite a hunk out of his ass, and the first thing he would know about it would be feeling his pants rip open and the air hit his balls.

Spinning around, Martin looked back toward the redneck on the backhoe, then at the one trying to balance himself exactly in the middle of the road as he looked for the alligator on one side of the road, then the other and then down at the ground behind his feet. Nothing. Yet.

"Keep your eyes open!" he yelled at the lookout. "That fucking lizard moves like lightning. You look away and it'll be chewing your goddamn leg off before you know it."

"Sir?"

"Don't look over here at me," Martin said, hopping off the roadbed into the marsh and making for the hole and the backhoe working at it. "I ain't the one you got to worry about. Look at that fucking mud hole. Keep doing it."

As he reached to within a few yards of the backhoe, lifting his feet high at each step to minimize the time they spent under water, Martin heard a new tone start up in the winch motor and saw the cable begin to move backward in short jerks as it wound onto the reel.

"It's coming, right?" he yelled at Cake Golson, bent over and playing the levers like a man hooked to a big fish. He nodded and said something Martin couldn't hear, and then pointed toward the hole with an index finger, not moving his hand from the control lever in the process.

An elongated shape was rising slowly from the edge of the hole, mud-covered and dripping water, its color slate gray beneath the streaks of dark earth. It was twisting slowly to one side under the strain of the steel cable, and as Martin floundered toward it through the marsh, he could see that a welded seam beginning at the tip of the pod was spit apart and gushing water as the cable pulled it up.

"Who gives a fuck," he chortled aloud, knowing things were back in place where they were ordered to be, and he stretched out his hand to pat the metal pod on its nose, telling himself not to slip down in the mud and fall in with the thing, when the load suddenly jerked, shuddered, and the cable made a high singing sound and ceased to move.

The engine of the backhoe beside him revved insanely as though its operator had for some reason given it all the fuel at his command, reached its highest level of revolution, stuck there and stayed. Stumbling away from the side of the machine, Martin fought to keep his balance as he turned to see what the dummy at the controls was up to.

Two floundering steps away to the side, he could see up to the platform where the seat was located, raised high above the body of the machine and enclosed by heavy yellow pipe. The four levers on the console were pushed all the way forward, and the metal seat for the operator, punched through with holes to allow for drainage, was empty.

The roar of the engine rose to a new high, shrieking now like a crazy woman, and Martin could smell hot metal and rubber burning, and he was running in place, feet churning, as he tried to turn toward the roadbed and still see behind him as he went. The mud sucked and pulled at his feet and calves, and the weeds wrapped themselves around his knees and thighs, and he was yelling at the man up on the road who had retreated all the way to the far side, his hands pushed out in front of him as though he were fending off somebody trying to sell him something he had no use for and did not want.

"It crawled up there," Martin said, scrambling up on the hard surface and moving so close to Dwayne the muddy front of his safari jacket rubbed against the man's shirt. "Right up on the fucking bulldozer like a monkey."

"Backhoe," Dwayne said, trying to move away from the man with his mouth two inches from his own as he crowded up against him on the margin of the road. "It's a backhoe. What did? Where's Cake?"

"I just told you. That goddamn big lizard got him. That fucking wet son of a bitch."

"The gator? I never seen him cross the road. I'd a hollered if I did."

"Snatched him like a piece of candy. One minute he's winching up the pod full of stuff, everything's going fine, the next thing the bastard's gone."

"Did you see him in the water over yonder?"

"No. I barely saved my own ass. And there's no use to go back to go look for him. The fucker's gone."

Behind Martin, the racing engine of the backhoe coughed, backfired twice with the sound of a small bomb going off, and quit. Both men turned and looked in the direction of the machine at the hole, the silence in Lost Man Marsh as sudden and jarring as a blow.

"Listen," Dwayne said. "Maybe we can hear Cake yelling or the gator wallowing around or something."

"Cake is past making noises, friend," Martin said, "and that damn lizard never makes a sound. Come on."

Breaking into a fast trot, Martin Utz headed for the blue pickup parked behind the trailer, his eyes fastened on the expanse of water surrounding the backhoe, Dwayne at his right elbow.

228

"What about the job?" Dwayne asked, looking down at the mudcovered shorter man puffing beside him. "That thing y'all are looking for?"

"That," Martin said, spacing his words between quavering breaths, "I'll think about later. I got to get out of here."

"I hate not to look for Cake first."

"You fucking dummy," Martin panted as they drew near the pickup, "he's in that damn lizard hole with Clarence and the runt by now. That son of a bitch is stocking up for the next three months. Start that truck and get me out of this swamp."

"I got to back it up for a long ways," Dwayne said after the two men had climbed into the pickup. "Way back before that place where we cut that red oak. Ain't no hard ground off this logging road to turn around none before then."

Martin finished locking his door and rolling the window up before he answered, his head swivelling from side to side as he spoke. "Do it. Give it the gas. Go on, go on."

The truck had traveled in reverse for about two-hundred yards, Dwayne twisted around to see through the rear window as he steered when Martin caught a flicker of movement ahead through the windshield toward the stalled backhoe in the marsh. A splash, a glint on the surface of the water. Something. Not pausing to speak, he lunged with his left leg and jammed his foot atop Dwayne's on the accelerator, putting as much pressure into it as he could muster in the confines of the truck's cab. The engine roared, and both men jerked forward as the tires dug into the roadbed and propelled the vehicle at its sudden new speed away from whatever Martin had seen a glimpse of in the mud and water of Lost Man Marsh.

Struggling for control of the wheel, which had come alive in his hands and which fought him now like a mad dog he was trying to pet, Dwayne cursed the man beside him and lashed out with his right elbow to knock him loose from what he was doing to the gas pedal.

He had caught Martin with two good elbow shots to the head, neither of which provided any benefit, when the window between the cab of the pickup and the bed exploded in a shower of dime-sized particles of safety glass. A hand, huge as a dinner plate, and covered with dirt and blood, closed over his face and began twisting his head so powerfully to the right and back that Dwayne felt the steering wheel slip from his fingers as his body lifted from the seat and began to move up toward the window opening as though he had discovered a new, impossible way to crawl backwards out of the truck.

How, he asked himself, as his head and shoulders moved through the opening into the rushing air outside, can that fucking asshole do this and still be sitting beside me in the passenger seat holding the pedal to the floor and screaming his lungs out? It ain't right, it can't be, he heard a voice say inside his head, no, and then he felt some better, relieved a little, right before all the red and black bloomed in his eyes, when he realized that some of what was happening was his, the screaming part, at least.

It was probably fifty miles an hour, maybe more, Austin Bullock judged, that the pickup was doing backwards when the rear end of it collided directly with the red oak tree the old people of the Nation called Thunder Man.

So many things happened at once that he did not understand later how it was that he had been able to see each part take place from where he lay behind the stand of palmetto bushes. Time had not stopped, and the scene before him in Lost Man Marsh had not shifted into video slow-motion. But he had seen the whole thing, of a piece, the way you witness a sunset in all its colors and changes without stopping to analyze each element of its natural constitution.

The bed of the pickup stopped moving when the rear bumper smashed into Thunder Man, but the cab did not. It closed upon the metal box of the truck bed, folding it instantly into a wad of metal like an empty cardboard container being stepped on by a heavy man. The rear wheels bounced into the air as the compressed bed climbed partway up the trunk of the red oak.

Above the level of the bed, out of the rear window of the cab came two bodies in instantaneous succession, flying backwards as though in pursuit of another shape which had risen from the bed of the truck at the moment of collision. That first one missed the tree cleanly, landing thirty feet away with a great splash in the marsh on the near side of the roadway. The other two did not. They joined the tree and each other in the same moment.

A shower of new pale March buds, detached from the tips of the red oak's branches by the force of the collision, sifted down upon everything below, the compressed bed of the truck, the two bodies crumpled against the bole of the tree, the ground beneath, the surface of the water of Lost Man Marsh beside the roadway.

Austin went first to the driver's side of the pickup and reached through the window to turn off the engine, popped out of gear and still running at top speed because of the shoe jammed atop the accelerator, and held in place by a fold of the rubber floor mat.

The first man out of the window had hit the red oak from the top of his head to his thighs, and he lay against it in a sitting position, his arms and legs spread as though he had intended to catch the other man in flight and cradle him against the blow to come. The back of his head was one with the black bark of Thunder Man, and his chin was forced up by the head of the other man who lay within the compass of his arms, now complexly a part of the first man's body, his flesh, blood and bone.

Tucker Pop-Eye was on his back in the mud and water of Lost Man Marsh, both arms sprawled at impossible angles to each side. One leg was crossed over the other at the knee as though he were sitting in a comfortable chair, at ease, waiting to take his turn in a conversation.

Austin could see him open his eyes as he approached.

"Tucker," he said in the language of the Nation, "that was a bad thing."

"I didn't get the tank," Tucker said in English.

"The tank?"

"Up there on the trail. Some kind of a new one that digs itself in. We ain't got one of them that I know of."

"No," Austin said. "Be still. Somebody will be here soon to pick you up."

"You called in a chopper? That's good. They better hurry, though."

"Thomas Fox Has Him went to old man Bronson Sings War's house. That's the closest place that has a phone where he can call the sheriff. They'll be here in a little while."

"You're the officer? I don't see no insignia."

"I guess so. Yeah. You know Fox Has Him, don't you?"

"Enlisted man? A gunner?"

"Yeah. That's what he is."

Tucker Pop-Eye shifted the leg supporting the one crossed over it and closed his eyes. "Hurts," he said. "You got a needle? Just until the chopper gets here."

"No," Austin said, moving to a spot in the mud near Tucker's right shoulder and squatting down to kneel beside him. "I'm sorry I don't. But I want to tell you a story I know you've heard before."

"A story? Is it about a mission?"

231

"Yeah. A real tough one, too."

"I took out the whole fucking NVA squad," Tucker Pop-Eye said. "A VC too. I made him let the nurse go. She's up there on that ridge across the rice paddy, about a klick, with the major and the chopper pilot. And the gunner, too. Just a kid."

"I know you did, Tucker Pop-Eye. You got them all."

"Yeah," Tucker said and closed his eyes. "But not the tank. Tell me about that mission. The tough one. Go ahead."

"There were six brothers," Austin began, "and they were living by a river. It was big water, this river, and it was before the Nation came to Texas. The brothers didn't have a canoe. They always wanted to see where the river went, where it led, but they couldn't.

"One day a stranger paddled up in a canoe, a beautiful one with designs and colors worked all down its sides with paints and carvings. He offered to let the brothers try it out on the river if they would let him spend the night and feed him a meal."

Austin Bullock closed his eyes and remembered the true words of the story of the six brothers who had outwitted the cannibal, and he told it all to Tucker Pop-Eye, broken there in the water of Lost Man Marsh. He had almost finished the telling of it when he heard the engines of the string of Coushatta County sheriff's department cars and the emergency medical vehicles coming down the logging road which runs by Thunder Man and Stone Woman, the huge red oaks which Dirty Boy used to fool the Big Man-Eater just after the Alabamas and Coushattas came to Texas in the Old Time.

Austin Bullock hurried the telling, but only a little, and he said the last words to Tucker Pop-Eye just before the first car door banged open and the chest of the broken man lying at the heart of Lost Man Marsh ceased its rise and fall.

32

Austin's ex-wife was sitting behind the wheel of the rental car with its engine running. Honey-Suckle, the Vietnamese pot-bellied pig, was beside her in the passenger's seat, propped up on a pillow from Walmart with a seat belt fastened around its body and a glazed look in its eyes caused by the sedative which the veterinarian had prescribed for the journey to come.

Honey-Suckle grunted twice when Austin leaned down to speak through the window, and Ellen patted her reassuringly on the head. "I know," she said to the pig. "I know."

"I'm sorry all this happened to you, Ellen," Austin said. "Are you sure you'll be able to drive to Houston by yourself?"

"That's the easy part," she said, "getting out of this warped, circular environment with all its curves and hidden places."

"Bad convergence, huh?" Austin said in a kind tone.

"No convergence at all. None. The lines of consequence never met at any point. Everything was completely parallel. Just doomed to vanish into infinity without coming a single bit closer."

"Well, yeah, I see what you're saying."

"And, Austin," Ellen said, turning in her seat to look more directly at the father of her child, "the one thing I do feel responsible for on my own is letting myself be taken in by that sawed-off little Native-American charlatan. I trusted a man again because I thought he was different. I thought he saw through the surface reality of curves and circles to the true lines of intersection beneath. He lied to me. I was just another woman to him, and he took advantage of my genetic bent toward truth."

"Yes," Austin said, looking away from Ellen's pale eyes toward the groggy animal strapped in the bucket seat for a safe ride to the airport. "He did for sure. He fooled a lot of people for a long time."

"But I learned two things," she went on. "You always learn something when you pursue the philosophy of Life Consequences, no matter what circle your path was forced into."

"That's good. I'm glad it wasn't a complete loss."

"I learned," Ellen said, raising her voice to a sterner level. "I learned that Laura is of me physically and historically, but not in a soulful sense. She must find her own way to consequence and conclusion."

"I agree. It's up to her now. She's all grown up, and I see the situation the same way you do, just like you said."

"And," Ellen said, speaking louder to cut off Austin if he was planning to add anything else verbal, "and I learned that my true companion through the journey is and will be Animal Presence."

"You mean the little hog," Austin said, glancing again at the tranquilized passenger on the front seat. "I guess."

"As an emblem, yes. The Vietnamese pot-bellied pig as symbol, not as hog per se," Ellen said. "Honey-Suckle. I have found my co-journeyer."

"Yes, you have got your little pig. Bless both your hearts." Austin straightened up to allow the car to pull away from the curb in front of his house. He watched the rental Ford Escort travel to the end of the block, its right signal light blinking, and he waved at the vehicle carrying his ex-wife and the pot-bellied pig until it was out of sight on the first leg of its journey to the Houston Intercontinental Airport and points west.

Laura was standing in the living room beside her packed bags when Austin entered the house.

"I'm going to always keep in touch with her, whether she wants me to right now or not," she said to him as he came inside. "She's my mother, no matter what she says or does."

"Of course you will. She'll always need for you to, and so will you."

"Well, I don't want to talk about it right now. She has things to do, and so do I."

"Yep," Austin said and started for the kitchen. "You want a Mister Sam's cola before Brandon comes to pick you up?"

"A beer," she said. "When do you leave for the state tournament?"

"Tomorrow morning, if Coach Mellard doesn't bust a blood vessel waiting until then."

"How will Annette do?"

"Depends on Thomas Fox Has Him, like always. But I expect the best. That Alabama is going to come through."

"I bet he does, too," Laura said, taking the beer can from Austin. "The People have a way of doing that."

"If the signs are right, and the medicine's good, they sometimes do," Austin agreed.

"Thomas Fox Has Him was the one who figured out that pod business, too, wasn't he? And it was just a big shipment of cocaine on its way somewhere," Laura said. "That's all the whole thing was about. All those dead people."

"That's right. And the Nation was lucky enough to have the damn plane from Colombia drop it at low level right into the edge of the Big Thicket. But, of course, according to Albert Had Two Mothers, Buzzard had a lot to do with it."

"I thought it was an accident the plane lost the pod in the marsh. Wasn't that what Fox Has Him found out on the Internet? How did Buzzard cause it to happen? Maybe I should get out my notebook."

"Thomas was wrong about that part—it being an accident the pod came loose. Buzzard, in the shape of a plane full of drugs, was being closely pursued by a DEA aircraft from where it had locked on down around Galveston, and, it turns out, dropped that pod on purpose. According to Albert Had Two Mothers, Buzzard was looking for a place to hide some rotten meat where nobody could find it and eat it up before he could. Opossum, maybe. Or Fox. So he made a deposit in Lost Man Marsh which immediately, of course, began to stink up that part of the Nation's territory. Until it was removed, the People were going to have this putrid stuff poisoning the air and having to be dealt with."

"But the people in the plane that dropped the pod in Lost Man Marsh knew what they were doing, you say."

"They had designed the pod so they could do just that if they had a need to dump it. The Nation just got unlucky, that's all, about where it landed. That's why it all took place here. According to what the DEA told Walker Lewis, anyway."

"That would explain Chief Emory and Charlie Sun-Singer trying to find out what it was and where it was located," Laura said. "But why did Tucker Pop-Eye kill those poor people? How does Abba Had Two Mothers fit that part into his interpretation?"

"He's still working on figuring out how the Buzzard story can accommodate that, I imagine. But if you're asking literally why it took place, I think it was because Tucker didn't know who he was or where he was at all anymore. He had lost himself a long time ago. And that little shaman son of a bitch figured out he'd be able to make him think and believe anything. So when Charlie found that cache of old Spanish medals near the place he had seen the pod go down into the swamp and showed them to Chief Emory, that bunch from Houston got scared everybody and his brother would go prospecting. So our little consultant went into action. At least that's the way Sheriff Lewis and the government guys figure it happened."

"And now the sheriff's a big hero, and Tucker Pop-Eye was the witch."

"You got to have a hero and a witch in every story, Laura, you know that. The narrative demands it. Whether it's the historical version or one that Albert Had Two Mothers would believe. And, of course, somebody's got to get credit. That's the biggest seizure of cocaine in this part of Texas, maybe even in the whole state."

"At least for a month or two," Laura said. "Until Buzzard comes back."

"Oh, you're becoming a cynic," her father said. "Where'd you learn that? At Rice University in an anthropology class?"

"No," she said. "Not in a classroom. I learned it from being around you." Laura paused and then she said one more thing as a car horn honked outside.

"Iskano," she said. "Abba Bullock."

Austin started to correct her pronunciation of the formal farewell a member of the Nation must make to the Stated Chief of the Alabama-Coushatta, but thought better of it, and instead told his daughter Colita, a woman of the People, to take her time and drive carefully on her way to Houston.

Albert Had Two Mothers scratched his forehead where he had worn the white paint for almost two weeks. With the help of his wife, he had had to take it off with turpentine, and the chemical had made his skin become sore and itchy. He looked at the eight young people seated before him on the damp earth at the heart of the Alabama-Coushatta Nation, five of them near the time for the manhood ceremony and the other three too young for that but interested in stories about the Old Time nonetheless.

He shifted to a more comfortable position on the section of cypress tree trunk on which he sat before the children and thought how to begin.

"This story," he started, "is about the longtime ago and the Close-Up time, too. It began in the Old Time when Dirty Boy was being chased by a Big Man-Eater that wanted to catch him and drag him off to the place where the water and the earth come together in a mix. Dirty Boy had a rock that wanted to be rescued from Big Man-Eater, you understand.

"Then it was that Thunder Man and Stone Woman they moved close together, see, so when Dirty Boy run between them then there was room for him all right, but not for Big Man-Eater. They looked like trees, big red oaks, Thunder Man and Stone Woman did, but they wasn't just that. No, they was human inside, but they made their outsides be trees, red oaks, thick and strong and tall.

"So when Dirty Boy come through there just running between them fast, see, the Big Man-Eater he tried to follow, and you know what he did? He knocked his brains out on Stone Woman and it made the water and the earth all red down in there, just like blood. It's still that way when you go look, and Dirty Boy he got away. You can check it out. That was the Old Time.

"It went along after that, it went along for a time, a time, a time. Then another Big Man-Eater he learned how to use a power saw, and he learned how to drive a truck and dig holes in the Nation with a machine, and he did all that, and he cut down Stone Woman. The reason he did, see, was so he wouldn't bust his head against that red oak tree like the Big Man-Eater did in the Old Time and then, see, he figured he could catch Dirty Boy this go-round.

237

"So he got to digging down in yonder in Lost Man Marsh to find something, an evil thing he wanted that Buzzard had buried down in there. Dirty Boy, he wasn't having none of that, so he commenced to work. He had learned how to do, understand, in the Close-Up time, too, just like the Big Man-Eater had, so he had a few tricks himself."

One of the children squatting on the dance ground before Albert Had Two Mothers said something to the one beside him in a low voice, and Had Two Mothers gave him a look. The boy hushed then, and the old man began to tell the rest of the story about how Dirty Boy learned to confuse Big Man-Eater so badly that he drove his pickup truck backward at an unsafe speed toward the body of Thunder Man waiting there to stop him. No other child interrupted or made another sound as the Second Chief of the Nation told the tale, and all listened attentively as the children of the Alabama-Coushatta should always do when an Elder tells of how the People deal with Big Man-Eaters, and cannibals, and ghosts, and witches, and Monster Lizards and all the creatures of darkness which have been trying since Abba Mikko first made the world to do wrong things to the Nation of the Alabama-Coushatta and to the men and women and children who live in Texas in peace in that place.

CPSIA information can be obtained
at www.ICGtesting.com
Printed in the USA
FFHW021130120319
50966389-56393FF

9 781942 956662